I0784758

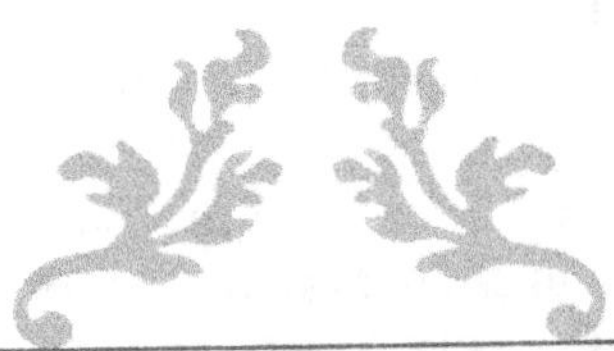

Billionaire Boss' Holiday Proposal

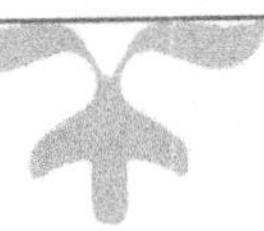

By Bonita Y. McCoy

ISBN-13:978-1-968792-48-0

Dedicated to Aaron, Akari, Adam, and Andrew

Behold, children are a heritage from the Lord,
offspring a reward from him.

Psalm 127:3

Prologue

A black plume of smoke rose high into the air above the stand of trees to the left of the trail. Brent Thibodeaux spotted the dark cloud as it lifted into the early morning sky— Fire!

His gut tightened as his training pushed him into action.

Picking up speed, he raced down the worn narrow path. He stumbled to a halt when he reached the tree line separating the woods from Fort Sam Houston. There before his eyes sat the base motor pool engulfed in flames.

He blinked in disbelief. Smoke billowed from every crevice along the east wall. The two large metal doors at the front of the structure stood wide open. His heart clinched. Was someone in there at this hour?

He raced toward the building. The smell of burning plastic and chemicals washed over him forcing him to cover his nose and mouth with his arm. When he neared the blaze, he grimaced against the wave of heat. The flames roared leaping out of one of the windows located at the front of the building, warning him not to come any closer.

Though the large front doors stood open, he couldn't see beyond the thick layer of black haze. Backing away, he pulled his cell phone from his shorts pocket and punched in the number for the emergency services on base.

"What is the nature of your emergency?"

"There's a fire in progress at the ARNORTH motor pool. I'm Brent Thibodeaux, Firefighter, badge number 715. The fire is contained but spreading. I believe there might be someone inside the building. Send a truck and rescue. You'd better contact the captain. He's going to want to know about this."

"Dispatching the truck and EMTs now."

Brent shoved his phone back into his pocket. He needed to find out if anyone was in the building. Jogging over to the west side of the structure, he assessed the situation. No flames jumped from the windows. The glass remained intact.

Peeking through one of the panes, he waited, hoping the haze inside would clear, so he could determine his next steps. The wide-open doors set off warning signals in his mind. He'd been a firefighter for too long to ignore them.

A gentle breeze swirled around him and the black smoke inside the building thinned. Thank goodness for those open doors. Scanning the wall closest to him, he spotted a man lying on the floor, motionless.

Should he open the window in front of him or find another way to the man? He didn't want to fuel the fire even more with a rush of fresh oxygen, or worse create a backdraft. No, he needed to find another way inside.

As he moved toward the front of the building, a

small series of explosions erupted from the back of the structure. The influx of oxygen brought in by the breeze had done the very thing he'd wanted to avoid. With all the chemicals in the shop, he didn't have long before the whole place blew. If the guy was alive, he needed to get him out now.

Brent covered his nose and mouth with the crook of his elbow and moved through the doors. The fire crawled towards him, but he dodged through the flames toward the perimeter. He hugged the wall making sure not to touch the hot metal and made his way around to the west side where he'd seen the man through the glass panes. As the black smoke thinned, Brent spotted a car on a lift about twenty feet from the window and a man crumpled on the floor nearby, clutching a wrench. The fire played dangerously close to his limp body.

The whine of the sirens in the distance caught Brent's attention. Help was on its way, but he didn't have time to wait. The fire inched closer to the man, lapping up the spilt liquid surrounding him.

Brent blinked back the tears that welled in his eyes from the sting of the smoke.

Lord, keep us safe. Without so much as a second thought, Brent moved into action.

Dashing towards the man on the floor, he bent over the figure to check for a pulse. Yes, there it was. Not strong, but he had one.

Tapping the man's cheeks, Brent waited for a response. "Hey, wake up. Open your eyes." Brent tapped the man's pale cheeks again. This time a slight moan rasped from the man's throat.

He didn't have time to wait for this guy to become coherent. He needed to get him out of here, now.

A loud boom rattled the metal structure. A glance over his shoulder told him the flames were igniting the accelerant now splashed all over the floor. This bad situation had just become his worst nightmare.

Brent sat back on his haunches and hovered over the man. Reaching out, he wrapped his arms around the guy's chest and pulled him forward. As Brent prepared to lift the guy onto his shoulder, the man regained consciousness.

"Oh no you don't," growled the man, ramming Brent with his full weight, sending him sprawling backwards into the flames.

Pain seared through him as the scent of his own flesh on fire filled his nostrils. He rolled out of the fire and continued to roll in the small space until he was sure the embers had been extinguished.

The dark-haired man, now alert, scooted toward him on his knees. "Oh no. What have I done? I thought you were that fool who broke in here. Let me help you."

Brent tried to push up with his left arm as the man grabbed his shoulder, but he crumbled under his own weight. His muscles throbbed in protest. The man's hands felt like acid on his skin.

Sirens sounded right outside the building. "Get me close to the front entrance, then go for help." That was all Brent could get out before the pain pushed him into the depths of the darkness creeping over him.

Chapter One

October 2022, Orange Blossom, Texas.

Brent Thibodeaux's heart thundered in his chest, echoing the sound of the Harley Davidson eating up the miles beneath him. He leaned into the curve and allowed gravity to do its work. The motor rumbled inches from the ground.

He straightened the machine, his mind drifting to the coming scene. What would Dan and Wade say when he arrived without warning, looking like he did? They hadn't seen him, not since … well, since several things had changed. He'd made them aware that he'd been injured, but he'd kept the details of the incident to himself, while he made some hard decisions.

He didn't need his older brothers jumping into the situation trying to help. No, the choices he needed to make about his future would be his. Well, his and the Lord's.

Brent tugged at the collar of the heavy jacket he wore more for protection than to ward off the cold. Even in late October, southern Texas sported a high of seventy degrees. Only in the evenings did the coolness of the fall season push its way through, giving a respite to the people of the small southern towns along the route.

He glanced into his rearview mirror and caught sight of his friend, John McAllister. The older man trailed behind him, his black leather jacket billowing out from his torso.

Brent chuckled. The crusty ex-soldier, who spoke his mind without hesitation or apology, didn't cut such a tough figure with the air dancing around him. He looked like one of those oversized, blow-up figures twisting and twirling outside a car dealership.

They were headed to Orange Blossom, Texas, to meet up with Rod Carson, the ranch manager of Silver Spur. Brent put in a good word for John when his oldest brother Dan mentioned needing another ranch hand in one of their more recent calls.

Why Rod wanted to meet in town instead of at the ranch was beyond him, but since he'd horned his way into coming with John, he hadn't argued the point. Brent figured now was as good a time as any to face his family. Besides, he had business to take care of with Tyler Kemp.

Brent pressed his lips together beneath the helmet's visor. What if his brothers reacted badly when they saw him? Or worse, what if they didn't even recognize him? He shook his head, flinging the ideas into the wind as it rushed past him. *Lord, protect my heart and theirs.*

John pulled closer, breaking into his thoughts, and Brent moved toward the yellow line in the middle of the two-lane highway, giving John enough room to pull alongside him. They had been on the road all day, stopping to take in a few sights and to rest and refuel when needed.

The ride from Fort Sam Houston in San Antonio to Orange Blossom normally took a few hours, but Brent hadn't regained his full strength. He eased up on the throttle and shifted into third, slowing his speed. Stretching his back, he relaxed his shoulders, willing the tension to leave his body.

Though the military hospital had pushed him further than he'd thought he could go, they had nothing left to give him. The fact he could handle his Harley was a testament to their determination. His rehabilitation now depended on time, patience, and the good Lord.

When they banked the turn, a bright yellow sign appeared ahead of them. The large white letters read "Welcome to Orange Blossom." Beneath the wooden sign hung a slightly lopsided banner announcing a weekend of fun at the Annual Harvest Festival.

Brent groaned. The Harvest Festival. He'd forgotten all about the annual event held on the last weekend of October. That must be the reason Rod wanted to meet in town. Silver Spur Ranch sponsored horse rides for the kids each year, along with hayrides in an ancient wagon. Rod always took charge of the hayrides, not trusting anyone else to handle the old rig with the respect it deserved.

If he'd remembered about the festival, Brent would've delayed his homecoming, giving the tourists and venders time to clear out of town. His heart raced at the thought of all those people milling about on Main Street. The idea of seeing his brothers for the first time since the fire was bad enough, but to face the whole town along with a brood of outsiders caused his palms to sweat even more in his leather gloves.

As they turned onto Main Street, he slowed, the rumble of his motorcycle vibrating through him. John fell in behind him to avoid the pedestrians moving from one side of the street to the other.

A group of children darted out in front of Brent. He clenched the brake and dropped his feet to the ground. The Harley lurched to a stop. None of the kids noticed his presence as they bounded onto the sidewalk outside Sweet Things Bakery.

A pretty brunette with ringlets cascading over her shoulders held out a cupcake to the smallest kid in the group. Stooping to meet his gaze, the woman smiled when the young boy took the cupcake from her hand. The kid, who was maybe four or five, ran his tongue across the chocolate icing leaving smudges of the sweet treat all over his face. The woman threw back her head laughing.

Brent couldn't take his eyes off her. He lifted his visor to get a better view. She must've felt his stare because at that moment she turned toward him and met his gaze. A smile made the corners of her eyes crinkle as she wiggled her fingers in a half wave in his direction. He nodded. Something seemed so familiar about her, but he couldn't place it.

Breaking eye contact, the lovely lady spoke to the children gathered around her, making them laugh. She stood and rumpled the little boy's hair before reaching for another cupcake. One by one, she handed each child the sweet treat covered in orange, white, or chocolate icing.

Brent waited the bike idling beneath him for the kids to dig their money from their pockets, but none did. That's when his gaze landed on the baking rack behind her, holding a variety of baked goodies and a poster that read *Free Cupcakes*.

Wrinkles threaded across his brow. No wonder Tyler had contacted him. Brent touched the letter tucked inside his jacket pocket along with his medical discharge papers. The letter had arrived at the precise moment he'd needed direction, as if it were an answer to his months of prayers.

A car horn blared, cutting off Brent's train of thought. He lifted his feet and motored down the street, searching for an open parking space.

Not finding one, he veered right onto Pine Street and hoped John would notice his turn signal. Halfway down the street, he found a spot. John pulled into the same space beside him and cut his engine. Swiping his foot along the side of the machine, John placed the bike on the kickstand. Reaching up, he removed his helmet, his salt and pepper hair plastered to his head from the sweat.

Brent followed suit, planting his kickstand on the pavement, but he hesitated before removing his helmet. The scars on his face from the flames had healed well enough so that no one should notice them, but the ones along his left jawline and down his neck looked like mismatched pieces of peach and red cloth.

The tee shirt he wore beneath the heavy jacket didn't do much to hide the crevices of the scars scattered across his upper body, but it worked to hide the cascade of deformed skin on his shoulder and upper back.

He toyed with the idea of wearing the jacket, but the heat made that an unbearable option.

"You coming?" John asked, setting his helmet on

the seat of his motorcycle and removing his black jacket. Opening his saddlebags that hung below the seat, John stuffed the heavy item inside.

"Yeah, I'm right behind you." Brent swung his leg over the seat and removed his helmet. The cool air touched his skin. He ran his hand through his hair hoping to make himself look a bit more presentable before surprising his brothers.

It'd been almost two years since he'd seen them. He'd come home for Easter to witness the dedication of the twins which had stirred a need inside him to reconnect with his family. The warm welcome and the growing numbers of the Thibodeaux clan acted like a magnet, pulling him back. He wanted to belong again. Not to a group like the Army who were bound together by a focused purpose, but to a family who would accept him no matter what. At least, that's what he hoped would happen.

John stood studying him. "Where's your mind today? Are you that wound up about seeing your family?" He detached his phone from the mount on the console of the bike and shoved it into his front pocket.

"Sorry." Brent pulled his leather gloves from his hands. Shrugging, he removed his jacket, the last piece of covering that kept the eyes of the crowd from knowing his secret. He couldn't hide the scars. They were forever a part of him.

"It's going to be fine. You've prayed about this. I've prayed about this. Shoot, we've even prayed about it together. God's got this." John met his gaze. The unmovable assurance in his friend's eyes put a stop to the whirling thoughts in Brent's mind.

"You're right. I have nothing to fear. Guess I'm

more concerned about the fine people of Orange Blossom and the cowhands at Silver Spur Ranch." Brent shook his head letting his gaze fall to his boots. "Remember what happened at the park, and what about the clerk at the gas station on the way here?"

"You're a bona fide hero, Brent Thibodeaux, and don't you forget it." John slapped him on the back. "Now let's go find Rod Carson before he gives my job away."

"I believe I know where we can find him." Brent led the way toward the town green, located beside City Hall a few blocks south on Main Street. Tables full of merchandise and crafts littered the sidewalks on both sides of Pine and Main. Brent dodged a gray-haired lady with a cane who stopped abruptly in front of him to admire a handmade quilt hanging on a display rack filled with other quilted items. John, however, bumped into her.

"Watch where you're going," she snapped. Turning to the vendor, she said, "People don't care who they run over."

The vendor smiled and nodded, not commenting on her complaint.

"Terribly sorry, ma'am." John's Texas twang added an air of authenticity to his apology.

The woman shrugged. "Guess it can't be helped. So many people are here this year. Clovis said he advertised the event in several online newspapers and on something called Myspace Market." She sniffed. "I'll never understand why we can't enjoy our town festival with our own folks."

John pressed his lips together to smother a smile.

Brent understood the older woman's concerns.

Change seemed to be the inevitable course of life.

As he rounded the corner back onto Main Street, Brent spotted a large bouncy slide reaching toward the sky. The colorful attraction stood further back on the green. That had to be the area where the horse rides would be located.

"Over there." He pointed. "I'm sure the corral will be set up near the slide. They try to keep all the kid activities together."

Brent weaved through the crowd with John close behind him, sidestepping strollers and grandmothers with more kids than hands. When he reached an open patch of grass, he stopped and scanned the layout of the rides and booths. Several children stood gathered around the face-painting table, waiting their turn while another group huddled inside a small tent, pushing beads onto strings. It didn't take Brent long to find the antique wagon with Rod Carson, the Silver Spur ranch manager, perched on the driver's seat holding the reins. Rod was facing the opposite direction, looking over his shoulder while Nikki helped a few of the younger kids get seated on the bales of hay.

A smile threaded its way across Brent's lips at the sight of his family. Man, he had sure missed them.

"That must be him." John stepped beside Brent and nodded in Rod's direction. "I'd know him anywhere from your description. Stout, older ..." He chuckled as Rod scooped up a boy who couldn't be more than three and seated him close to his side, draping a protective arm over the child's shoulder. "Maybe a bit of a teddy bear."

Brent laughed. "Yeah, he's an old softy. Rod insists on driving the wagon every year. He swears it's because of safety issues, but it's mainly because he enjoys the kiddos so much."

As Brent stepped toward the wagon, he heard his name called above the hum of the crowd. Turning, he looked over the top of the individuals around him, his six-foot three frame making the task easier.

"Brent, wait," a female voice shouted from somewhere to his left.

He searched the sea of people for a familiar face. A hand shot up into the air and waved at him. "You go ahead, John. I'll catch up in a minute."

"Sure thing." John slapped his back. "Remember, God's got this."

As John moved off, Brent repeated under his breath, "God's got this."

A red headed woman with a passel of kids in tow emerged from around the group of teenagers in front of him. "Oh, my word, what are you doing here? When did you arrive? Does Wade know you're here?" Bernadette, Brent's sister-in-law, shifted the toddler from one hip to the other. Freeing an arm, she snaked it around Brent's middle and hugged him tight. "Why didn't you let us know you were coming? You could've mentioned it to Wade when you talked last week."

Brent returned the hug. As far as he was concerned, Wade had married one of the last good women on the planet. "I wasn't sure. It's been so long since I've visited."

"Yeah, almost two years ago, Easter, right?" A gentle smile lifted her lips.

A pang of guilt twisted his gut. "I didn't know how to explain what happened to me the last several months over the phone."

Bernadette stepped back to examine him. The blond-haired little girl she held looked up at him from under her light-colored lashes. Her pale blue eyes met his, then she ducked her head into Bernadette's shoulder. "It's all right, Lani. This is Uncle Brent. He's a fireman in the Army." Bernadette rubbed the child's back, but her attention never left Brent.

"Hello there, little lady," Brent addressed the sweet child, trying to redirect Bernie's focus.

Instead, Bernadette inspected him, making him feel like a germ under a microscope. "Are you sure you're okay?" Her brows furrowed.

"Yeah, I'm good." Brent pushed his hand through his hair and pulled a smile onto his face.

She pursed her lips as if deciding whether he was telling the whole truth.

"Really, Bernie, if I wasn't doing much better, I wouldn't be here."

"So, what happened? What kept you away from Orange Blossom for so long?"

Brent's mind balked at the question. He didn't have the energy or the inclination to go into his story in the middle of a crowded festival while five children waited for her. "Can I tell you later? Maybe when we're all together? It'd be easier for me to go through it once instead of having to repeat the story." Some story. He'd come close to dying. The thought of reliving those moments in the raging fire again did not appeal to him.

"Sure, that makes sense." A boy of about six pulled on Bernadette's shirttail. He sported a big green balloon painted on his cheek. She drew him close to her hip and draped her free hand over his shoulder without looking down.

He tugged on her shirt once more, his eyes big and full of hope. "Bernie, can Rebecca take me to ride the horses again?"

"I'll take you, but first, let me introduce you to your Uncle Brent."

"You mean our fake Uncle Brent. Like you're our fake mom." The older boy who spoke crossed his arms over his chest with exaggerated effort. The lion's mane painted on his face in shades of yellow and gold creased between his eyebrows.

Brent gritted his teeth. He had no time for disrespectful kids and even less for someone who would wound Bernadette.

For a split second, a twinge of pain played on Bernadette's face. Turning, she touched the boy's forearm. "Love doesn't recognize real or fake. If people care about you then they care."

"He doesn't even know my name," the teen spit out the words, meeting Brent's gaze. He read the challenge being issued to him by the lanky youth.

"You're right." Brent swallowed his irritations and followed Bernie's lead by showing compassion. "But I'd like to get to know you."

Bernie stepped aside so Brent had a full view of all the children. "This young man is Duncan." She squeezed the little boy's shoulder next to her. "This tall young woman is Rebecca. She will be finishing middle school this year." She pointed to a lean girl with straight black hair.

"Nice to meet you." Brent smiled at the shy young teen.

"Simon is new to our home. He joined our foster family last week. He's eleven."

"Twelve," he corrected. "Geeze."

It took every fiber in his being not to yank Simon by the shoulders and make him apologize to Bernie. The kid in the middle lifted his hand and waved. "I'm Noah. So, you're Uncle Brent. What's it like being a firefighter and a soldier? Did you get to shoot a gun? Have you gone to other countries on secret missions? Have you ever saved someone from a fire?"

Brent's heart stuttered at the last question, but before he could answer the boy, Bernadette corrected him.

"Noah, what have we said about asking too many questions all at once?" Bernie cut her eyes toward him and grinned. "Let's take Duncan over to the horses, and we can deliver Uncle Brent to the rest of the family as well."

"Yes ma'am," he answered, his tone flat like a pancake.

Brent chuckled at the irony. She'd done the same exact thing when she'd first seen him, pelting him with questions. "And this little cutie?" He leaned over, so he was eye to eye with the girl in Bernadette's arms.

"This is Lani. She's two and rather fussy. Her molars are coming in." Bernadette hugged her closer. "There's been a lot of crying and not much sleep, if you know what I mean."

Brent followed Bernadette and her brood of foster kids to the corral scanning the area for people he might know. He hoped to avoid any encounters like the one he'd experienced with the gas station clerk earlier. She hadn't meant anything by it, but her startled expression along with her "What happened to you?" question had fueled his fears about seeing his family today.

Lost in thought, he missed the fact Bernadette had stopped short.

Motioning with her free hand, Bernadette whispered, "Squat down."

"What?" he asked, confused by her instructions.

Nailing him with a stern glare, she said, "Just do it."

Not wanting to incur the anger of the red head, he folded his long frame behind Bernadette. She gathered Noah, Rebecca, and Duncan close to her, creating a wall. Stretching her arm around the other kids, she snatched Simon's sleeve and pulled him next to Noah.

"Hey honey." Brent recognized the low timber of his brother Wade's voice. "I see you guys found the face painting tent."

"We found something else as well," Bernadette teased. "Or rather someone else."

With a quick movement, she stepped aside to reveal his presence. Brent straightened, allowing a smile to spread across his lips.

"Well, knock me over with a feather and tickle me pink." Wade chuckled and stepped forward to embrace Brent. Thumping his back, Wade pushed him forward, holding him by his shoulders. His eyes lingered on Brent's scars that showed above his neckline.

Brent fought the urge to touch the crinkled skin. "I can knock you over, but I'm not sure about the pink part." He laughed hoping to distract Wade from the peach and red patches.

"Man, it is so good to see you. I had hoped you'd come with John for a visit."

"Actually, it's not a visit," Brent said.

From somewhere behind him, Dan yelled, "It can't

be. Is that my littlest brother?"

Brent turned to find Dan jogging toward him, holding his cowboy hat in place on top of his head as his long legs ate up the distance between them.

"Dan the Man." Brent took a few steps forward to greet his eldest brother.

"I told Wade you'd come." Dan grabbed Brent and whisked him into a tight bear hug that ended with another thump on his back. His brother let go of him, joy shining from his eyes. "It's so good to see you. Wade and I were wondering if you'd tag along with John. How long are you here for?"

"He was getting to that part when you interrupted." Wade glanced at Dan.

Dan tilted his head in Wade's direction. "If you stick around long enough, you'll find he's as bossy as ever."

Brent laughed. Relief flooded through him. His brothers were the same. The same loyal men who stood with him when their parents were killed. The same loyal men who encouraged him when he went into the military, and the same loyal men who supported his decision to stay in the military as a firefighter.

"I thought the oldest sibling was supposed to be the bossy one," Bernadette snickered. "How come the middle child is the bossy one with you guys?"

"Because he was always the one who came up with a plan and dared us to execute it. He led us on more missions—" Dan made air quotes, "then I can count. Besides, one of us needed to be the sensible one, and that'd be me." Dan pointed to his chest with his thumb as a smile crinkled the corners of his eyes. "So, how long are you here for, little brother?"

Chapter Two

Monday morning, Maggie Kemp Bishop struggled to slide open the door on one of the three glass display cases that held a variety of mouthwatering treats in Sweet Things Bakery. She'd been the manager and head baker in her brother Tyler's business for the last three years and had complained more than once about this particular door, but Tyler never seemed to have the time to fix it.

Blowing a strand of her curly brunette hair out of her eyes, she balanced the warm metal tray of cookies between her mitten-covered hand and her left knee. With her other hand, she rattled the case door to force it to move. "For the love of Pete," she mumbled.

The bell above the door rang. Without glancing up, she greeted the customer. "Be right with you." Squatting, she wrapped her hand tighter around the handle letting the edge of the tray lay tilted across her knee while holding the other end in her mitted hand. *They'll just have to wait.*

Giving a firm yank, the door on the antiquated piece of equipment slammed back against its twin on the other end of the case, pulling her along with it. Juggling the warm tray of cookies, she tumbled backwards, losing her grip. Almost in slow-motion, the tray and all its contents flew into the air. From her squatting position, Maggie lunged forward, trying to save her morning's work.

Cookies with pumpkin faces artfully iced on them dropped to the ground like dead leaves in the fall. When she tried to catch the wayward tray, the broken cookies acted like marbles sending her feet in every direction but the right one.

The tray banged against the tile floor, but she couldn't stop her forward motion. Arms whirling, Maggie's left foot landed squarely on the tin tray, sending her sailing to the ground.

Out of nowhere, two strong arms caught her from behind under her shoulders.

"Here, let me help." The customer pulled her to a standing position and turned her toward him, holding her close. "Are you all right?"

"I think so." With her hands resting on his chest, she glanced over her shoulder at the mess on the floor. "Thank you." She took a step back then turned her attention to her tall rescuer.

The instant she looked into the man's eyes she recognized him. Brent Parker Thibodeaux, her junior high crush, her brother's best friend. She'd know those misty green eyes anywhere.

A grin eased across her lips as heat crept up the back of her neck. *Of all the days for him to step into this bakery.*

"Brent, when did you get back into town?" The last she'd heard he was still in the military. The haircut and firm chest under her hands gave weight to that notion. Plus, she had insider information as part of the Bible

Babes. "Nikki didn't mention you were coming home to visit."

"She didn't know. A friend and I rode our motorcycles into town Saturday during the Harvest Festival." He frowned, but he didn't let go of her. Tilting his head, he studied her. Her cheeks warmed under his scrutiny. "I saw you outside on the sidewalk, handing out cupcakes."

Her heart kicked up a notch. "Oh, that was you. I didn't recognize you with the helmet on," she teased. *Like you don't recognize me, now*. But of course, he wouldn't. She'd been fourteen the last time he'd seen her right before he left for Texas A&M and the ROTC program.

She pressed her hand against his taut frame. Boy, a lot had changed in the last fifteen years.

A smile grew on his lips at her touch. "So, you know my sister-in-law, Nikki. I suppose you know Bernadette, too."

"I do. They're both part of the Bible Babes. We meet out at Silver Spur ranch every month." She lifted her hand to his left cheek, amused by the confusion on his face.

The instant her hand settled on the curve of his jaw she could feel the crags of uneven skin. A spark flared in his eyes. Reaching up, he moved her hand away from the red splotches.

"Don't tell me you don't know who I am," she prodded, trying to resurrect the lightheartedness that had been prevalent moments ago.

He shook his head as a boyish grin lifted one corner of his lips. "Nope, I'm afraid I don't, but if it counts, I'd like to get to know you." A twinkle played in his eye.

Relief rushed through her as she played along, her momentary discomfort passing. "You only say that because I'm a mystery to you."

"I like mysteries."

"If you knew who I was, you'd think twice about that offer." Most men turned tail once they found out she was a mom, but she'd let herself enjoy this moment of flirting with an old crush. As silly as it was, at least one of her teenage daydreams had come true. She'd adored him, but he thought of her as a pest—a chatterbox.

Brent chuckled. "I'm not so sure about that. I'm not easily scared off. Taking a risk has always been in my wheelhouse."

"Um, I'm a pretty big risk." She tightened her hold on his arms and toyed with the idea of giving her rescuer a peck on the cheek.

Before she could, the kitchen doors swung open. "Hey, when did you get into town?" Tyler Kemp blurted out as he spotted Brent and Maggie, standing only inches apart with Brent's arms around her.

Maggie groaned. Tyler the ever-protective big brother.

Stopping short, he glared at Brent then at the mess on the floor. "What on earth happened here?" Scowling, he crossed his arms over his chest. "And why are you holding my sister?"

Brent let go so fast Maggie struggled to keep her footing and grabbed the counter to regain her balance. "Maggie? Little Magpie? It can't be."

Maggie watched as all the bravado and flirting evaporated.

Looking past her to Tyler, Brent said, "I didn't know. She was falling and needed help."

"Oh, I see." Tyler grinned. "That explains why the cookies are on the floor but not the part about my sister."

Maggie, embarrassed by Tyler's behavior, cut into her brother's prying. "No, the reason the cookies are on the floor is because you refuse to do anything about that stupid door." She pointed to the display case. Walking around Brent, she moved through the mess to go fetch the broom and the dustpan from the kitchen. Careful not to slip again, she maneuvered her way through the crumbled cookies and smeared icing.

Brent shrugged. "I didn't know that was Magpie. I thought she was happily married and living somewhere in California."

"She was. It's a long story," Tyler said.

Maggie pressed her lips together to keep from commenting. Happily married, another interrupted daydream. *And we know that all things work together for good to those who love God, to those who are called according to His purpose.* How she had clung to that verse three years ago when her world turned upside down. When she'd lost Ted.

"I'm sorry. I thought she was a clerk." Brent glanced her way.

Maggie rolled her eyes then stepped over the pumpkin shaped cookies splayed on the floor near the end of the counter. That's all any woman wanted to hear, a man apologizing for saving her.

"No problem, man." Tyler moved toward one of the two tables, near the floor-length windows at the front of the shop. "She's changed a lot since the last time you saw her."

Brent followed Tyler's lead and took a seat at the small round table. "Yes, she has."

Maggie stopped at the kitchen doors, fed up with feeling invisible. "I'm standing right here, people. And Brent—" She glanced over her shoulder, surprised to find a twinkle still in his eyes when he met her gaze. "Don't call me Magpie."

She'd been crazy about Brent Thibodeaux, but he hadn't given her the time of day. He'd considered her nothing more than his friend's little sister. The four-year age gap between them had seemed as large as the Pacific Ocean, but now, the difference had dried up and vanished with the years. With the warmth of his touch still lingering on her arms, she allowed herself one last glance at her old crush before retrieving the broom.

~

To the best of his ability, Brent tried to pay attention as Tyler Kemp, his business partner, went over last quarter's numbers for the bakery. After all, the man was briefing him on his next career move, but no matter how hard Brent tried, he couldn't concentrate.

Too distracted by his encounter with Maggie to follow what Tyler was explaining, he stuck his legs into the walkway and crossed them at the ankles, letting his gaze drift over the layout of the bakery.

Two glass cases full of cookies, cakes, and cupcakes decorated for Halloween stood anchored close to the back of the store. The order counter sat between them and held an electronic pad for receiving payments. A set of swinging doors hung to the left of the counters, leading into the kitchen. A third glass case ran the length of the adjacent wall and held a variety of Danish, donuts, and other pastries. The bakery even offered a small selection of gluten-free sweets for those who couldn't eat regular flour. A coffee bar separated the front area from the back, giving customers a place to prep their coffee without holding up the line at the register.

Brent sat in a hard wrought iron, ornate chair. His body spilled over in uncomfortable places, making him aware of his long legs and muscular frame. Tucking his knees beneath the dainty table that looked as if it were knit from lace and not made of metal, he bumped the edge. The slight tremor shook the napkin holder sitting on the plexiglass surface. Wincing, he rubbed his knee.

Six wrought-iron tables covered with plexiglass sat scattered throughout the front near the full-length windows. All of them ringed with tiny, antiquated chairs like his. The place hadn't changed much since Brent hung out at the shop as a teen.

Maggie entered the room, leaving the doors swinging in her wake. She carried a broom and a dustpan, mumbling something under her breath. Tyler stopped talking and watched her work.

Brent followed her movements. He couldn't believe the beauty he held earlier was Tyler's little sister. A grin crept across his lips as he remembered the lanky teen with freckles and braces who chased after them, wanting to be a part of whatever they were doing. Unlike the old bakery, Magnolia had changed considerably and for the better. Heat flared on his cheeks.

The soft curved lines of her body no longer resembled those of a teen but rather those of a mature woman. She'd turned into quite a beauty.

She must've felt him staring because in the middle of a broom stroke, she stopped and frowned at him. Her expression told Brent all he needed to know. The brunette with curly tendrils framing her face wanted nothing to do with him. He'd blown his chances with her before he'd ever started. Not that he would've pursued her— after all she was Magpie, the chatter bug. Tyler's little sister, a strictly hands-off situation.

Rolling her eyes, she turned from him and finished cleaning up the mess behind the counter. Done, she walked back through the doors to the kitchen, holding the full dustpan. Not a word passed her lips.

Once Maggie disappeared into the kitchen, Tyler picked up where he had left off. "I know I should be making a bigger profit, but it seems the more business we get the more it costs to keep up." He shifted in his seat, keeping his voice low. "I hate that I don't have better news to tell you."

"I knew when I bought half of this business it was more about the welfare of the town than about making money. What's a town without a local bakery, right?"

Brent glanced toward the kitchen then straightened and leaned over the plexiglass top closer to Tyler. "It's just that I saw Maggie giving away cupcakes at the Harvest Festival. Is that prudent right now?"

Tyler shook his head. "I understand your concerns, which brings me to the real reason I wanted to meet with you in person before the wedding." Tyler rubbed the back of his neck— a tale-tale sign he had bad news.

"Spit it out. I'm a big boy. I can take it." Brent chuckled, trying to relieve the tension radiating from his friend.

"Well, with me getting married..." Tyler leaned his

elbow on the table and cupped his chin in his hand. Worry played across his features.

"I can't believe Nadine finally convinced you to propose." Brent jested, confused by Tyler's demeanor. "Seriously, congratulations, man." Brent hoped his friend knew how happy he was for him. "You guys make a great team. Have you set a date, yet?"

"Nadine wanted a Christmas wedding, so we settled on Christmas Eve." Tyler rubbed his neck again. "You see, the fact is we're not only getting married, but we've also decided to move to Atlanta and start our own graphics design business. We figured with my business experience and her design talent it'd be crazy for us not to try. That's why I wrote to you about selling my share of the bakery."

"Oh." Understanding washed over Brent. "I see." Brent leaned back in the small uncomfortable chair, churning over this new information. After a moment, he asked, "So, when were you thinking of selling?"

"We're not moving until after the new year. We still have a few details to work out, like where we're going to live." Tyler chuckled. "So, I'd like to get the bakery side of things wrapped up as soon as possible. The money would be a big help in determining our housing options."

Brent ran his hand down his jawline. He'd been praying about his next steps since the accident, aware his time in the Army's fire brigade was over. Now with his medical discharge in hand, maybe this was his answer. He could take over the bakery and use his business marketing degree Pops Harris had encouraged him to get. "You know this could be a good thing." He leaned forward. "It'll take me some time to get the money together. I don't have a lump sum laying around, but I'll have my accountants working on it. We should be able to make it happen by the end of November. Will that work?"

Tyler grimaced. "That's not what I wanted to discuss with you. There's something else I need to tell you." He snatched a glance at the kitchen door then drew closer to Brent, their elbows almost touching like two little boys up to mischief. "I already have someone who wants to buy my half of the business."

"That does put a new twist on things." Brent stroked his left jawline, aware of the scars. He'd thought this was a new opportunity, that he and Tyler could run the bakery together. There'd be no more silent partnership, but he didn't know if he wanted to take on someone new. What if they clashed, or had different ideas of how to drive the business? "Would this buyer of yours consider backing out?" Brent shifted to keep the metal chair from cutting into his legs.

"No, I'm certain they won't. They've had their eye on the bakery for a while." Tyler shook his head and released a long sigh. "That's why I'm telling you now. I don't want you to agree to anything without all the facts."

"Maybe if I talked with him, he might consider investing in something else." Brent wanted this to work, not only so he could be near his family, but also for Tyler's sake as well. His friend needed the money for his own new beginning. "I mean as the silent partner shouldn't I have been approached with the offer before anyone else?"

"First, let me stop you there. The *he* you're talking about— is a *she*," Tyler corrected. "Maggie's the one who wants to buy my half of the business. She'd be your new partner."

"Maggie?" Brent motioned with his thumb toward the kitchen doors. *Magpie would be his new partner.* He blinked, taking in this fact.

"Yeah, when she moved back from California three years ago, I hired her as shop manager and my head baker. Maggie's been through culinary school and man can the woman bake. She needed a job." Tyler shrugged. "She's my little sister. I had to help after all she'd been through."

"So, you felt the need to offer her your half of the business?"

"Actually, it was part of the deal she made with me when I hired her that I'd give her first crack at buying me out." Tyler shrugged. "So, I agreed if and when the time ever came, she'd be the first to know. Who knew it'd be so soon?"

"So, she wants to own half of the bakery?"

"Actually, she wants to own all of it." Tyler squirmed in his seat.

"What do you mean?" Brent straightened. So far, this conversation hadn't gone in the direction he had anticipated, at all.

"Maggie doesn't know you're a silent partner in the business. She thinks she's buying the whole thing, lock, stock, and barrel."

"Then you'll need to set her straight. I already have a few marketing ideas to help move the shop to a place where it's making more of a profit." *Which would include not giving away the merchandise for free and changing out these ridiculous chairs.* "I made some plans of my own for this place, and if we're going to be working together, she needs to hear what's on the agenda."

"I haven't said anything yet because she's still trying to come up with the capital." Tyler shook his head. "I'm not sure she'll be able to raise it in time."

"So, I'm the backup plan?" Brent asked.

Tyler shrugged. "She's worked her fingers to the bone the last three years, making this place into the success that it is. Without her, we wouldn't even be breaking even. She's the reason most folks come to Sweet Things."

"Maybe, I should talk to her. Let her know she doesn't have to worry that we'll work things out together if I should have to buy your part," Brent offered.

"Nope, not going to work. She doesn't know about you, remember?" Tyler sighed. "And I haven't discussed other options with her—if she can't come up with the funds."

"Well, I guess it's time for you to tell her about me, Tyler, so, we can come up with a plan together."

"I know. I know." Tyler leaned back, holding his hands up in surrender. "It never seems like the right time."

"Then, find the right time." Brent tapped his chest with his thumb. "Or I will." He stood to go, causing the legs of the hideous chair to scrape against the white tile.

"Wait a minute, will you? I have an idea." Tyler motioned to the seat Brent had vacated. "Maybe there's another way to break this to her gently. Hear me out."

"Gently?" Brent repeated the word, doubtful. He didn't want to arrive on the scene charging in and taking over, but he needed everyone on the same page, which included Maggie. Brent crossed his arms and widened his stance. He'd hear Tyler out, then make the call. "What exactly do you have in mind?"

Chapter Three

Why had he agreed to Tyler's crazy plan? One minute he was standing firm on his principles, and the next Tyler handed him an apron with the Sweet Things logo on it and told him to report for work Friday afternoon.

"This way," Tyler said. "You can start on the weekend shift and give Maggie time to warm up to you, get reacquainted, before I tell her you're going to be her new partner. Once we see how things go, I'll move you to full time, weekdays." A smile spread across Tyler's face and spilled into his eyes. "Besides, it'll give you a chance to see how the two of you work together. You might not want to do so after you spend a little time mixing dough and cleaning the glass cases."

He'd agreed to the outrageous plan even though his gut told him it would end in disaster. Brent hated dealing in deception, but Tyler had begged for a little more time while he figured out how to tell his sister about their business arrangement. Now, seeing his family's reaction to his predicament, he feared he should've listened to his gut.

Dan laughed and slapped his thigh. "That's one of the funniest things I've heard in a long time. Being hired at your own company." He wiped the tears from his eyes. "How do you get yourself into these situations?" Dan shook his head, plunking down his glass beside his bowl of warm homemade vegetable soup.

"Remember, not a word to Maggie until Tyler has time to tell her about me." Brent gave his sister-in-law a sideways glance as he lifted the soup spoon to his lips, wishing he hadn't shared so openly about his position at the bakery.

"That's going to be hard," Nikki said. "I'll see her next week at the Bible Babes meeting. You know I hate keeping secrets from my prayer buddies."

Rod Carson, the manager of Silver Spur Ranch, and John McAllister, Brent's friend and the ranch's newest hire, snorted and guffawed at Brent's predicament.

"Reminds me of that TV show *Undercover Boss*," John said as the laughter slowed. "I can see you now. A fake wig, a goatee, wearing a tie-dyed tee-shirt with a bandana around your head." Another round of chortles made the loop around the kitchen table.

Nikki, who sat between her three-year-old twins, Danielle and David, at the end of the table pressed her lips together. "That is a bit much. Maybe as an undercover boss, you can learn a few of the hidden secrets, like how much vanilla Maggie puts into the butter cream frosting." She chuckled while righting an overturned sippy cup.

"So, you won a coveted position on the weekend shift?" Dan asked.

"What do you mean?" Brent shifted in his seat, ready to move the spotlight from the crazy image John had conjured up in his mind to something more solid. He'd worked weekends all his adult life. The Army didn't take the weekends off. Military life trained him to accept his assignment whatever it might be, especially on the fire brigade.

"It's the least desirable shift given to teenagers and older employees with grown children." Nikki's eyes softened as she met his glance. "You'll do fine. Maggie is one of the sweetest women I know. She's changed a lot since she and Matt returned to Orange Blossom a couple of years ago."

Brent frowned. He hadn't heard Maggie or Tyler mention her husband being in the picture. For some reason, he'd gotten the impression she was no longer married. She hadn't been wearing a ring, a fact he hadn't missed. "Who is Matt?"

"Oh, I thought you knew. Maggie has a little boy named Matthew, but everybody calls him Matt. He's the most precious thing. Well," she glanced at her own children. "Besides our two." She rumpled her son's hair as he took another bite from his sandwich.

"Momma more juice, peas," Danielle asked, holding her sippy cup out by the handle with one small hand.

Brent pushed back his chair from the oval table that seated eight. "I'll get it for you, little lady." He moved across the kitchen to the refrigerator. "So, Maggie has a son."

"Yeah, when she returned to Orange Blossom about three years ago, she was expecting. The Blossom Bible Babes adopted her into our group. We worked to provide some much-needed encouragement since she was on her own with no husband. Plus, we gathered the necessary supplies for when the baby arrived."

"That was nice of you gals," Rod said. "It's never easy when you lose a spouse."

"We did what we could. My two were babies at the time, so I had firsthand experience that being a mom was a lot of hard work, and I had help from a proud dad. I can't imagine doing this alone." She smiled at Danielle who squirmed in her seat, waiting for her juice. "So, we pitched in and did what we could. Bernadette gave her a baby shower, and her Aunt Marilyn helped find her a place to live."

"Why didn't she stay with Tyler?" Handing Danielle her sippy cup, Brent slid back into his seat glad the spotlight had swung away from him and his new "undercover" boss-employee position.

"She didn't think it would be fair to make Tyler take on the responsibility for her and Matt. Besides, she needed her own space to sort out a few personal issues." Nikki pushed back in her chair, lending an air of finality to her words.

"I know the feeling." John leaned his elbow on the table, propping his chin on his fisted hand. "I've lived on someone else's property for my entire life. First my parents, then the Army, and now here. I understand why Maggie didn't want to stay with her brother. Sometimes a body just needs some breathing room, to do what you want without requiring someone else's permission. Shoot, I'm close to fifty and haven't ever had my own place." His brows furrowed as he squinted at Nikki. "Who'd you say helped Maggie find a place?'

"Her aunt, Marilyn Kemp. She's a realtor with William Keys Realtors in Orange Blossom. They manage several of the properties throughout Reseda

County."

Dan met John's gaze. "What? Our bunkhouse doesn't meet your standards?" He joked with the older man.

"No, your outfit is fine, real fine, but just because I'm single doesn't mean I can't have a little slice of Texas heaven for myself." A twinkle glistened in John's eye. "You wouldn't want to be greedy now, would you? Besides, I've been considering getting my own place for a while."

"I couldn't agree with you more. Every man needs a little land, a little lady, and a little one to add to his joy." Dan waggled his eyebrows, catching Nikki's attention.

She blushed a sweet shade of pink. Turning to John, she said, "I'll find her card for you. There's one stuck in a file somewhere in the office. Stop back later this evening, and I'll have it for you." Wiping the mayonnaise from David's cheek, she lifted him out of his booster seat. The little boy ran straight around the corner where a couple of barks and a yelp sounded. "Don't let Blue out of the mud room," she yelled after him. Glancing toward Dan, she said, "I swear he loves that dog more than either one of us."

Dan grinned. "We can't fault him for it. If not for Blue, who knows if we would've ever met." He rose and circled the table to where Nikki sat. Bracing his hand on the table, he leaned over and kissed her cheek. "After all, if we hadn't met, David and Danielle wouldn't be around. So, in a way, they owe him."

Nikki leaned back and lifted her face to Dan. Her husband brushed her lips with his. "That would've been a shame, but we owe our meeting more to the Lord's timing than to a pup."

"I don't know about that. God can use anything to accomplish his will. Look at Balaam and his talking donkey Pastor Connor mentioned last Sunday."

"Well, if Blue starts talking, I'll be sure to let you know." Nikki patted Dan's hand.

Regret washed over Brent while he watched the scene play out before him, a family in motion. He'd missed so much over the years, like Nikki and Dan's wedding and the birth of his niece and nephew. He'd been overseas for those events. Worse though, in his early years, he'd missed saying good-bye to Pops Harris because of his Officer's Basic Course.

A lump formed in his throat at the thought of the man who'd taken him under his wing after his parents' death. His stomach lurched, causing his appetite to wane. "I need to get ready for work." Standing, he grabbed his bowl of soup and the plate that held the remnants of his sandwich and carried them to the sink.

"Yeah, we need to get back to it, as well," Dan said.

The other two men at the table took their cue and rose to their feet. Rod snatched the half of sandwich still sitting on his plate and wrapped it in a napkin to take with him.

Dan stopped at the hat rack on the kitchen wall near the back door. Grabbing his cowboy hat, he perched it on his head. Turning, he met Brent's gaze. A broad, toothy smile spread across his face. "Don't forget your wig and goatee." He chuckled and strolled out the back door followed by the other two men.

Rod hesitated at the threshold, catching ahold of the doorknob. "And that tie-dyed shirt. I'm sure no one will recognize you Mr. Undercover Bossman." Rod chortled as he closed the door with a thud.

Brent groaned. *What had he gotten himself into?*

Maggie bit her tongue when Brent helped a woman in her late twenties who was obviously more interested in him than she was in the cookies in the display case. "So, these don't have peanuts?" She pressed her fingertip against the glass.

"Right. They have macadamia nuts but no peanuts." Brent rested his forearms on the top of the case and clasped his hands together. Meeting the woman's twinkling gaze, he gave her a half-grin.

Maggie could see the exchange through the glass of the third display case where she knelt cleaning the bottom shelf. She recognized the boyish, rugged half-grin, the one that used to make her teen heart do somersaults. No more of that nonsense. As far as she was concerned, Brent Thibodeaux was enemy number one, waltzing in here trying to buy her beloved bakery right out from under her nose. Why else would he be here?

She'd tolerated his presence over the last week, but what had her brother been thinking? That traitor. She rolled her eyes and swiped the damp rag over the white metal. *It's not like he needs the money. And so far, this was the third woman today who flirted with him.*

"I'm asking because I'm allergic to peanuts, and I'm planning to go to the movies tomorrow night to see *Ticket to Paradise* with a few of my friends." The brunette pushed a strand of her long hair behind her ear, a coy smile playing on her lips. "We agreed to meet at the Peabody Theater around seven, and I'd hate to miss it."

Could she be more obvious? Maggie shook her head.

"Sounds like fun. I'm sure you'll enjoy it." Straightening, he added, "How many cookies would you like?" He swung open the case door and picked up the tongs. At least, Brent had made himself useful and fixed the display door.

The woman ignored his question. "I heard Julia Roberts is wonderful in it, and who doesn't like George Clooney? Several of the ladies in my office say they have real chemistry. That's so important whether on the movie screen or in real life. Wouldn't you agree?" A light shade of pink crept onto her cheeks as she fluttered her eyelashes.

Maggie snickered, the empty case magnifying the sound.

The woman scowled at her through the glass as if she were a cream cheese Danish gone bad.

"Did you want three or four?" Brent pulled one of the small white paper bags from the basket sitting on top of the case. "You can't go wrong with macadamia and white chocolate. I hear it's one of our baker's specialties."

Turning, the woman smiled at Brent. "Four please. I told the ladies at the office I'd share. I work at Cane and Bailey Law, right around the corner on Pine."

"Oh, I know Bill Cane. He handles our family legal business from time to time." Brent walked to the electronic tablet set up to act as the cash register and rang up the order. "Cash or card?"

"Card," the woman answered as she pulled a small leather card holder from her pocket. "You should stop by and say hello. I know Bill would love to see you."

"Maybe I will." Brent took the card and touched it on the screen. The machine beeped. "Do you want an emailed receipt or print."

The stylish brunette hesitated. "E-mail, please. It preserves our trees."

Rather it gives her a reason to give him her contact information. Maggie rose and lifted one of the decorative cake plates, moving it back into the now pristine case, while keeping one eye on the vulture circling Brent. A bang rang out as she hit the glass stem against the metal. Pushing down her irritation, she slowed her movements and checked to make sure the plate hadn't been damaged.

The woman rattled off her email as Brent tapped it into the tablet. "FlyRobinFly@ gmail.net."

Brent chuckled. "I take it you're Robin."

"Yes, Robin Tate." She extended her hand over the counter between them. Brent took it, giving her arm a pump.

Maggie thought she might lose her lunch. Even the woman's email oozed cuteness.

"Nice to meet you, Robin. I'm Brent Thibodeaux." He handed her the bag with the cookies.

"Yes, I know who you are." Taking the bag, she flipped her hair over her shoulder. "I saw you ride into town on your motorcycle during the Harvest Festival. Nice bike, by the way." She turned and sashayed to the door, letting the cookie bag dangle from her hand. Pushing the glass door open with her hip, she wiggled her fingers with their perfectly painted nails at Brent. "See ya soon."

The door swung close. "Not if I see you first,"

Maggie muttered and picked up the spray bottle filled with cleaner from the top of the case.

"Why'd you say that?" Brent asked.

"Do I really need to explain to you the facts of life?" Maggie pushed past him and slammed her hip against the kitchen doors sending them swinging open. Irritation rushed through her. There was no way Mr. Flirty Pants could understand what the bakery meant to her. It was more than a livelihood for her and Matt. She believed it to be part of God's plan. He'd used it to rescue her when she was drowning in grief.

Brent followed her into the kitchen. "Why are you so angry that Robin introduced herself? From what she said, it sounds like she could become a regular customer. Has she ever been in the shop before?"

"No," Maggie admitted before kneeling to place the bottle of cleaner on the rack beneath the large sink. Using the sink's edge, she pulled herself back to standing, putting her toe-to-toe with Brent. The scent of his woodsy musk drifted around her, causing her heart to skip a beat.

"Who knows? Maybe me being here will draw in some new customers. Isn't that a good thing? After all, Tyler said you guys are barely keeping up with payroll."

Aha, she had him. "Why would Tyler tell you about the business?" Maggie crossed her arms and took a step back, willing her treacherous heart to behave itself.

From the moment her brother told her about hiring Brent, her mind twisted into a tangle of worry, curiosity, and suspicion.

Brent's eyes widened, "He ... he wanted my

opinion on some of the marketing tactics. Since I have a degree in business marketing and finance. Remember, I wasn't in the military all my life, just most of it."

His knee-weakening half-grin reappeared along with a small dimple on his right cheek. His left cheek wore a peachy splotch where the dimples mate had once resided. "Oh, I'd forgotten about your time at Texas A&M." She hoped his opinion was all Tyler wanted from Brent. Surely her brother wouldn't sell to someone else without giving her the opportunity to find the money, though she had no idea where to begin the hunt. Even with the insurance money left from Ted's accident, she didn't have enough to purchase Sweet Things.

Scowling at the thought, she moved to one of the three silver metal tables that stood in the center of the open space. Lights hung above the tables bathing them in warm, bright light. Kristen Hall, her dear friend and one of the two other bakers who worked in the shop, stood at one of the tables cutting out turkey-shaped cookies. "Hey Brent, hand me one of those trays." She nodded toward the shelf beneath the table nearest him.

"Sure." He knelt and pulled out one of the trays, handing it to Kristen.

Maggie grabbed the mitts from the table in front of her, stuffing her hands inside. Mumbling, she walked to the stack of three free-standing ovens.

"What's wrong with her?" Kristen asked Brent. "She's been testy all week."

"I heard that. Nothing's wrong with me." Opening the oven, she slid out the pan full of pilgrim-shaped sugar cookies and carried it to one of the racks to cool. She needed to decorate them before putting them out in the morning. As shop manager and head baker, she still had a specialty order to fill and inventory to take before she called it a day.

Sliding the pan into place, she snatched off the mitts and tossed them onto the counter next to the ovens. "Shouldn't you be out front?" She asked Brent, who stood staring at her, his dark green eyes filled with concern.

"Yes, but I didn't want to leave without resolving whatever is bothering you." Brent bent his chin to his chest and met her gaze. "So, what's this about? Because if I didn't know better, I'd say you were a little bit jealous." His eyebrows rose as he bit back a grin.

"Oh brother," she scoffed. "Of course you would. Leave it to a man to make it all about him." She wanted to take the words back the instant they left her lips.

Hurt played on Brent's face before his jaw tightened. "Fine. You're not jealous. What is it then?"

"Honestly, I can't figure out why you're here." Maggie propped her hand on her hip.

"I'm here to work." Brent crossed his arms over the bright green apron that hugged his broad chest.

"So, you've said." But it was all the things he didn't say that bugged her. "Why on earth would a billionaire need to work? What do you think, Kristen?"

"I think it's time for me to go home. I'll put these cuties in the oven. Will you take them out in about twenty-five minutes?" Kristen whisked the pan of turkey-shaped cookies to the oven and slipped them in, then set the timer. "Are you working tomorrow, Brent?"

"If I still have a job after this conversation." He glanced toward Maggie, widening his stance.

She shifted her weight and let her hands drop to her

sides, trying to remain calm. The fact her brother had so little faith in her ability to gather the funds grated on her last nerve. That had to be the reason for Brent Thibodeaux's presence. He wanted to learn the ins and outs of running the bakery, so when she failed, Tyler would have a second choice in place.

Kristen hustled to the coat rack by the back door that led to the alley and grabbed her purse. Slipping the strap over her head, she let the small pouch hang across her body. Facing Brent, she said, "Good luck and may the force be with you." She formed a V sign from *Star Trek* with her fingers and darted out the door.

Brent chuckled. "She has her movies mixed up."

"Yeah, she does." Maggie laughed, letting the tension of the moment drain from her. "I'm sorry I put you on the spot with Kristen. That was unfair. I'm sure if Tyler told you about our numbers, then he's also told you he wants to sell Sweet Things."

Brent cast his gaze to the floor. "Yeah, he told me. He and Nadine want to start a graphics design business in Atlanta."

"I'm happy for them, but that leaves things up in the air for me. I want to buy the bakery. It's what I've dreamed of my whole life." Maggie sighed. "In truth, it's always been more my dream than Tyler's, but I'm not sure how I'll come up with the capital. I have some of it, but …"

"I didn't know you loved to cook and that owning a bakery was a dream of yours. It surprised me when Tyler told me you moved to California to go to culinary school."

"Don't you remember all those nights you ate over at our house and we served dessert?" Maggie let the memories from the past sweep into her mind. The cute boy who hung out with Tyler and let her play video games with them. The one who stood up for her against Hank Potts, the middle school bully. "Who do you think made them?"

"I assumed your mom did." Brent tilted his head, studying her. "I guess there are a lot of things I assumed at eighteen which turned out to be wrong." A light flickered in his eyes.

Maggie's heart raced. "That does tend to be the case. We make assumptions and then later discover they were wrong." A picture of Ted dropped unbidden into her thoughts. She'd expected they'd be together forever, but that hadn't been God's plan. No, instead a helicopter accident during a training session took him without warning—shattering their future.

She cleared her throat wanting her words to sound lighter and less accusatory. "So, let me be blunt Mr. Thibodeaux. Are you here to learn the business, so you can buy Sweet Things, or do you have other undisclosed motives?" She forced a smile onto her lips, dreading his answer.

Brent's Adam's apple bobbed. "If at all possible, your brother wants to sell to you. He's firm on the point. I'm here because I need a job, or should I say, a purpose. Your brother has given me an opportunity to make myself useful, to help get the shop to a place where it's making a clear-cut profit."

Maggie frowned. He hadn't really answered her question.

Brent stepped closer to her. "So, let me ask you a question. What are your plans for obtaining the money for the purchase of the shop?"

"Well, I don't have a *plan* per se, at least not yet." Maggie hated sounding so unprofessional. Hesitating, she added, "I have money put back, but I'm thirty thousand short of Tyler's asking price."

"Oh, that's not so much."

Maggie bit her lip. Sure, to him, a billionaire with connections, thirty thousand probably sounded like loose change, but to her, Tyler might as well be asking for all of Fort Knox.

"Can I make a suggestion?" The right side of Brent's lip pulled into a smile.

"Sure, why not?" She shrugged one shoulder, willing to hear him out.

"Put me to use. I've bought and sold several businesses, and I'm pretty good at drawing up a business proposal to present to a bank or an investor."

Maggie swallowed the guilt, rising in her. Here she thought of Brent as an interloper, a Judas of sorts trying to horn in on her precious bakery, and now, he stood there offering to help her. "Wow, you'd do that for me?"

"Of course, but we will need to get the shop on better footing. Barely getting by won't help to secure the financing you need." Brent closed the distance between them and placed his hands on her shoulders. "We're going to need to show any potential investors they can make a profit."

She tensed under his touch, little prickles skittering across her skin. Her emotions warred within her. Every time she looked at him, she saw her teen crush, the boy who had rescued her from a middle school bully.

But he was no boy, and she had no clue about the man who stood before her. Fifteen years lay between then and now. Could she trust him?

"What do you say, Magpie? Let me help you grab your dream."

Chapter Four

Brent had replayed his conversation with Maggie a thousand times over the last few days. How he'd gotten himself into such a fix, promising his competition he'd help her win the big prize—the bakery—was beyond him.

If truth be known, he felt pretty sure guilt had played a big part. He hated keeping the truth from her. She needed to know he was a partner, that she couldn't own the whole bakery, but Tyler hadn't told her yet, and waiting to tell her no longer worked for him. Torn between his friend, and Maggie, Brent struggled to do the right thing. Hearing the door open, he pushed these thoughts aside to tend to the customer.

"What can I get you, John?" Brent asked as he scooted one of the chairs under the empty table before giving the top a swipe.

"I heard you had a carrot cake that would put Paula Dean to shame." John strolled to the counter where the cakes were displayed and pointed to the desired dessert that sported several little carrot-shaped decorations.

Brent finished arranging the chairs around the two empty tables before hustling behind the counter to get John's order. For a Wednesday afternoon, the shop hummed with a steady stream of customers. "Anything else? How about a cup of coffee to go with it?"

"Sounds good but make it two of both, the coffee and the cake."

Eyes wide, Brent smirked. "Oh, you must have a hot date. You big spender," Brent joked. "Anyone I know?" He leaned over and pulled two slices of the cake from the case, placing them on the white ceramic plates.

John lifted his chin. "It's not a date. It's business. Nikki gave me the number for Maggie's aunt who's a realtor. She suggested we meet here to discuss my options and talk about what I'm looking for in a home. She's the one who recommended the cake."

"Oh," Brent straightened. "I didn't realize how serious you were the other day about getting your own place."

"I'm dead serious." An easy smile touched his lips. "I've been living with other people so long I'm not sure how I'll fare in my own company."

Brent turned to the coffee dispensers behind him. He'd found working at the bakery also included learning a thing or two about being a barista. Filling the white mugs, he asked, "Want any creamer or sugar?" He slid the mugs onto the counter in front of John.

"I'd better take some of both. I'm not sure what Marilyn will be in the mood for." John struggled to get his hands wrapped around everything.

"Leave the mugs," Brent offered. "I'll bring them to the table for you along with a variety of sweeteners and some flavored creamers from the coffee bar."

"Thanks." John walked to the free-standing coffee bar where the napkins, silverware, and coffee paraphernalia were kept and grabbed a wad of napkins. Picking up the plates, he carried them to the table Brent had cleaned. "This should be good."

Brent deposited the mugs onto the plexiglass then realized John didn't have any silverware. Shaking his head, he returned to the free-standing counter and got two plastic forks. *Boy, John must be rattled.* As an Army major acting as the primary staff officer for the logistics task force, his job had been to make sure everybody had what they needed. John never forgot anything when it came to being prepared.

"So, are you nervous about this meeting?" Brent asked.

John ran his hand down his face before planting his chin on his fist. "Yeah, you could say I'm a bit nervous." John plopped back against the small white chair. "It's one thing to take orders and make do with what you're given, but now, I have a chance to decide what I'd like to have in a home."

Pulling out one of the other chairs, Brent took a seat. "So, what do you want? A ranch? A condo? Shoot, you could even get one of those tiny houses and be able to make the bed while scrambling your eggs."

John chuckled. "Could you imagine me in a house that size? I'd have to fold in half to fit."

"No, I couldn't, but it shows you the number of options that are available out there."

"Yeah, maybe too many." John sighed.

Shrugging, Brent stood. "I guess you'll have to narrow it down."

"That's what I'm hoping Marilyn can help me do. Narrow it down to one." John picked up a plain creamer and added it to his mug then used the handle of his fork to stir the brown liquid. "I forgot the spoons."

"Don't worry. I'll get them for you." Brent retraced his steps to the condiment bar and grabbed two spoons. Just then, the bell above the door jingled, and Marilyn Kemp, Maggie's aunt, stepped across the threshold, wearing a dark yellow pants suit which matched her bottle blond hair she'd pulled back into a loose bun.

Marilyn scanned the dining area. The instant she spotted John her bright red lips lifted into a smile. Brent chuckled. John had no clue what was about to hit him.

As Marilyn strolled across the tile, her three-inch heels clacked against the hard surface as the expensive-looking leather satchel she carried swung in time with her movements. Her demeaner oozed professionalism.

Brent shook his head as she passed him. His friend sat at the table wearing a short-sleeved tee shirt with the Harley Davidson logo on it, a pair of dusty jeans, and a bandana wrapped around his curly salt and pepper hair.

When John saw her, he rose to greet her.

Never had Brent seen two people so different from one another. Scowling, Brent wondered if they could work together to find John the house he wanted. From what he knew about Marilyn, it'd take a miracle, since wardrobe wasn't the only difference between these two.

His brother, Dan, had met Marilyn years earlier. She'd been the one to help him find a rental house after Hurricane Harvey. At the time, he'd described her as flirty, self-absorbed, and way over the top. Dan had stopped short of calling her a barracuda, but barely.

Brent's experience with the woman hadn't been much better. Though he'd been a teen at the time, he vividly remembered her ability to commandeer any and all conversations when attending family functions at the

Kemp household, making sure the chats pivoted back to her favorite topic — her.

But Nikki swore to him she'd changed. The Marilyn of old was no more. She'd grown in the Lord, and everyone considered her a valued member of their Bible study group, The Bible Babes. Brent wanted to believe Nikki for John's sake, but he'd have to see it for himself.

"Good afternoon," Marilyn stuck out her hand to shake John's. "You must be John McAllister, I'm Marilyn Kemp."

John gave her petite hand a firm pump. "Nice to meet you. I appreciate you coming today." Moving around the table, he pulled out the seat across from his own.

A smile lit Marilyn's face. "Oh, thank you." She scooted into the chair and plopped her satchel into the empty one next to her. "I'm so glad you called me. Nikki gave you a glowing report. She went on and on about how well you've taken to your new position at the ranch." Marilyn rested her crossed arms on the table and leaned in close. "Seems you've made quite the impression on everyone at Silver Spur Ranch."

Brent could've sworn he saw his friend blush under her praise. He headed over to place the spoons he'd retrieved on the table. "Good afternoon, Marilyn. How are you doing today?"

"Well, Brent Thibodeaux. My, how you've changed since the last time I saw you. You were nothing but a gangly teen, then. I heard through the grapevine you'd started working here at Sweet Things." Marilyn leaned back in her chair to meet his gaze. "I thought for sure the rumors had to be wrong."

"Nope, it's true." Brent plastered a smile on his face and reminded himself she was here to help his friend.

"For the life of me, I couldn't fathom why on earth you'd want to work, here, or anywhere for that matter. There's so much you could do with your money." She gave him an innocent look. "And time."

Brent's muscles tightened. Did Marilyn know about his interest in the bakery? That he acted as a silent partner? He couldn't imagine under what circumstances Tyler would've told his aunt but not his sister. He'd never considered others might know about their arrangement.

He needed to talk to Tyler and urge him to tell Maggie before someone else beat him to the punch. If Maggie found out about his partnership in the business, she'd look at his offer to help her as some sort of ploy. Which it wasn't. Nothing would make him happier than seeing Magpie's dream come true. His concern centered on how she'd feel about having him as her partner.

The bell above the door jangled pulling his attention back to business. Brent glanced over his shoulder and saw a group of women gather around the case with the cupcakes. "I better go see what they need." Turning to his friend, he said, "Good luck."

Brent hurried to the group of ladies but couldn't keep his mind on the task. Once he'd finished with their orders, he hurried back to the front dining area to check on the progress of the couple looking at the sample book of wedding cakes.

"Did you find anything you liked?" Brent asked the couple, half listening to the conversation going on behind him at John's table. He let his glance drift in that direction and discovered Marilyn laughing as she cut into her piece of cake for another bite.

The couple stood and handed Brent the book of glossy pictures.

"She does such wonderful work," said the woman.

"But we're meeting with another caterer on Friday." The young man gave the woman a sideways glance. "Can you tell Maggie we'll let her know once we make a decision?"

"Sure can," Brent added, "Again, she's sorry she couldn't be here today. A family emergency."

"Tell her we hope little Matt gets to feeling better," the young woman said.

"I will." Brent placed the book on the table and watched the couple step out onto the sidewalk. Pushing the chairs back in place, he homed in on the exchange going on beside him.

"So, you're looking for at least a three bedroom," Marilyn said.

"I believe so." John furrowed his brow. "I guess that's why I need your help. I'm still not a hundred percent sure about all the details, but there are some aspects I'm firm on when it comes to a house."

"And what would those be?" Marilyn opened her pad of paper and fished out a pen from her satchel.

"For starters, I don't want a new build. I want something that has been lived in and seen some life. A house with a bit of character. Maybe a couple of trees in the yard."

"Okay, no new builds. Something with character and age." She jotted down some notes.

"And I want a piece of land. Nothing like the ranch, mind you, but a little elbow room. I want something that can change as I change. A place where I can grow old without having to move to somewhere different."

"Got it." Marilyn's pen scribbled across the page. "Elbow room. A place you can grow old with."

"Well, eventually grow old." John grinned, causing the corners of his eyes to crinkle. "I plan on living a full life here in Orange Blossom. They say fifty-five is the new forty."

Marilyn peeked over her paper and returned his smile. "Of course, a man, like you, has a long life ahead of him." She pursed her red lips. "Do you mind if I ask you a personal question?"

Brent froze. *Don't do it*. He curbed the urge to jump into the conversation to save his friend from a grave mistake. The Marilyn of old could use any scrap of information against her prey, even the most innocuous tidbit. He wanted to scream stop, but Nikki's voice played in his head, reassuring him Marilyn had changed.

"No, go ahead," John said.

"What led you to retire from the Army at this point in your life?"

John glanced down at the mug on the table, hesitating before answering. "I got injured on duty and messed up my knee. It left me with a slight limp and the choice of retiring or taking a medical discharge. With more than twenty years in my pocket, I opted to retire." John lifted his cup to his lips and sipped his coffee. "Best decision I ever made."

"So, you're happy here in our little Texas town?" Marilyn laid her pen down and pulled her mug close, wrapping both hands around it. "We do have a lot to offer. You saw our Harvest Festival. Wait until you see Christmas. We deck the whole town out with wreaths, window displays in all the shops, and even the light posts receive tinsel decorations in the shape of snowflakes or sprigs of holly. During that time of year, the town glows." Marilyn's voice filled with childlike wonder then she sighed. "Christmas is spectacular here in Orange Blossom."

Brent scowled. This didn't seem like the Marilyn he'd known.

"You sound proud of your town." John chuckled. "I can't wait to see it at Christmas. You make it sound like a wonderland without the snow and ice or the need for tire chains."

Marilyn laughed. "I am proud of our little town. It's changed a lot over the years since I've been a realtor, and some of the changes have been for the better."

"Then I'm glad I've moved here." John leaned forward, drawing closer to Marilyn.

Their eyes met and for a moment, Brent couldn't tell if this was a business meeting or a date. He frowned, picking up the wedding cake album.

"Speaking of moving, let's see if I've jotted everything down, so I can narrow our potential prospects when I get back to the office. Then we can pick a day to go look at the houses that make the cut." Marilyn set her cup beside her empty plate and picked up her note pad. "You want something with age and character, that you can grow old with, that has some elbow room, but not too much."

"Yeah, something that fits me and will compliment my lifestyle. Nothing fancy, but something warm and inviting. A real gem."

"Warm and inviting." Marilyn scribbled the words on her pad. "It'll be my job to make sure it's a gem."

Brent's eyes widened as he listened to Marilyn read over John's list. Turning, he found the pair leaning toward one another across the plexiglass on the small metal table. They looked so comfortable. Unable to resist having a little fun with his friend, he asked, "You know what your list sounds like to me, don't you?"

John straightened, and Marilyn looked up from her notes.

"No, what?" John asked.

They both stared, waiting for his answer.

"Like a list for a potential wife."

John's brow furrowed, then a slow smile spread across his lips. "I guess it does sound like a list of qualities for a wife. Hmm, I've never thought of it that way. I suppose finding a house and finding a wife are similar. They're both big commitments." John's gaze landed on Marilyn and a slight twinkle danced in them.

Brent shook his head. Apparently, the man was smitten.

Marilyn, to her credit, blushed. "Well, I can only help you with a house," she said, but the pink in her cheeks made a different statement. Standing, she retrieved her satchel from the other chair, tucking her note pad and pen in the side pocket. Meeting John's gaze, she said, "I'll call you once I narrow down the listings. "Without a word to Brent, she hurried to the exit with her three-inch high heels clicking on the tile as she retreated.

Brent smirked. He'd never seen Marilyn Kemp flustered, let alone embarrassed. *Would wonders never cease?*

~

Maggie closed her eyes and tried to pray along with Nikki.

"Father, direct our discussion this evening and teach us more about your Son and You," Nikki said.

Amens floated out from the circle of women gathered for the Blossom Bible Babe meeting at Silver Spur ranch.

Maggie blinked her heavy eyelids. Matt had kept her up crying with an earache last night, and she'd spent the bulk of the day at the pediatrician's office verifying it was, in fact, another ear infection. Doc Patterson gave her the prescriptions needed, but this was Matt's third ear infection in the last six months. The doctor recommended putting in tubes. She couldn't bear the thought of her little man having surgery, but she didn't like seeing him in pain either.

Plus, the expense. Of course, she'd do anything for him, but how would she ever afford to buy Sweet Things Bakery if she struggled to handle the normal emergencies of life?

Sighing, Maggie forced her mind to focus on Nikki as the hostess's gaze drifted around the circle of ladies sitting in her living room. "First, I want to thank all of you for coming this evening. I know it's difficult for some of us to get away from our other responsibilities, but our time together in the Word of God is worth it."

"I wasn't sure Wade could handle all the kids alone. Since we've added two new faces to our crew this month, it's been harder to keep the peace." Bernadette sagged into the winged back chair. "I'm grateful Wade loves the kids as much as I do. We both feel like the Lord led us into this ministry."

"Fostering kids is definitely a ministry." Purdy Thomas, the sixty-something secretary of Cowboy Community Church, nodded. "You and Wade are making a difference."

Maggie admired both Bernadette and Wade. She barely mustered the strength to handle one two-year-old, and they'd taken on five kids of varying ages and abilities. How they did it, she had no idea. She squirmed on the soft sofa, stifling a yawn.

Nikki picked up her Bible and notebook. "Last time we discussed Ruth and her faithfulness to Naomi. This month I wanted to discuss God's faithfulness to the two women. Did everyone finish the chapters in Ruth?"

"There weren't that many," Marilyn remarked as she flipped the pages of her Bible.

"True, but what a message." Regan Perez, a Reseda County Sherrif's deputy and the newest member of the Bible Babes, grinned. "I found myself wondering how I'd handle picking up everything and moving to a place I'd never seen. I couldn't do it."

Maggie remembered how difficult the move had been for her when she'd decided to leave California and come back to Orange Blossom. She'd been three months pregnant with Matt and barely showing. Leaving behind the home she'd shared with Ted rated as one of the hardest things she'd ever done. The guilt of starting a new life without him still haunted her.

Marilyn glanced up. "As a realtor, I meet the bulk of the people who move into our area, and you're right, most of them do come visit the town and do some research online before moving here. Today I met someone who came sight unseen to Orange Blossom. And he said he's glad he moved here."

"I couldn't do it." Sarah Thomas, Purdy's granddaughter, said. "I couldn't move without checking out the new town first."

"Hence all the college visits." A sadness settled in Purdy's eyes.

Maggie couldn't imagine the struggle Purdy was having letting go of her eldest grandchild.

"Grams, you know this is all part of my plan. First the internship, to make sure being a vet is what I want, then off to one of the four-year colleges with the curriculum I'm looking for." Sarah sat on the floor, her back propped against the oversized cushion leaning against the wall with her legs stretched out in front of her. "I have to move away to get the degree I want."

"I know, I know. But it doesn't mean I have to be happy about it." Purdy blinked several times before swiping under her eyes.

"Aww, Grams. We have time before I go. I'm not leaving until next fall." Sarah sat up and slipped her hand over her grandmother's.

Nikki reached over to the coffee table and pulled out two tissues from a box sitting near her. She handed them to Purdy who dabbed away the tears.

"I agree with you ladies. Ruth was brave to follow Naomi into a strange land, but she trusted the God of Naomi, who became her God." Nikki pulled on the bookmark in her Bible and let the pages fall open to the Book of Ruth. "Tonight, I want to point out God's wonderful provision for these two women. When they had no means of providing for themselves, the Lord sent Ruth into the fields of Boaz, a near kinsman of her deceased father-in-law, to walk behind the harvesters, gathering what grain they left for the poor."

"I love that it said, 'As it happened,' when it referred to Ruth choosing to harvest grain in Boaz's fields." Sarah giggled. "And then Boaz *just happens* to come in from Bethlehem. God is so good. He sent her to a man who was kind and would help her."

Maggie squirmed again trying to keep her focus on the discussion. "And to someone who would keep her safe." The unbidden thought of her late husband, Theodore Bishop, flooded into her mind. He'd kept her safe, providing love and encouragement. She missed being part of a partnership, the feeling of working and planning together to build a life.

Now, everything seemed empty. She understood why Naomi wanted to be called Mara. Life tasted bitter when the one you loved with your whole heart died. Her one bright spot was her son. Even when she was worn out, she treasured her little boy.

"Yes, God provided Ruth a safe place to gather grain, which allowed her to provide food and money for the care of Naomi. Even better than that, God gave them a permanent place of safety and provision through Boaz, as their kinsman redeemer."

"A redeemer like Jesus, our redeemer." Bernadette tucked her foot under her in the chair.

"We all need a redeemer," Purdy said. "Someone to pay the price we can't pay."

JoJo Meyers, who worked at *The Daily Blossom*, threw her hands into the air. "Amen, sister. I know I do."

Maggie frowned. She knew they were speaking about salvation through Jesus and the fact he'd paid the price no one could pay for their sins, but needing someone to pay for what she couldn't struck too close to home tonight. A picture of Brent wearing a bright green apron popped into her brain.

Annoyed, she leaned forward in her seat, trying to dislodge the image. She still hadn't figured out a way to purchase Sweet Things Bakery, and she couldn't fathom having it sold to someone else right out from under her.

She didn't accept Brent's excuse about being there to help with the marketing, at least not all of it. Plus, his appearance at the bakery seemed too convenient. Straightening her Bible on her lap, she tried to focus on the discussion going on around her, but the image of Brent, smiling his boyish grin and handing some blond a cupcake consumed her thoughts.

An hour later, the meeting broke up. Maggie lingered, wanting to talk with Nikki. She trusted her to keep her concerns confidential. She needed some good advice and well … prayer.

Once everyone had said their goodbyes, Nikki invited Maggie into the kitchen for a cup of herbal tea. "I'd offer you coffee, but it keeps me up if I drink it after four in the afternoon. You'd think with twins nothing would rob me of my sleep." She chuckled as she pulled down a canister and placed a kettle on one of the eyes of the stove.

Maggie slid into one of the chairs at the oval table. "Thanks for letting me stay to talk. I know you've got tons of other things to do."

"Nonsense. I'm happy to help if I can." Nikki held out the canister to her. "Which flavor would you like?"

Taking the white canister, she chose a red

raspberry zinger she loved and handed it along with the canister back to Nikki.

"So, what's on your mind?" Nikki selected a flavor and placed a tea bag into each mug sitting next to the stove. Leaning her back against the counter, she faced Maggie.

Maggie pursed her lips, considering where to start. "You may have heard that Tyler wants to sell the business."

"Yeah, Brent mentioned it." Nikki's gaze fell to the floor.

"I thought he might've. But what you may not know is I'd like to buy it."

"That doesn't surprise me. I know how much you love baking and owning the shop would be wonderful source of security for you and Matt. Plus, you and Tyler put a lot of energy and time into building up your reputation in the community." Nikki turned when she heard the whistle of the kettle. Pouring the water into the mugs, she pulled two spoons out of a drawer. "Honey or sugar?"

"Honey, please," Maggie answered, wondering how to get to the point of her concerns.

Nikki picked up a small plastic bear that held the golden liquid and put all the items on a small tray which she carried to the table. Sitting in the chair across from Maggie, Nikki gave her one of the mugs with a spoon in it and the plastic honey bear. "It would be odd if you didn't want to keep the business."

"I'd love to keep it, but I have no idea how to get the financing I'd need to buy out Tyler. It wouldn't be fair to him and Nadine for me to ask for a payment plan with them. They'll need the money from the sale to start their graphic design business in Atlanta." Maggie wrapped her fingers around the mug letting the warmth soak into her hands. "I can't ask them to put their dream on hold while I pursue my own."

"No, that wouldn't be fair." Nikki stirred her tea. Her brow furrowed. "How much do you need? I don't mean to be nosey."

"It's all right. I asked for advice. You should know the state of things. I have most of the money, but I need thirty thousand more to meet his asking price. It would cover Tyler's initial investment in equipment, renovations, and inventory. Then I'd take over the rent for the building and all the utilities." Maggie bit her bottom lip. "I'm hoping what comes in each month at the bakery would cover those items and replenish the stock and of course, payroll."

Nikki kept her gaze on her mug. "Have you spoken to Tyler about wanting to buy him out?"

"I have, but he won't commit." Maggie pushed her tea mug out of the way and crossed her arms on the table. "He won't give me a straight answer. Tyler's worried I'm getting myself in over my head, and to be honest, he's right. Buying the bakery would wipe out my savings and what's left of Ted's insurance money. Who would want to lend money to a single mom with no collateral?"

"The shop is collateral." Nikki reached over and patted Maggie's arm. "God has a plan. Remember, I worked two part-time jobs to make ends meet. I understand what you mean about no savings and no security. Compared to me, you're way ahead of the curve."

"I know I should be grateful, but I can't help

wondering what's going to happen if Tyler sells to someone else." Maggie ran her finger around the rim of her mug and swiped a drop of honey from it. "What if we clash or they want to make changes I don't agree with? Even worse, what if they want to replace me?"

Nikki studied her friend's face for a full ten seconds, making Maggie nervous. Shrugging, Nikki said, "Maybe you need a partner right now. Have you thought of that? Someone who can pull the load when you have a crisis on your hands."

"What do you mean?" Maggie crossed her arms on the table in front of her, trying to guard against this thought.

"You know … like when Matt is sick, or your parents need help. Or for that matter, when you're the one needing help. I'm simply saying a partner doesn't have to be a bad thing. You might find having one rather useful." Nikki drained the last drops of her tea from the mug. "Look at Naomi. At the beginning of the book, she can only see one way to solve the problem, and she's so unsure of the outcome she tries to send her daughters-in-law back to their people."

"Yeah, so?" Maggie tilted her head, waiting to see where Nikki would go with this line of thinking.

"So, God proved her wrong. He had a completely different plan for both Ruth and Naomi. A good plan. One much better than they could've hoped or imagined." Leaning forward and squeezing Maggie's hand, Nikki added, "God has a plan for you, too. Just lean into it."

Maggie sighed. Her friend was right as usual. She needed to trust that if God wanted her to buy Tyler's business, he'd provide a way. Then without warning, the earlier image of Brent drifted into her mind. He had offered to help her write up a business proposal. Maybe Brent was her Boaz. Maybe God sent him to help her find the funding. After all, he had a degree in this stuff, and his family did business with half of the state of Texas.

A smile crept across her lips as she warmed up to the idea. Yeah, Brent Thibodeaux could be exactly what she needed. Someone to help with her business proposal, so she'd start out on the right foot. But partner? Why had Nikki chosen that word?

Chapter Five

Maggie moved the green and black dinosaur out of the way with her foot. Balancing Matt on her hip, she unlocked the bolt on the front door and swung it wide. Her mom, Libby Kemp, entered the small rental house carrying her purse and a plastic bag stuffed with goodies from the supermarket around the corner. Maggie shut the door behind her.

Libby tossed her purse and the grocery bag onto the couch. "Hey there. How's my little man?" She held out both her hands, and Matt slid toward her.

"He's doing better, now that the antibiotics have kicked into gear. We both got some much-needed sleep last night."

"Oh, I'm so glad to hear that. He needs his rest if he's going to get better soon." Libby applied an abundance of kisses to her grandson's chubby cheeks. "Grandma wants you well for the holidays," she baby talked.

"Gand Gand," Matt squealed, delight radiating from his eyes.

"Oh, my sweetie." Libby squeezed Matt to her, placing her cheek next to his. "Isn't he brilliant?"

Maggie stifled a groan as a hint of a smile

emerged. Her mother and father insisted on being called Grandma and Granddad two very hard names for a two-year-old. Of course, they were thrilled with any attempt, even if his rendition sounded more like 'Gandolf' the name of the wizard from *Lord of the Rings* than grandma.

"Come on Gand-Gand. Let's unload your bag in the kitchen." Picking up the grocery bag, Maggie walked around the small half wall that separated the living room and dining room which she used as Matt's playroom. It held a changing table, a toy box so full it overflowed, and a hard plastic climbing fort with a short slide attached. Passing through the cluttered area, she entered the kitchen. "Don't mind the dirty dishes or the pots on the stove."

"I know I taught you better." Libby shook her head and gave Maggie a sour look.

"By the time I get home from the bakery, I barely have time to bathe Matt and fix dinner. I don't have time to have a spotless house, too. I'd rather spend my time with Matt. He won't be little, long." At least that's what everyone kept telling her.

"No, you're right. You need to spend what time you have at home being a mom. The house can wait." Libby slipped Matt into his highchair and gave him the chunky, soft plastic train sitting on the kitchen table in front of him. "There you go."

"Tank you." Matt squeezed the toy to his chest. "Choo-choo." He ran the engine across the tray.

"The Cheerios are on the bottom shelf in the upper cabinet, and his bowl is in the dishwasher." Maggie pointed, tamping down her feelings about the state of her home. "I do appreciate this, Mom. The daycare doesn't allow anyone who's been ill to return until after they've been fever free for twenty-four hours."

"No problem sweetheart, I've got this." Libby pulled a can of chicken noodle soup out of the plastic store bag, placing it in the only empty spot on the counter. "You know if I could, I'd watch Matty every day, but Dad and I both need our jobs, even if mine is part-time."

"At least you're lucky you've both been able to have jobs you love."

"Blessed like you. You're able to do what you love." Libby emptied the grocery bag. Opening the door beneath the sink, she tossed the bag into the garbage.

At least she'd taken out the trash last night. Glancing at the clock on the microwave above the stove, Maggie straightened and moved to the doorway. She needed to change, or she'd be late.

Libby glanced at the clock as well. "I know you need to get to the bakery, but I wanted to ask about your hunt for a bridesmaid's dress. How is it going? Are you having any trouble finding the color Nadine wants to use?"

Maggie grimaced. "I haven't had the chance to look for a dress yet, but the color shouldn't be an issue. It's a Christmas Eve wedding, so there should be plenty of nice red knee length dresses to choose from out there."

Libby frowned and stopped stacking the dishes in the sink. "It's not any red. It's a true Christmas red. You know bright and cheery like Rudolph's nose."

"I know, Mom. Bright and cheery. Got it." Maggie heard the impatience in her tone and pressed her lips together to keep from adding anything else to the sharp remark. The hurt expression that crossed her mother's face pinged her conscience.

"I only want Tyler and Nadine's wedding to be as lovely and wonderful as your and Ted's. That's all."

Guilt swelled inside Maggie's chest. Thanks to her family, her wedding day had exceeded all her hopes, and it was due in large part to her mother's efforts.

"I'm sorry." Maggie moved toward Libby with her arms open wide and pulled her in for a quick hug. Taking hold of her hand, Maggie stepped back and met her mother's gaze. "The color isn't my problem. It's just that I'm not ready to let go of the money yet. I might need it for other … things." Like full ownership of the bakery. A dress or a bakery? Maggie shrugged, yet another loose end dangling in the wind of her life. "I'll be sure to buy the dress in plenty of time for the wedding."

Libby smiled and squeezed her hand. "I'm sure you will but be certain to get it early enough to be altered if needed."

Looking past her mother at the microwave clock, Maggie said, "I do need to hustle if I'm going to be on time. And as you pointed out, I need all my pennies for a dress." Maggie squeezed her mom's hand one last time.

"Fine, fine." Libby turned and opened the utensil drawer.

Just as Maggie turned to leave, her mom spoke up, "So, who opened for you this morning?"

Maggie stopped. Taking a deep breath, she walked back to the doorway. "Ranita and Brent. Ranita's a morning person, so she didn't mind starting the pastries. Today, though, we have a catering order for the

Methodist Women's Thanksgiving Luncheon for a hundred cupcakes. She'll need help to finish them in time." Maggie hoped her mother would catch her meaning.

"Oh, that's good. A nice big order for the bakery." Her mother leaned her head into the dishwasher to fish out Matt's favorite dinosaur bowl before reaching up into the cabinet to retrieve the Cheerios. "Did you say Brent opened this morning?"

"Yeah, I figured since he insists on working at Sweet Things, I might as well treat him like any other employee." Maggie stood in the doorway, summoning her patience. After all, her mother was doing her a favor.

"Don't you find it strange Brent came to work at Sweet Things around the same time your brother announced he's going to sell? I mean it's not like the man needs the job. I'm sure the Thibodeaux family owns Silver Spur Ranch, free and clear along with several other properties. Unlike your dad and I, who still have a year and half before our mortgage is paid off."

"I agree it's strange, but he's not there to buy the business. If he were, why would he offer to help me write a business proposal, so I—" Maggie's eyes grew wide.

Her mother froze. Turning toward her, she met Maggie's gaze. "A business proposal? Are you wanting to buy the bakery?"

"I had considered it." She crossed her arms, leaning against the door-jamb, giving up on leaving any time soon. Her mother wouldn't take this news well. "It makes sense I'd want to own the bakery, doesn't it? I mean it's been my dream."

Pity crept into her mother's eyes. "Honey, how in the world are you going to swing something like that? With a toddler growing out of his clothes every two seconds and rent you're barely making ends meet. Maybe Tyler will let you pay in installments."

"No, I don't want him putting his life with Nadine on hold for me." Maggie shook her head. "It wouldn't be fair to them."

"Well, I'm sure if you talked it over with Tyler, he'd work out something with you." Her mother rinsed the bowl and dried it before pouring in the small round pieces of cereal.

"Mom, I'm not going to do that. I'd rather see if Brent can help through some of his channels. He told me he's written numerous business proposals and has received several over the years. He knows what he's doing."

"Even in the Army?"

Maggie chuckled. "Even in the Army. Apparently, serving your country doesn't make you exempt from doing business." Straightening, she stood to her full height. "So, are we good?"

"Yeah, we're good."

"Great." Turning, Maggie stepped into the play area, but not before her mother added, "Still it doesn't make sense why Brent would want to work at Sweet Things."

"I know, but Tyler wants him there."

"Mark my words. If you're not careful, Brent Thibodeaux may be your new boss." A glint shone in her mother's eyes. "It could be worse, though. At least, he's nice-looking." A playful grin spread across

Libby's lips. "If you have to work for someone, why not someone rich with rugged good looks, right?"

"Mother." Maggie scolded heat sweeping up the back of her neck. She'd never heard her mom talk about any man that way. For a minute, she sounded like her Aunt Marilyn. Who was this woman masquerading as her mother?

"You'd better get going," Her mother set the dinosaur bowl filled with Cheerios in front of Matt. "We wouldn't want the Methodist Women's Thanksgiving Luncheon to miss out on your famous cupcakes."

Maggie squeezed past Ranita who stood behind one of the counters of the bakery helping a group of customers. Leaning over, Maggie stashed her purse and grabbed a clean apron from the pile in the cubby under the counter. She'd left hers at home in the dryer in her mad dash to be on time.

Pulling the loop of the green apron over her head, she wrapped the strings around her waist and tied it in the front. The Sweet Things logo, a white wedding cake surrounded by other delicious treats centered in a large pink heart, decorated the bib of the apron. She forced a smile onto her face and moved to the adjoining counter to help the next customer.

"What can I get for you today?" While she waited for the middle-aged construction worker with tattoos on her arms to place her order, Maggie scanned the seating area looking for Brent.

She'd come through the back-alley entrance through the kitchen and hadn't seen him. He should be helping with the cupcakes for the luncheon. Where could he be? Didn't he realize Ranita needed help?

Before she could locate him, the sound of his laugh rose above the clamor of the customers waiting in line. She spotted him seated at the far table with his back to her, talking with Curtis Wagner, the advertising manager for *The Daily Blossom*, the local newspaper.

"I'll take two of your blueberry scones and four of your banana muffins." The lady in the orange vest pointed to the muffins in front of her. "And I'd better get six coffees black, and would you throw in some of those little creamers? I'd appreciate it. Marvin hates his coffee black." The woman smirked. "He's all tough talk when he's complaining about his supervisor, but give him black coffee and he whines like a baby."

Maggie nodded, keeping her smile in place. She recognized the woman as a repeat customer. She'd been frequenting the bakery ever since construction started on a building a few blocks down on Pine Street. Maggie wanted to make sure she continued to come to the bakery for the construction crew's morning java fix. So she pushed down the impulse to march around the counter and give Brent Thibodeaux an earful.

Grabbing one of the bakery's bags, she snapped it open with a flick of her wrist. Maggie snatched two sheets of white paper out of the box on top of the counter and tossed the blueberry scones into the bag with gusto. Then she repeated the action with the banana muffins. Glancing past the customer, she watched Brent stand and shake Curtis's hand. What nerve! Gabbing with a friend while customers stood waiting. Work hours weren't the time for a reunion, and the instant they were alone, she would make that fact crystal clear.

Brent escorted Curtis to the front door still

chatting, thumping Curtis on the back before opening the door for him. "Thanks for coming, today. I can't wait to see your ideas for the holiday ads. I'm sure they'll be great."

"My pleasure doing business with you." Curtis chuckled, poking a notepad into his shirt pocket. "I'll give you a call as soon as JoJo and I have something to show you."

After placing the six cups of coffee into a couple of to-go holders, Maggie slid the hot beverages toward the woman with the orange construction vest. "Here you go," she said never taking her eyes off Brent. Had she heard Curtis correctly? The words *doing business* clanged in her ears.

"Don't forget the creamer. You don't want Marvin to come get it. He'll make such a scene." The woman shook her head. "What a baby."

Maggie glanced at the customer. "Oh, sure. Sorry." She dug out a handful, tossing them into a separate bag. "Here you are. Have a great day." Maggie broadened her smile.

When Orange Vest moved away from the counter, the next person in line stepped forward. Maggie listened as the young mom gave her order, but she never took her eyes off Brent, who strolled toward the kitchen door with a goofy grin on his face, as if he were pleased with himself.

"I'll go work on those cupcakes," he called to Ranita then pushed against the swinging doors and disappeared behind them.

Maggie couldn't keep her swirling tempest of emotions contained any longer. "I'm sorry. Can you excuse me for a minute? I'll be right back." Again, she forced a smile across her lips before pivoting on her heels and marching toward the kitchen.

Stopping in front of the stainless-steel table where Brent stood stirring the plain white icing, she crossed her arms and glared. "Didn't you notice Ranita was overrun with customers?"

"I know. Isn't it great?" Brent stirred the color into the white frosting turning it tan. "Business has picked up a lot according to Tyler."

"That's not the point."

Brent looked up from his task. "Oh? What is your point?" He placed the bowl he held in his hands onto the tabletop and met her gaze.

"That you were sitting around gabbing with a friend when you should've been helping behind the counter." Maggie pointed over her shoulder toward the front of the store. "You can't ignore the customers. You're an employee now. Not some hotshot billionaire who owns the joint." She pressed her lips together before any of her other fears popped out in her words. For a moment, silence dangled between them.

Brent straightened, a strange look crossing his face, then one of those boyish half-grins appeared to replace it. Maggie frowned, unsure of what had happened.

"You're right, Magpie. I need to be more aware of what's going on in the shop. I'll do better." Brent picked up one of the bags of icing and squished the red clump down to the tip.

This seemed way too easy. Something didn't add up.

Brent pushed the icing through the tip onto a cutting board. The curves of the tip stood out, but he failed to flick his wrist as he moved the tip to make

Tom Turkey's wattle that hung from his neck. His efforts looked more like a red glob then a piece of turkey anatomy.

"Here I'd better do that." She'd decorated hundreds of cupcakes with turkey faces over the span of her baking career. Taking the icing bag from his hands, her fingers brushed against his skin. A tingle danced through her. Surprised, she ducked her head, concentrating on the cutting board in front of her to keep from making eye contact.

Moving the curvy tip across the board in a few short snips, she tested the thickness of the icing and her technique. Ranita had finished the tail feathers as the background. Orange, yellow, and red teardrops flared across the small spaces. She'd also added a brown drop for the faces. All that needed to be added to complete Tom Turkey were the eyes, beak, and wattle.

"I'd better start with the eyes." Maggie picked up the black one sitting ready to use. As she moved around the long table squirting two little dots on each long face of the turkeys, she peeked over at Brent who stood studying her hands.

"You're very good at this." Glancing over at his own attempt, he chuckled. "I guess it's harder than it looks."

She shrugged. "I've been at it a while." Clearing her throat and keeping her gaze locked on the desserts in front of her, she asked, "What did Curtis mean when he said, 'Nice doing business with you'?"

Brent rubbed his hand down the left side of his cheek over his scar. "I asked him to …" He hesitated. "Now, don't get mad."

She lowered the icing bag to the table and scowled.

"What, Brent? Tell me."

"I asked him to work up some ads to run in the paper over the next two weeks until Thanksgiving. I thought we could feature your awesome Dutch apple pie and that creamy pumpkin pie you used to make. I still have dreams about that pie." He grinned.

"The one you thought my mom made. That creamy one?" She planted her fist on her hip.

"Yes," He beamed. "That one."

She could feel the irritation rising in her and fought to keep her tone professional. "Brent, we don't have the money for extra ads. Besides, don't you think you ought to talk to the owner or at least the shop manager before you spend that kind of money?" She shot him a sideways glance before squeezing out the next set of turkey eyes.

Brent pulled to his full height and crossed his arms, his gaze settling on his boots. "I did talk to Tyler yesterday. While you were out taking care of Matt."

Maggie pressed her lips together. She should've known Brent would run it by Tyler. The two were as thick as thieves since Brent started working at the bakery. "I guess I jumped to conclusions. Of course, you talked with Tyler and of course, he okayed it. Why not?"

"Look Maggie, I know you've poured your heart and soul into this bakery for the last three years. I'm not going to do anything to jeopardize your hard work." He moved around the table to her side.

His nearness flustered her. The delicate black dot she intended to make, came out more like a misshaped eyepatch. Putting down the bag of icing, she picked up a small knife and used the tip to remove the blob.

"Magpie," her childhood nickname rang with tenderness, completely disarming her. She turned to him, lifting her eyes to meet his gaze, afraid of what she might find.

The scent of his musk drifted around her as he cupped her shoulders. "You can trust me. I'm going to do everything I can to help you. If we can get the revenue up with a few ads, you'll have a better chance of getting the rest of the funding you need."

Her heart wanted to trust him, but she was no longer a lovesick teen. She wasn't willing to follow him around without question. Maggie had responsibilities, she had Matt. She still didn't trust his intentions. Why would a billionaire be working at a bakery? Why was he so keen on helping her? Searching his eyes, she hunted for the answer.

The calm assurance she found in their depth gave her the peace she needed. "I trust you, Brent. I know you ran the ads to help me." She'd lost her dream of having forever with Ted. She couldn't afford to lose her dream of owning Sweet Things.

Chapter Six

"You have to tell her." Brent squirmed in the folding chair opposite Tyler, who lounged in the large leather chair behind his desk. Shifting, Brent tried to get comfortable on the metal contraption, but like the office, it squeezed in on him. The clatter of the pots and pans in the kitchen told him Maggie and Ranita were still working.

Tyler sprang to the door, peered into the kitchen then closed it. "I know. I know." He sighed, strolling back to his chair that squeaked under his weight.

Brent frowned. He didn't like keeping Maggie in the dark. She already distrusted him. His gut told him the longer they kept his partnership in the business a secret, the harder it would be to make things right with her. That didn't set well with him. "Maggie knows something is up. She keeps asking me why I'm here. I feel like a heel keeping this from her. She has a right to know I might be her partner and that she's only buying half of the business."

"What have you told her?"

"That I needed a purpose and thought I could help you with the financial bottom line— do some advertising and marketing." Brent rolled his shoulders to relieve the tension he'd been carrying all day, ever since his conversation with Maggie. "I told her I wanted to put my degree to use after all this time, and I thought it would be better to start small." All of this was true, but these reasons weren't the complete picture. They were half-truths which meant they were also half-lies. The knot in his stomach tightened, causing him to adjust his position in the chair. Pushing hard against the back, he tried to move it an inch or two so he could stretch out his legs, but the contraption wouldn't budge, thanks to the worn-out brown carpet.

"Speaking of advertisements, I like the idea of having a Crazy Pie Day right before Thanksgiving. Did you meet with Curtis yet?"

"I saw him earlier today. He said he and JoJo would have something worked up for the event along with some other ads by Tuesday." Brent straightened in his seat and leaned his forearms on his knees. "Have you talked to Maggie about the idea of a Crazy Pie Day?"

"No, but I will." Tyler tapped his fingers on the wooden surface of his desk before letting out another long sigh. "I'd better do it this evening before she leaves."

"Yeah, that'd be best." Brent's heart pinged with a hint of guilt. He should be the one to talk to Maggie about both the Crazy Pie Day and his part in the business. After all, both involved him.

"I guess I'm finding it difficult. The Crazy Pie Day won't be so hard but telling her about your interest in the business is going to crush her." Tyler shook his head. "I hate to be the one to kill her dream of owning the business solo, but I don't see how she can swing it without a partner."

"Why don't you let me tell her— about Crazy Pie Day, since it was my idea? We don't need her to find out from the ads in the paper. Especially, since she's the one baking the pies." Brent thought of Tyler as another brother. He'd helped him through one of the toughest points in his life, the year he'd lost his parents in a car accident. But at the moment, his patience with the guy hung by a thread.

Tyler's eyes widened. "No, we don't want that. She'd kill me. I'd literally be dead. Nadine would be a widow before she became a bride."

"Okay, while I'm discussing Crazy Pie Day with her, I can tell her about me. I don't like keeping secrets from her. You said I needed to work here for a while, so she could warm up to me, and I could get to know the staff, and I have. It's time to bring her in on the situation. She needs to know I'm your partner and your backup plan for the bakery."

A flash of remorse glimmered in Tyler's eyes, then a smile bloomed on his lips. "You must admit, my plan is working beautifully. She seems much more comfortable having you around than she did the first week." Tyler tilted his head. A gleam of mischief danced in his eyes. "Another week or two and she won't be so put off at the thought of having you as a partner. She might even like the idea."

"Maybe, but I'm not waiting another week or two. Maggie needs to know now. She's trying to put together the financing to buy this place, and she can't do that without all the facts."

Tyler shook his head. "There's no way she'll ever get enough backing to take on the whole shop." He rubbed his hand across the back of his neck, a habit he repeated often when stressed.

"Then I'd better tell you I've agreed to help her draw up a business proposal. I have some contacts who might be willing to invest in an up-and-coming business with a great bakery chef."

"You've agreed to help her? Have you gone nuts? That means you're in competition for ownership against yourself. Too crazy, bro." Confusion clouded Tyler's face but then it cleared as a glint of understanding shown from his eyes. "Oh, I see. You have a soft spot for my sister."

Brent straightened. "I do not. I mean, no more than I should." He stumbled over his words. "After all she's your sister. We're all friends, and I want to help her." Flustered, Brent stood to leave.

"Look, it's okay if you have a soft spot for her. It'd be weird if you didn't since we were all kids together. You hung out as much with her as you did with me our senior year of high school."

"She did follow us around a lot." Brent chuckled.

"Right, she did." Tyler's smile faded. "I guess I didn't want to overwhelm her. She has a lot on her plate. Maybe, you can approach her with the Crazy Pie Day idea tonight. If she likes it, take the credit and talk it up. Then later next week, we can tell her about you."

Tyler was right. Maggie had a lot going on right now with Matt being sick and her long hours. How she kept all the plates spinning dumbfounded him. From what he'd heard from Nikki and Bernadette, Maggie worked hard to be a great mom, and he admired her strength. Maybe Tyler was right. Maybe now wasn't the best time to spring his partnership in the shop on her.

Then an image of Maggie at fourteen popped into his head. She stood on the steps of the library trembling in front of Henry Potts, the junior high bully, looking vulnerable. No, Brent wouldn't do that to Maggie—take advantage of her by buying the shop. He wouldn't put her in a position of vulnerability. "I'm telling her tonight before she leaves. She deserves to know."

Tyler studied his face. Brent hoped he couldn't read the truth. He did have a soft spot for Maggie, but as Tyler's best friend, he'd have to keep his feelings for her under wraps.

Shrugging, Tyler fell back against the leather chair, surrender written on his face. "Agreed. Now to more important matters. Have you thought about what to do for my bachelor party?" A smile spread across his lips. "You do know that's part of being the best man, right?"

"I am aware of my duties as best man. Don't worry." Brent had been honored when Tyler asked him to stand with him on his big day. Meeting Tyler's gaze, he asked, "So, what did you have in mind? Maybe a little get-together Friday night before your Christmas Eve wedding?" He planted his hands in his pockets. "How about a night out camping like we did our senior year over winter break?"

"Sounds good. You know a couple of fellows hanging out around a campfire, eating whatever junk food we can get our hands on." Tyler beamed. "It'll be nice to see some of the old gang. I heard from Ryan, and he's going to be here the weekend before the wedding to visit his parents."

"That should work then. We'll ask Ryan and Chuck."

"Yeah, Chuck. He's always good for a laugh. The stories he tells." Tyler shook his head.

"Right? And Nadine's brother, Karl," Brent added.

"What about your friend John? You should invite him. It'll give him a chance to get to know those of us who live here a little better."

"Yeah, he'd like to be included. Besides, we need someone who is a little older and wiser to keep us in line." Brent rocked back on his heels, chuckling at the memories racing through his mind of their high school camping trip.

Tyler's face lit up. "But we won't be stealing any road signs this time around, will we?"

A trace of heat rose on Brent's neck. "Correction. Allegedly stole."

Tyler hee-hawed. "I still remember the rush of panic when Sheriff McCain drove by in his cruiser. I thought I'd have a heart attack."

"I know. It scared me to death."

"I've never seen anyone shrink to the size of a steel pole and become invisible the way you did."

"Yeah, and I've never seen anyone dive into a hedge the way the three of you did." Brent chuckled. "I still can't believe I held the sign up where it should've been." Brent crossed his arms and shook his head at the foolishness he'd gotten himself into thanks to his buddies. "It's the only reason I didn't get caught. Well, that and it was dark."

"What did you ever do with the sign?" Tyler asked.

"You know me. I put it back the next morning after everyone went home. No way would I steal something. Not with Pop Harris waiting for me at home." Brent checked the time on his phone. "I guess I'd better get moving if I'm going to catch Maggie before she leaves. She may not be too pleased with me if I don't."

"Why is that?" Tyler asked.

Brent dug in his front pocket and produced a wad of keys. "Found them on the floor near the register. I meant to give them to her earlier, but maybe, this will work out better."

"She can't leave before you talk to her." Tyler rolled his eyes. "So, that's why you volunteered."

"No, but it's a happy coincidence." Brent shrugged.

"You better get going then," Tyler said. "And thanks for helping Maggie. I still think it's nuts, but I appreciate the fact you're willing to put her interest first. That means a lot to me."

The gleam in Tyler's eyes made Brent feel exposed. Moving toward the door, he settled his hand on the knob. "No problem. I want to see her make a success of this place." More than that, he wanted Maggie to have the desires of her heart, the bakery and anything else she may want.

~

"Serves me right. Worrying about other people's business," she mumbled as she took out the spray bottles and paper towels used to clean the windows and the display cases. "Where are you, you little imps?" She ran her hand along the shelf. Nothing.

Maggie dug around in the cubby under the counter below the register, searching for her keys. The contents of her purse had spilled out that morning in her rush to help Ranita, but she'd been too busy being aggravated with Brent to notice.

Pulling her phone from her back pocket, she turned

on the flashlight app. The light flicked bright against the darkness of the store. Everyone had gone except Tyler and Brent. For well over an hour, the two had sat huddled in Tyler's office with the door closed, most likely conspiring together. They were still in there when she'd finished in the kitchen.

She'd considered marching into Tyler's office and planting herself in one of the metal chairs, but what good would that do? He'd left her out of the meeting, even though she was the shop manager. Annoyance and something akin to fear warred within her.

Why did she let Brent get to her? So, he ran a few ideas by Tyler about ads and marketing. That's why he was here, right? It didn't mean he wanted to purchase the bakery. A frown pulled at the corners of her mouth. It didn't mean he wasn't trying to buy the shop either.

"He said he wasn't, so, let it go," she muttered. She worked to take all her thoughts captive and give them to the Lord. Not an easy task for her even on a good day.

Shining the light into the cubby, she scanned the shelf for the keys. Not seeing them, she reached as far back as her arm would go and patted the shelf with her hand while trying to hold her phone with the light in the other. Her search produced some flyers from the recent Harvest Festival, a Tootsie Roll Pop wrapper, and three pennies, but no keys.

"What'cha doing?" Brent's voice boomed in the quiet.

Maggie jumped, bumping her shoulder against the edge of the counter. The surge of pain caused her to fall backward landing on her rear. "Are you trying to give me a heart attack?"

"What are you doing in here in the dark? I know

you're trying to save money, but this is ridiculous." Brent walked to the light switches on the wall by the kitchen doors and flipped the center one. The lights flickered on.

Strolling back to Maggie, he extended his hand to help her up.

"No thank you." She grabbed the edge of the counter to balance herself. In one swift move, she regained her footing, swiping the back of her faded jeans to remove any dust from sitting on the floor. Leaning over, she retrieved her floppy cloth purse and plopped it onto the counter next to the register. "I was looking for my keys. Apparently, my purse toppled over." She gestured to the cubby. "When I got to my car, I couldn't find them."

"And you thought being in the dark would help, how?" Brent's lips lifted into a one-sided smile.

Her heart thudded, but she refused to give it any notice. The blow to her pride still stung from not being included in their little pow-wow. "I didn't want to take the time to turn the lights back on. The fluorescents take so long to heat up. I figured by the time the lights were on enough to help, I'd have found them."

The grin spread across his face drifting into his eyes. "I agree with you. The lights wouldn't have helped you."

"And why is that, exactly?" She planted one hand on her hip and drummed her fingers on the counter.

Brent stuck his hand in his pocket and retrieved a large key ring in the shape of a heart which read *Today is a gift from God*. Her key ring.

"What are you doing with that?" She stopped drumming her finger and nailed him with a glare.

"I found them on the floor." He nodded to the area beneath the register as he dangled the key ring a few inches out of her reach.

She raised an eyebrow. "Thank you. Now, may I have them?" Stepping forward, she lunged at the keys but missed.

Brent palmed them and held them close to his chest. "No, you may not."

Maggie huffed. "What? Are you twelve? I don't have time for a game of keep-away. Give me *my* keys."

He opened his hand, his grin widening.

She lunged forward, but he backed away, holding the key ring above his head.

Frustration filled her. She refused to flirt with the enemy. Okay, maybe not an enemy, but the guy sent mixed messages. One minute he talked about helping her find the funding she needed, the next, he held clandestine meetings with her brother.

Stopping in front of him, she said, "You know my mom is waiting for me at home, right? And I still need to make dinner for Matt?" She rose onto her tiptoes and took a swipe at the keys.

"That's a good point," Brent conceded and lowered his hand. He looked like a deflated balloon. "Here you go. I did want to speak to you about an idea I have for an event."

Maggie snagged the keys from Brent's palm and tucked them into her pocket for safekeeping. How he could act like a kid one minute then talk business the next, baffled her. Three years of single parenthood had planted her feet squarely in adulthood.

"Okay, I'm listening. What's going on?"

"Let's sit down. This might take a minute or two."

Brent headed into the seating area and pulled out a chair for her. The glow from the overhead lights near the display cases bathed him in the soft gray hues of shadows. His six-foot three silhouette towered above the chair.

Maggie slid into the seat, still unwilling to let go of her irritation. "Okay, now that we're seated, what's on your mind?" Her heart quickened at Brent's serious expression when he took the seat across from her. Even in the dim lighting, she could see he struggled to find the words.

"I have something I need to tell you."

The firmness of his jaw didn't help the foreboding that flooded over her. "So, what's so dire? Let me guess. You've changed your mind about helping me." She pressed her lips together, bracing for what he might say.

"I haven't been completely honest with you." Brent grimaced, rubbing his hand across the tabletop before making eye contact.

Her heart pounded, not sure what to expect. "You haven't been honest?" She parroted his words, unsure where this conversation was headed. "What do you mean? Is the business doing worse than Tyler's let on?"

"No." His brow furrowed as he wet his lips. "It's—"

Then a memory returned from earlier in the day. "Look, I saw Curtis here this morning, if that's what you're trying to tell me. You told me you'd talked with Tyler about some advertising ideas." Maggie studied his face. "So, if you think I'm mad because you and Tyler didn't include me, I'm not, okay? But I would like to be included from now on in any decisions, as you move forward with this ad campaign." Maggie rose before he could respond. "I need to get home, but we can talk about your ideas tomorrow and make some decisions." What Maggie really needed was the night to cool her ire before talking over anything with Brent. She feared she'd say something she'd regret if he pressed the point, and she didn't want to make a business decision based on her emotions.

"That's not it. Well, not entirely. One of my ideas was to have a Crazy Pie Day, the Tuesday before Thanksgiving. You know offer a bunch of marked down traditional pies and maybe add one or two specialty pies to the menu. Something creative."

Maggie stiffened. Her posture mimicked a runway model, shoulders back, spine straight, with her head held high. "You want to do what? Have you lost your mind? Do you know how busy it gets that close to Thanksgiving, and now you and my brilliant brother want to add to the madness? No, absolutely not." Crossing her arms, she clucked her tongue. "Crazy Pie Day is right."

"I know it will be a lot of work, but we'll have the whole crew here all week, and the previous week, so you can focus on the pies. We'll take care of the rest."

She shook her head. The workload for the event alone would be daunting, and the days leading up to Thanksgiving were already chaos on skates.

"I believe it'll bring in more business, and the profits will cover the staff's pay for the extra hours."

"Nope, it's too much. We can't handle that volume of customers."

Brent leaned back in his chair. His gaze glued to the table in front of him. "I've already placed the ads for the event. They should start running next week. It'll be in *The Daily Blossom* as well as a couple of local papers in the nearby towns."

Maggie's jaw dropped. Was she hearing right? Tyler, who always passed any big decision about the business by her, had already put this idea into motion without even mentioning it to her? An idea that would require her to work longer hours and come up with new pies … by next week … if she even had the time to experiment with the ingredients before the actual day.

"You … I can't … What were you two thinking?" Anger tied her tongue. Closing her eyes, she pushed down the hurt. What good was it being the manager if her brother kept her in the dark? Whipping around, she marched to the counter and scooped up her purse.

Brent stood, sending the legs of his chair scraping against the floor. "Wait, Maggie. I need to tell you something else."

She stopped, extended her arm and held out her palm. "I've heard all I need to hear. Anything else can wait."

Crossing the space between them, Brent took her by her shoulders and turned her toward him. "Oh, Maggie."

His voice mollified the hurt in an instant. She gazed into his eyes and found them full of compassion. The tears she'd been fighting welled up, blurring her vision. "I don't want to hear any more about how you and Tyler are making plans. I know you're going to buy the bakery. That's what you wanted to tell me, right? And why not?"

"Not exactly," Brent said. "The truth is …" He stammered. "I already own part of the bakery. I've been a silent partner from the time Tyler opened the shop. He needed the capital, and I wanted to help him."

"You what?" Hot tears streamed down her face as all the worry and agitation of the past month came rolling out. "You own half the bakery? Why didn't Tyler tell me?" Maggie wanted to step away from Brent, but her legs felt like Jello.

"I guess he didn't expect to sell. Then he got serious with Nadine." Brent tightened his hold on her shoulders. "At that point, he didn't know how to tell you. So, we thought if you worked with me and got to know me, you might not totally hate the idea of being my business partner."

"You must think I'm such an idiot. The two of you played me." A rush of anger swept over her, and she pulled away from his touch.

"No, Maggie. I have the utmost respect for you. I've watched you run this bakery and take care of your son Matt. I don't know how you do it."

She averted her gaze. "So, I suppose you won't be helping me with the business proposal. Why would you? If I don't get the backing, I suppose you'll buy out Tyler, and why not? You already have a stake in the business." She sobbed.

Brent drew her to him. She resisted at first, then gave in, leaning her forehead on his chest. "Besides, who's going to back someone like me?" Swiping at the renegade teardrops, she pressed her lips together to keep the negative thoughts swirling in her head to herself.

Brent wrapped his arms around her. "It's going to be okay."

She leaned into his hug and allowed herself to cry

until all the fire in her subsided. Then she stepped back, away from his reach. "I'm sorry. This has been my dream ever since I started working for Tyler and it's so close to becoming a reality it's hard to know Sweet Things won't be mine."

Brent grabbed a few napkins from a nearby dispenser and offered them to Maggie. "No, it'll be ours, and if you ever want to buy me out, I'll let you."

Taking the napkins, she patted under her eyes and sniffled, feeling more like Tyler's baby sister than an adult who could handle the ups and downs of owning a business.

A pang of embarrassment zipped through her as she met Brent's gaze.

"I'm sorry Magpie. I should've told you the truth from the get-go. Don't know why I went along with Tyler's stupid scheme."

"Yes, you should've." She allowed her gaze to drift to the ground, knowing if she didn't break the connection, she'd be tempted to return to his strong arms.

"So, when I talked with Tyler tonight, I told him I intended to help you find the funds you need. That we planned to work on a business proposal together."

"What did he say?" Maggie sniffled again, raising the wad of napkins to her nose.

"He said I was crazy for competing against myself." Brent laughed.

Maggie giggled and dabbed her cheeks. She had to admit it was kind of crazy but very sweet.

"You should know, he wants to sell his half to you." Brent crooked his finger beneath her chin and lifted her face, so her eyes met his. "I'm the backup plan, Maggie. I'm still going to do everything within my power to get you the dream of your heart."

Chapter Seven

Maggie slipped into the last pew in the back of the sanctuary of Cowboy Community Church with her two-year-old in tow. She'd thought about staying home when she woke up late, but with it being the service before Thanksgiving, she made the effort to be here. Getting both her and Matt ready had proven to be more challenging than she'd anticipated. Who knew a shoe could fit into the crack between the wall and the refrigerator?

Picking Matt up, she settled him on her lap. Dropping the overstuffed diaper bag to the floor, she pushed it under the wooden seat with the heel of her foot, brushing against the leg of the man seated next to her.

He scowled in her direction before scooting further toward the center and sliding his arm around the woman sitting next to him.

Maggie shrugged, feeling helpless as she turned her attention to the front of the sanctuary. The choir sang the words to the hymn, 'We Gather Together,' a favorite for this time of year. Thanksgiving loomed before her, but before she could even give the holiday any consideration, she needed to survive Crazy Pie Day thanks to Brent. A spark of irritation flared in her.

But irritation wasn't the only emotion that sprang to life when she thought of Brent Thibodeaux. The flutter in her stomach sent tingles through her like butterflies dancing around marigolds. At times, the swirl of emotions threatened to overtake her good sense. They were all tangled together – irritation, suspicion, attraction, respect. She stopped the process right there with a frown. Brent was her competition, but he could also be the answer to her problem. What a tangled mess! It didn't help that every time they were together, she found herself in his arms, those strong, capable arms.

Wanting to think about anything else but him, she glanced around the sanctuary, looking for her mom and dad. She spotted them sitting closer to the front of the packed church. Many of the people she recognized as regular members of the congregation, but some new faces stood out to her.

Matt squirmed, sending his stuffed dinosaur falling to the ground, dragging her attention back to him. Maggie tried to catch the toy but missed, causing the dino to hit the knee of the gentleman beside her. He glanced her way, his furrowed brow and the downward pull of his mouth let her know his patience wouldn't hold out much longer.

"Dino, dino." Matt stretched his chubby arms toward his favorite toy now located on the floor.

Maggie moved Matt to the other side of her lap. Leaning over, she maneuvered her shoulder between the pew in front of her and the edge of her own seat. Her fingertips brushed against the soft fur pushing the toy further away. It lay just out of reach, under the seat of the man in the black suit sitting next to her. She glanced his way, but he avoided making eye contact.

"Dino," Matt hollered.

"Shhh …" Maggie patted Matt's back and produced a different toy from her purse beside her.

Matt squeezed his eyes closed and puckered his lips. "I wan' dino."

The teen sitting in front of them glanced over his shoulder.

Knowing there would be no consoling Matt until she got the dino, Maggie made a second attempt at retrieving the toy. As she straightened, someone brushed past her forcing the man in the black suit to inch further down the line.

Maggie frowned. The pew couldn't hold another person.

"Excuse me. I believe there's a toy under your foot. Do you mind?"

The man in the suit grunted something but lifted his leg. Two broad shoulders leaned forward and scooped up the green dinosaur.

Turning, Brent Thibodeaux handed Matt his toy. "I believe this is yours."

Matt grabbed the toy from Brent's hand and hugged it to his chest. Smiling, he laid his head on her shoulder, staring at Brent.

"You looked like you could use some help, and I needed a seat. Man, this place is packed. I bet Pastor Connor is thrilled. He loves a big crowd," Brent whispered close to her ear as he ran his arm along the back of the pew behind her.

Those incorrigible butterflies took flight.

She could smell the woodsy scent of his musk. It

wafted around her like a breeze from the deep woods. "Thank you." Rattled by his appearance, she concentrated on settling Matt back in her lap, letting him rest his head against her chest.

"Let's stand and sing "Come Ye Thankful People Come" on page 797 of the hymnal," the choir director instructed.

"Here let me help you." Brent stood and reached for Matt.

Before she could warn him that taking Matt might not be a good idea, Brent swung him from her arms and up into his. "Hey there buddy. You want to sing?"

Matt grinned at the hulk of a man. "Sing." he threw back his head.

Brent laughed. "Aren't you full of energy today. You must be feeling better."

The sound of pages rustling drifted through the room. The piano player hit the first notes of the hymn. Maggie pulled the hymnal from the holder on the back of the pew and flipped to the page. Holding the book with both hands, she stood and centered it, so Brent could also see the words.

As he sang the notes, his voice came out strong. It held a silky quality like melted chocolate, rich and sweet. For a moment, Maggie stood listening, but once he glanced at her with that half grin tugging on his lips, she dropped her gaze to the page in front of her and joined him in singing the chorus.

A strange sensation washed over her while they stood together, singing the old familiar hymn. It felt right to be standing here with Brent and Matt, like they belonged together. It'd been a long time since she'd experienced this feeling. Not since Ted, and then it had been on those rare occasions when he was home and not deployed overseas. Then all parts of life converged into one fulfilling moment. Rare moments indeed.

Her gaze moved from the words on the page to the man who stood beside her. Matt laid his head on Brent's shoulder and wiggled the dino's arms, content. So often, she'd wondered how it would be for Matt to grow up without the influence of his dad. She'd put pictures of Ted all around the house and picked one to put on the nightstand beside Matt's toddler bed, but she held no illusions it would make any difference.

He'd never even seen his father, and what stories she could tell him wouldn't mean much to him without a connection. Ted would be an idea, a mirky image at best, and an idea couldn't play catch or go on picnics or buy Matt ice cream to cheer him up.

The congregation sang the word, "amen," interrupting her thoughts. The heat of embarrassment crept up her cheeks. She'd been staring at Brent throughout the entire song. She jerked her focus back to the front of the sanctuary, hoping he hadn't noticed. The choir director motioned for everyone to be seated.

Pushing her purse aside, she slid onto the cushion. As Brent sat, Matt reached out to her, and she plucked him out of Brent's hands, the motion so smooth it seemed as if they'd been trading the child back and forth all his life.

Brent slipped his arm along the back of the pew again and rubbed Matt's cheek. "He's a great kid, Maggie. You're doing a fine job."

His words sent a burst of tingles zipping through her. Why did she care what he thought of her parenting, but she couldn't keep the warmth from her cheeks at his praise.

"Thank you. I try."

"You do more than try," He whispered in her ear. "You succeed." His nearness and kind words made that unwanted tangle of emotions rise in her and expand.

Daring to glance into his face, she caught her breath at the intensity in his green eyes. Usually, they held a teasing sparkle, but now, they looked more like stormy waves, dark and dangerous.

~

Brent struggled to keep his eyes off Maggie. She wore a beautiful blue dress that made her eyes shine. When she glanced at him during the last hymn, his heart revved like the motor on his Harley. The dark ringlets of her hair that had escaped from her bun dangled precariously around the curve of her neck, drawing his gaze. If they'd been anywhere else but church, he'd have thought of kissing her.

Maggie closed the hymnal and leaned forward, placing it in the holder. The movement snapped Brent back to reality.

Kissing her? Magpie?

He pulled his arm back to his side and trained his eyes on the minister. *Kissing.* Had he lost his mind? Sitting next to the dark-haired beauty clouded his judgement. This was his best friend's sister, he was talking about, not some random person. Not that he tended to go around kissing random people. Shaking his head, he attempted to derail his thoughts and get them back in line.

Now, he realized his mistake. He should have kept his distance. Hadn't his head and heart been in a wrestling match ever since the first day when he'd caught her in his arms?

His pulse pounded in his ears, drowning out Pastor Connor, and with every breath he took, the sweet fragrance of her perfume engulfed his senses. All he wanted was to chat with her after church, so he'd sat next to her, figuring she'd be impossible to find once the service ended. How had he gotten to the point of wanting to kiss her?

Glancing to his side, he took one last look at the beauty and told himself she was off-limits. No if, ands, or buts about it. He'd been in the military for goodness' sake. He could show some self-discipline. Then, without warning, Matt lunged at him.

Brent held up his hands and caught the little guy before he plummeted into the man in the black suit. The boy giggled, then turned and lunged towards his mother. For the next few minutes, Matt kept them on their toes until Maggie distracted him with some crayons and paper.

By the end of the sermon, Matt slept in Maggie's lap. He looked so peaceful. Brent fought the urge to take him from his mother to give her a break. He didn't want to wake the boy, but her arms had to be tired from holding the child's full weight. His father, Ted Bishop, must've been a big man because his son was a chunk. A definite football player in the making.

Brent waited for the man in the black suit to exit the row, then he stood and unwedged the diaper bag from under the pew. Without thinking about it, he tossed the dino and the pad of paper into the large open compartment.

"Oh, you don't have to do that." Maggie moved Matt from her lap to her shoulder. Placing her hand on the seat in front of her, she steadied herself as she rose. Matt didn't budge. A dribble of spittle clung to the boy's cheek.

"It's all right. I do it for Nikki all the time with the twins. You can imagine the load she has to carry for two." Brent picked up the crayons and replaced them one by one in the box. Tucking the yellow container inside, he lifted the bag to his shoulder. "Ready to go? I'll walk you out. I have some news I want to share with you."

"Interesting. Can I ask what it's about?" Maggie's brows furrowed.

He needed to tread lightly. She had no reason to trust him. After all, he was her competition for Tyler's share of the bakery. The enemy. But he hoped with this news she'd change her opinion about him.

"It's about the business proposal." He followed her into the aisle.

"You mean the non-existent one." She wagged her head. "I have to find the time to put that together."

Matt let out a sigh as he turned his head on his mother's shoulder, never opening his eyes.

"I guess all that coloring wore him out." Brent chuckled, watching Maggie move into the church foyer. The hem of her blue floral dress swished with her steps.

Eyes up, Thibodeaux. He followed her to the side of the room, out of the way of the people heading for the front doors.

Turning, she faced him. "What did you want to tell me?"

"Well, I made a few calls like I promised, and I've found two possible investors. But we'll need to act soon and get the proposal squared away."

Maggie sighed, a look of distress sweeping across her face.

"I thought you'd be excited."

"I am excited," but her tone held a hint of weariness. "How soon do you need it?"

"No later than the first week of December." Brent hurried on without waiting for her to respond. "I know that's soon, but remember, I said I'd help you pull it all together. You don't have to do this alone."

"It's not only the proposal. It's Crazy Pie Day." She frowned. "Along with the orders for Thanksgiving. Then the doctors told me Matt needs tubes in his ears. I don't know when I'm going to fit that in, but it needs to be soon. Writing a proposal ..." Maggie pressed her lips together.

Tears of frustration pooled in her bright hazel eyes. Brent's heart melted to his toes. "Oh, Maggie, I didn't mean to overwhelm you with Crazy Pie Day. I should've discussed it with you first before I ever mentioned it to Tyler."

Matt stirred, groaning.

"Yes, you should have." She patted Matt's back. "But there's nothing we can do about that now."

"Look, let me make it up to you. What can I do?" Brent asked.

The foyer continued to fill with people from the sanctuary. Several groups formed as individuals gathered to chat with one another. Conversations like their own buzzed throughout the large space.

Something caught Maggie's attention. She lifted a hand and waved. Brent followed her gaze. Maggie's mom and dad threaded their way around the clusters of people toward them.

"There you are. I'm so glad I caught you."

"Hi, Mom," Maggie said.

Maggie's dad, Stuart, trailed his wife. The intense look on his face caused Brent to do a double take. He'd known Mr. Kemp long enough to notice when something was bothering him, but the moment the man caught sight of his grandson, his face bloomed into a beam of light. "Let me take the little man." Before Maggie could protest, her dad swooped Matt into his arms and snuggled him close.

The little boy stretched his whole body, his legs extending to his grandfather's belt. Yep, the boy would grow to be a big man.

"That's a nice look for you." Stuart grinned, pointing toward Brent, who stood holding the diaper bag.

"Hey, I'm an uncle now. I'm used to being a pack mule." He chuckled. "Besides, the little man isn't so little. He's solid, so, I thought I'd offer Maggie a hand to her car."

Stuart glanced at Brent, a twinkle of understanding dancing in his eyes. "Oh, how thoughtful of you. I guess chivalry isn't as dead as it's been rumored to be."

Brent fidgeted with the strap of the bag. He didn't like being under Maggie's dad's scrutiny. If Stuart looked too closely, he might discover how much Brent cared for his daughter. Shrugging, Brent downplayed his actions. "Everybody needs a little help now and then."

"I remember not too long ago when you and Tyler did everything you could to get away from Maggie. She hounded you boys like a dog on the scent of a rabbit."

Brent laughed. "She could be pretty persistent." He

cut his eyes in Maggie's direction. Deep in conversation, she and her mother huddled together off to the side. Maggie did not look pleased.

"It's nice now that the two of you don't mind having her around." Stuart's eyebrows winged up. Mischief played in his hazel-colored eyes that gleamed a few shades darker than Maggie's.

"Gand, Gand," Matt said, pumping his legs, trying to get down. "Momma." He leaned over his grandfather's arm almost falling backward, reaching his arms toward Maggie.

"Nope, you need to stay with me." Stuart walked his fingers up the boy's exposed tummy to his chin then tweaked his pink cheek. The boy giggled and scrunched his shoulders.

As the women rejoined them, Maggie said, "It's fine, Mom. You do so much for me already. I hated to ask for your Sunday afternoon."

"You know, if this emergency meeting of the Women's Auxiliary hadn't been called, I'd have been happy to have our little guy with us this afternoon." Libby sighed and rubbed her hand over Matt's blond hair. "But if we're going to have everything ready for Thursday for the shelter, I need to be at the meeting."

"What's going on?" Brent asked.

"Mom had planned to watch Matt for me this afternoon, so I could work on some recipes for Crazy Pie Day. You know, something unique for this event." She frowned.

He'd messed up by not getting her approval for Crazy Pie Day first. Even though he was certain it'd bring in new customers, he'd put Maggie in a tight spot, and now he'd added a business proposal to the mix.

"Listen, I'm free this afternoon. I could watch Matt."

"No." Maggie let her gaze fall to the carpeted floor. "I couldn't ask you to do that. Besides, Nikki would wind up doing the lion's share because it's what we mom's do. I can't infringe on their family time."

"What if I watched him at the bakery? I can entertain him while you work your culinary magic on some flour and sugar, and if anything goes wrong, you'll be right there to tell me what to do." A smile spread across Brent's lips. "Besides, we all know you've loved bossing me around since we were teens."

Libby and Stuart chuckled.

"Yeah, but now you're the boss." The words came out snarky. Maggie pressed her lips together. Brent could read the regret on her face. She could never hide her feelings very well.

Stuart stared at Maggie. "What do you mean?"

"Nothing. Just an inside joke." Maggie shrugged.

A knot formed in Brent's stomach as he realized how much he'd hurt her. Tyler and his idiotic ideas. The knot tightened at the prick of his conscience. He couldn't place the blame on Tyler. He was the one who agreed to go along with the scheme. Undercover Boss, more like Undercover Blockhead.

"Come on, Maggie. What do you have to lose? Besides, while you work on the pies, I can start working on the proposal. Maybe I can get a rough draft going for you to look over before we lock up."

Confusion washed over Stuart's face. He leaned close to his wife and whispered, "What proposal? And what boss? I feel like I've walked into the middle of a conversation being spoken in French."

"I'll explain on the way home." Libby gave her husband an understanding glance.

Maggie pursed her lips and let her gaze rest on Brent. Crossing her arms, she tilted her head. "So, you think we can watch Matt, work on recipes, and come up with a proposal all this afternoon?"

"Yeah, I know it's going to be hard, but we might manage a rough draft by this evening." Brent shifted the diaper bag from one shoulder to the other then pulled Matt from Stuart's arms. He needed to make things right with Maggie. "You said you wanted my help. This is me helping. Nanny Brent, reporting for duty."

A wide smile swept up from Maggie's lips all the way to her eyes and replaced the clouds of doubt he'd seen earlier.

Brent caught his breath. Man, when she smiled, she transformed into a radiant beauty.

Matt wiggled in Brent's grip, pulling his attention away from Maggie. The boy slid his hand around Brent's neck but paused to pat the scars on Brent's left jaw with his small hand. Brent smiled down at him, aware of the child's touch, but the usual discomfort did not come.

"Booboo?" Matt asked.

"No. Scar." Brent rubbed his hand down the little boy's back, letting the tyke touch the dimpled skin.

"Car?" Matt patted the area one last time before leaning his weight against Brent's arm and turning to his mother. "Go. Go."

All four adults laughed at Matt's connection of words. "He's right," Brent said. "We need to go, go, if we want to get everything done, done."

Chapter Eight

Maggie glanced over her shoulder toward the bakery office after she rolled out the last pie crust she'd mixed. Brent sat holding Matt on his lap typing one-handed on the keyboard.

"Okay, buddy. Here's where we want to tell the investors how talented Mommy is at cooking." Brent's voice carried across the quiet room.

"Mommy cooking," Matt parroted.

"That's right. Mommy's cooking right now."

"Go Mommy," Matt said.

"Not yet, little man. Give me another minute, and we'll go say hi."

Maggie grinned. She had to give him kudos for winning over Matt. The way he stepped in to help her when she felt nothing but overwhelmed at the mention of the proposal, edged toward the heroic. Brent was right. She needed to finish the proposal if she intended to buy Tyler's half of the bakery. Time wouldn't stand still for her just because her plate overflowed with a thousand responsibilities.

Glancing once more at the man chatting with her son, she pushed down the feelings of regret from earlier in the church foyer. Why had she made the remark about him being her boss? Sure, it was true, considering what he'd told her, but that wasn't how he treated her. Deep down, she knew he'd never look down on her, even if she didn't come up with the financing for the bakery.

"Potty, now." Matt clamored down from Brent's lap.

Putting her rolling pin down, she grabbed a towel to wipe off the flour on her hands. "Here's my big boy." She squatted to hug him.

Brent followed. "He needs to use the restroom, and that is definitely a mom thing."

"He's been potty trained now for a few weeks, but I can see where that line has to be drawn." She giggled. "Boundaries." She stood and took Matt's hand.

When they returned, she found Brent back at Tyler's desk typing away on the computer. He'd been keeping Matt occupied since two o'clock when they'd first arrived. Now, looking at the clock, she discovered it to be a little after four.

Pressing her lips together, she hesitated outside the office door. The proposal was important toward securing a future for her and Matt. She needed the business plan to get the funding, but she also needed to work on the recipes for Tuesday.

Brent muttered something under his breath as he leaned closer to the screen.

With a nod, she made her decision. She'd keep an eye on Matt and give Brent an hour or so to work on the proposal.

"Come on, Matt. Let's set you up in the kitchen." Maggie held the boy's hand and strolled to the small window near the back door. Pushing open the curtains, she let in a sliver of late afternoon light from the back alley. Locating the diaper bag, she pulled out a blanket, snapping it into the air and letting it drift down to the floor where the sunlight played. "Now, choose three toys."

The little boy stuck his hand deep into the bag and fished around. She had a fair idea which three toys Matt would grab from the bag— the dino, a fire engine he'd received as a gift last Christmas, and a clunky hard plastic robot. Sure enough, the first one out of the bag was the fire engine. He plunged his chubby hand in again and withdrew the robot. Finally, he squatted next to the bag mimicking her own position and looked inside to retrieve the dino. Hugging it close, he plopped onto the large, quilted blanket.

"Okay, big guy, you stay here and play." Maggie leaned forward on her knees and kissed the top of her son's head. "I'll be right over there." She pointed to the table.

"Okay."

With Matt settled, Maggie rose and walked to the metal table where her four pie crusts sat waiting. Out of desperation to make things easier for Crazy Pie Day, she'd picked a theme, and what better theme for the fall season than apples. She'd found a recipe for an Apple Blossom Tart that starred the crisp, sweet Pink Lady variety of apples. Her mouth watered at the thought of the cream cheese and light brown sugar mixed with the taste of the apple.

She'd also found a recipe for an apple and cheddar pie that would be a big hit with the customers. The warm gooey cheese wrapped around the sweet tangy apples screamed comfort food. She also wanted to use one of the crusts for her basic apple pie, the one she'd perfected over the last three years. It always sold well during Thanksgiving week, so she wanted to nail down the recipe.

The crown jewel of her themed Crazy Pie Day though was her late grandmother's apple pie recipe which added tart cranberries and a splash of lemon juice to the ingredients. She'd loved the subtle tanginess as a kid and thought it would be fun to share the unorthodox pie with the community. Well, actually, with three or four communities in either direction of Orange Blossom, Texas, since Brent and her blockhead of a brother made sure to advertise their little scheme far and wide.

Maggie sighed and worked on coring the Pink Ladies for the tart. Determined to keep a good attitude, she hummed as she worked. Her mind drifted to the church service earlier that morning and the familiar hymns. Boy, Brent had looked good in his blue suit and tie. She glanced toward the doorway of the office and caught sight of the man scowling at the screen in front of him.

Shaking her head, she dragged her attention back to the task in front of her. These pies wouldn't make themselves.

An hour later, she popped two of the four pies into the oven to bake. She set the timer for fifty minutes and let her thoughts wander to food of another sort— dinner. With all the running around after church to secure her ingredients, she'd only had time to feed Matt his lunch. Now, her stomach grumbled in complaint.

Maggie peeked at her son who had helped himself to two of the pots from the bottom shelf of the metal table closest to him. The two-year-old sat on the quilted blanket making swishing noises as he plunged his dinosaur into the large pot. "Whoosh, whoosh," he said as he dipped the green tailed monster into the empty pot.

The filling for her All-American apple pie bubbled in the pot on the stove. It's aroma wafting through the kitchen. She reached for a ladle and stirred the mixture of sugar, apples, and cinnamon. Replacing the lid, she tilted it slightly, so the steam could escape.

Wiping her hands on her apron, she strolled to the office then leaned against the jamb in the doorway and waited for Brent to notice her.

He sat with his back toward her, thumbing through the finance ledger for the bakery.

"What'cha got there?"

He swiveled the large leather chair in her direction. "I was going over the finances for the last quarter. Tyler gave me a run down my first week back in town." He met her gaze. "But at the time, I was too distracted to pay attention." A smile wove its way up his cheeks and landed in his eyes. A spark caught in his gaze that made her knees wobble.

"Distracted. By what?" Maggie moved to the metal chair in front of the wooden desk and slipped into the seat to keep her shaky legs from their treacherous design.

"A certain brunette who flung cookies all over the floor."

Maggie laughed. "Please don't remind me." She leaned forward resting her elbows on her knees. "I try to forget those kinds of moments. It might surprise you to know I've had more than my fair share of them."

"Nooo ..." Brent chuckled. "I'd never guess."

His teasing sent flutters rippling through her. She'd distracted him that first day. If she were honest, she'd have to admit to being a little distracted too. "Let's see you try being light of foot and still get a hundred baked goods out every morning by six."

"I'm not a morning person. That's why I need you to get this financing. I need a partner who *is* a morning person and a dough person and a pie person." Brent placed the ledger on top of the desk and leaned forward, a playful grin tugging at the corners of those full lips of his. "I need you, Maggie Bishop."

Another little flutter zipped through her. Was he flirting with her? "Oh, so you're helping me solely for your own benefit?"

"Maybe."

Leaning back in his chair, Brent crinkled his nose. "Is something burning?" Smoke floated in wisps into the office.

Maggie leapt to her feet. "My filling!" Dashing to the kitchen, she grabbed the mitts from the table near the stove. Brent rushed past her.

Flames danced around the outside of the pot where the sticky filling boiled over onto the eye, causing the flames to roar. Shocked, Maggie froze in place. The smoke in the kitchen grew thicker, making her eyes water.

"Get Matt and go out the back door." Brent jerked the fire extinguisher from the holder on the wall. "Now, Maggie. Move."

The sharp tone of Brent's voice snapped Maggie out of her stupor. Without hesitating, Maggie scooped up Matt and raced to the back door. How did this happen? She could have sworn she lowered the flame under the pot before stepping into the office to chat with Brent. She tucked Matt's head in the crook of her neck, slipping out the back door that stood ajar. Matt coughed against her shoulder. The fresh air filled her lungs the moment she stepped across the threshold into the back alley of the shop where the dumpster and recycled cardboard waited to be picked up. The roar of a truck engine caught her attention. She turned her head in time to see the vehicle fly past on the side street. Shaken, she clutched Matt tight to her chest.

~

Brent yanked the pin unlocking the fire extinguisher. Rushing toward the stove, his firefighter training kicked into gear. Aiming the extinguisher toward the flames, he squeezed the handle. The blaze crackled to life and rose toward the vent hanging above the stove top.

For a moment the heat of the fire pushed his thoughts to the last fire he'd worked. The flames of which had left him scared on the outside and compromised on the inside. The sizzling sound of the pie filling turning into blacken residue produced the memory of the pain of the flames on his skin. Fear gripped his heart, causing him to faulter and let go of the handle. The extinguisher slipped, bumping against the metal table behind him. *Thibodeaux, you can do this. Maggie needs you.*

Brent set his jaw and held the extinguisher at the proper height. Squeezing the handles, he swept the nozzle from side to side, making sure he covered the fire's base, so it wouldn't reignite. The white foam spewing from the nozzle covered the entire top of the industrial-sized stove.

The fire hissed and spit but the foam did its job, leaving a black concoction of ashes mixed with the white fluff. Brent huffed, released a long breath, and forced his muscles to relax. The memories of that morning a year and a half ago washed over him. The fire, the man, the smell of the diesel burning.

Setting the fire extinguisher on the table behind him, he inspected the mess. The plastic ladle Maggie had left in the pot now looked like a piece of modern art, twisted and misshapen. *This could have been the whole shop.*

Fear froze him to the spot. What about Maggie and Matt? If anything had happened to them, he'd never forgive himself. He'd trained for these situations, but his own bad experience got in the way today. His own battles almost put the business and the people he cared about in peril.

~

Impatience and worry plagued Maggie while she held Matt tight against her chest. The few minutes she'd been in the alley seemed like hours. What was happening in her bakery? Did Brent need her?

A thump rang from inside the kitchen. Setting Matt's feet on the ground, she took his hand and moved to the doorway to check on Brent. She'd left the back door open behind her in case the fire got out of control and Brent needed to make a quick escape.

She should have known better. After all, he was a seasoned firefighter, a real-life hero. He could handle a stove fire, no problem.

Stepping over the threshold into the kitchen, she surveyed the stove covered in black ashes and white foam. The vent hanging above the stove wore black marks where the flames had licked the metal. If Brent hadn't been there, what would've happened? The question rang in her heart. He'd saved her two most precious treasures, her son and the bakery.

She shook her head to dispel the thought and moved toward Brent with Matt clutching her hand.

The instant she saw his face, her heart wrenched. "Oh Brent, are you okay?" Letting go of Matt, she placed her hands on Brent's shoulders, forcing him to meet her gaze. "Talk to me. What is it?"

Brent met her gaze and a faint smile tilted his lips. "I guess I'm a little out of practice. It's been a while since I've dealt with a fire." He glanced toward the mess.

He might be out of practice, but Maggie had a feeling there was more to the story than he wanted to share. "A seasoned professional like you? It must be second nature, like brushing your teeth."

"Nah, I still have to work at it." Brent's Adam's apple bobbed as he swallowed. His muscles tensed under her touch. "My last fire with the brigade. It didn't just leave the scars you can see. It left a few you can't see."

She reached up and touched the scar running down his left jaw. The skin felt bumpy but soft. His gaze connected with hers, and he covered her hand with his. "That's why I'm here Maggie. I needed a change. A new direction. And I thought the bakery might be the place where I could start over."

Her pulse raced as his dark green eyes softened. She could get lost in those eyes.

"I understand." Maggie curled her fingers around

his hand but didn't let go. She held on, hoping her touch would comfort the wounded places in his heart. "I came back to Orange Blossom for the same reason. I needed a new start. With Ted's death, I couldn't bear to be away from family. The loneliness nearly did me in."

Brent squeezed her hand. "I'm so sorry for your loss, Maggie, but you've done such a great job with Matt and the bakery. According to Tyler, your baking skills pretty much saved the shop single handedly. I guess I have you to thank for saving my investment."

She shook her head. "If it hadn't been for Tyler and my parents and those persistent Bible Babes, I wouldn't have made it out of the fog. It nearly consumed me. If it hadn't been for the baby I was carrying, I wouldn't have made it." She turned her gaze on her son.

The little blond hair boy ran to her and wrapped his arms around her legs. Looking up, he said, "Mommy, ohs."

Brent let go of her hand. "Sounds like the little man's hungry." He rumpled the boy's hair.

Stepping back, she walked to the stove, studying it. "This doesn't make sense."

"What?" Brent leaned his hip against the metal table and faced the warped stove hood.

"I know I put the burner on low. This shouldn't have happened." Glancing toward the back door, she said, "And the back door was unlocked and partly open."

Brent followed her gaze. They hadn't gone out the back until the fire. "You're right. That doesn't make any sense."

Chapter Nine

When the tenderness of the moment faded, Maggie scooped up Matt and settled him on the quilt. Digging around in the diaper bag, she found the plastic container with the cereal in it. "Here you go, sweetie."

She grabbed the sippy cup from the side pocket and moved to the refrigerator. Swinging the door open, she fished out a jug of apple juice she kept on hand. "This should help to ease his tummy troubles."

"I can't blame him. My stomach seems to be giving me fits as well." Brent's lighthearted tone eased her worry. "Tell you what. I'll take you guys to The Flying Pig for dinner. My treat."

"What about this mess? I can't leave it. It wouldn't be fair to Kristen and Millie since they're the ones opening in the morning. Matt has another doctor's appointment."

"You're right. We should clean up. How about I call in the order, then we tackle this mess? If we aren't done by the time the food is ready, you can go pick it up while I finish the cleaning."

Maggie considered his suggestion. They did have to eat after all. "Okay, sounds good."

After Brent phoned in their order, they scraped and

wiped and scrubbed until the timer went off on Brent's phone the whole idea of making any more pies forgotten. "You head out to get the food, and I'll sweep up the residue," Brent said.

"Be sure to put the trash out. Pick up's tomorrow."

"Sure will, honey." Brent's playful tone caught Maggie off guard. She glanced over her shoulder in time to see him wink at her before he lugged the 50-gallon trash can from its usual spot over to the stove.

She lifted Matt into her arms cereal and all, trying not to spill the sippy cup. "Don't hurt yourself with that load."

"Don't worry about me. Remember, I'm a professional bakery owner, now." He flexed his bicep. "I've got it covered."

Maggie giggled at his antics. "What? Are you twelve?"

"Only on my good days." He stopped and locked onto her gaze. The half grin that caused her knees to go weak emerged.

She couldn't help herself as her lips curled into a smile. The heat of a blush threatened to bloom on her cheeks. Boy, the man could flirt. Then she remembered the cute girl from the lawyer's office. Flirting, that's all it was, and she needed to remember that fact.

"I'll be back," she said, looking away, breaking the connection. Matt wiggled in her arms as she walked to the door.

Brent shifted his weight, his voice taking on a low gentle timbre. "I'll be waiting for you, Maggie." The sweetness of the words hinted at a promise, a possibility that she didn't dare consider.

When Maggie returned, she found one of the tables

in the front area of the bakery set with silverware and plates for three. Brent had replaced a regular chair with a highchair for Matt. She loved the way he included her son as if it were second nature.

"Hope this is all right."

"It's perfect." Maggie released Matt and placed the bags with the Styrofoam containers on a nearby table. When she pulled the containers out, they rubbed together, making a squeaky sound that sent shivers up her spin. "I hate that noise. It's like fingernails on a chalkboard, but worse."

Brent chuckled and picked up Matt, depositing him in the highchair. "Do you have a bib?"

"It's in the diaper bag in the kitchen."

"Give me a second." Brent jogged toward the back.

Maggie watched as Brent's well-formed shape hustled through the swinging doors. A man of action who likes kids, rare indeed. Shaking her head, she instructed her heart to keep it professional. After all, they were going to be business partners, that is if she ever finished putting together a proposal.

Brent pushed through the doors carrying the diaper bag. "I figured it'd be easier to bring all Matt's gear in here."

"Smart." Maggie continued unpacking the bags. "So, how far did you get with the proposal today? You know, before I tried to burn down the joint." She shot Brent a so-sorry look.

Brent pulled the bib from the diaper bag and snapped it around Matt's neck. "Pretty far. If you will fill in some information about your career as a pastry chef before you worked here and your schooling, that would go a long way."

Maggie widened her eyes. "Really? You got that far today?"

"I told you I've got experience writing business proposals. I've done a lot of them over the years, and it helped that we worked here, so I had everything at my fingertips. Plus, I've been at the receiving end of the proposal, since I like to see my money work for the community. People asking for funding for one venture or another."

"So how much more time do you estimate it will take us to finish the proposal?"

"Maybe another afternoon or two." Brent grabbed one of the foam containers and scooped out a nice size helping of the macaroni and cheese onto a plate. Flipping open the top of the other box, he dished a few pieces of honey barbequed pork next to the mac and cheese. Then he placed the plate on the tray in front of Matt. "Didn't you say earlier Matt has a doctor's appointment tomorrow?"

"Yeah, why?"

"Are you planning to take the whole day off?"

"I wish I could. I'd love the time to look over the rest of the recipes since I only made two of the four pies I'd planned to make. I want to taste test the other recipes before I sell them." Maggie scooted the plate closer to Matt. "I'll need every minute tomorrow to get ready for Tuesday. Guess I'll have to taste test as I go." A lopsided grin stretched across her lips.

"Oh, I thought if you were taking the day off, we could work on the proposal but how about Wednesday evening? The bakery closes early, so that should give us more time." Brent lifted a plate from the table and handed it to her. "Maybe I could swing by your house, and we could finish it up. That way, next week, I can make appointments for you with the four interested investors."

A rush of tangled emotions washed over Maggie. Why was he helping her? She'd treated him with such anger and suspicion when he first arrived, and she'd made his transition to working at the bakery as hard as possible. Now, he was going above and beyond to help her become his partner when he could easily buy out her brother, making Sweet Things his own.

Gratitude swirled through her. She thrust the plate in her hands to the table and took two steps forward. Wrapping her arms around Brent's middle, she squeezed. "Oh, Brent, I don't know how I can thank you for helping me with this. When you mentioned the proposal this morning, I wanted to crumble like an over-baked cookie."

Brent eased his arms around Maggie and leaned his head on the top of hers. His touch calmed her thoughts, and she settled into his embrace.

They stood for a moment holding each other before Matt's voice broke through the stillness. "Momma, more juice. Peas."

Maggie stepped back, letting her hands run down Brent's arms. She squeezed his hands before she let go.

Brent grabbed the sippy cup from Matt's highchair. "Let me get it for him. You go ahead and fix your plate before the food gets cold."

When he left the room, Maggie picked up her plate, but the somersaults in her stomach left her hungry for more of Brent's embrace and less for her dinner.

The food tasted delicious, and she savored each bite. Matt ate most of the macaroni and cheese, but

Brent took his fair share of that dish as well. The barbeque pulled pork sandwich melted on her tongue.

"Oh, Freida says 'hi', by the way." Maggie bit into the barbeque.

"How is she? I haven't seen her since I've been back."

"She's doing fine. I told her about our adventure today. The fire and all. She said she couldn't imagine having a better person on the scene then you. With all your experience and such."

Brent's smile faded. He grunted his acknowledgement, adding a sharp nod.

Maggie dropped her fork onto her plate. "All right, what is it? I know you've been through a lot, but this is more than something from your past."

"I almost lost it today. I knew what to do, but I froze. If you hadn't been here with Matt, I don't know if I would have been able to pull it together."

She reached across the table and touched his arm. "Brent, we all have moments …"

"But this was the first time I've dealt with a fire since I left the brigade. Fact is, I hesitated. What if it had been a real fire—you know, a bad one?"

"A real fire? That was a real fire." Maggie squeezed his arm. "And a real firefighter put it out. You saved the bakery, for both of us."

Brent leaned back in his chair, a scowl forming between his brows. "You don't understand. I let my own fear and pain put you in danger."

"No, you didn't. You reacted with swift and accurate action." Reading the frustration on his face, she decided to try another tactic. "Why don't you tell me what happened? Make me understand how you feel."

~

Brent grabbed his napkin and wiped his mouth, stalling another minute. He didn't want to tell Maggie about the fire in the base motor pool. He'd done everything in his power to forget that day and the days that followed. The pain, the sound of the fire, the acrid odors. He'd worked hard to regain full use of his left arm after surgery and rehab. Then he met John, a fellow patient, who reminded him he wasn't alone. That none of us are alone.

As if reading his mind, Maggie gave him an out. "It's all right if you'd rather not talk about it."

"It's not that I don't want you to know. It's hard for me." Brent pressed his lips together.

"I get it. The fire changed your life." Maggie wiped Matt's chubby cheeks with a napkin to remove some wayward sauce. "It's like Ted's death. So unexpected, but it changed everything."

"Yeah, you do understand." Brent made a quick decision, inhaling he steadied his nerves. "I went out for an early morning run on a trail behind Fort Sam Houston. When I came around the bend, I saw a plume of smoke rising into the air. I knew the motor pool sat on the edge of the property. I hustled to the scene. The blaze had spread, so I called it in. But before the fire trucks arrived, I spotted someone inside unconscious."

Maggie touched his hand lying on the table. "Oh no, how awful. You must've been terrified for the person."

"I was. So, I went in without gear which was a stupid mistake." Brent shook his head, trying to push the disappointment down deeper into the dark crevice of his heart. He'd known better, yet he still went inside. "All the training and years of experience didn't prepare me for what happened."

"What did happen?"

"The guy regained consciousness, and in a state of panic, he pushed me into the fire."

Maggie lifted her hand to cover her mouth as a small gasp escaped. "Oh, Brent. I had no idea. The recovery must've been brutal."

"I don't like to talk about it." Brent shifted in his chair. "The worst part is the guy who set the fire got away with it."

"Someone set the fire? You mean it wasn't an accident but arson?"

"That's exactly what I mean. The military police suspected one of the men who worked in the motor pool, but they couldn't prove it, and the man who I found in the fire couldn't identify his assailant."

"What happened to the suspect?" Maggie asked.

"I'm not sure, but I heard they discharged him from the Army because of some other issues." Brent took a sip of the sweet tea from the foam cup before he continued. "I ran into him once at the hospital during my rehab. He had the gall to ask me about my recovery."

"Are you sure he was the one?" Maggie leaned her elbow on the table, placing her chin on her hand. He held her attention. Her hazel eyes stayed on him. "I mean maybe the police concentrated on the wrong man."

Brent shook his head, letting his gaze drop from hers. "No, I don't think so because after he asked me about my recovery, he made a cryptic remark about the fire. Said he could still smell it on me."

"Wow, that does sound suspicious." Maggie sat straight in the metal heart-shaped chair.

"Yes, it does. But not enough to do anything about it." Brent leaned back with a shrug. "Now, you know what happened, and how I got my cool scars." He joked, trying to lighten the mood. Talking about arson wasn't exactly the way to win points with a woman who baked cupcakes to give away and spent her evenings playing with toy dinos. He raised his eyes, expecting to find pity lingering in her gaze, but instead, he found the glow of acceptance.

"I love your scars. They add character. A bit of depth from your adventurous life."

He chuckled. "I've never considered them in that light."

"More bar-q." Matt tugged on his bib and rubbed his sauce-covered fingers through his hair before either Brent or Maggie could stop him.

Maggie shot out of her seat. "Oh, Matt." She clucked her tongue. "What a mess." Grabbing a handful of napkins, Maggie attempted to wipe the sticky honey barbeque sauce out of his blond locks.

Brent pulled the two-year-old out of the highchair. "This calls for an emergency bath. When the twins look this bad, Nikki douses them." Grinning, he held Matt out in front of him. Waltzing through the swinging doors, he headed toward the industrial sized, double-sided sink.

"Down. Me, down."

Maggie hurried behind him with the diaper bag that he considered to be a Mary Poppin's bag. It held everything, never grew, and magically produced what was needed. He was sure Maggie could conjure up her own parrot-headed parasol from its chasm if necessary.

Once the water reached the right height, Maggie plopped her toddler into the deep sink.

Matt splashed Maggie while she wrestled to get soap in all the right spots. Brent made the mistake of leaning too close to the action. The toddler slapped the water with both hands sending a wave up Brent's nose and down the front of his shirt.

Giggling, Matt said, "again, again."

Using a dish towel, Brent dried his face and handed Maggie a towel from the stack. While Maggie slipped a pair of pajama bottoms over Matt's legs, Brent cut three slices from the Apple Blossom Tart she made earlier. After dressing Matt, Maggie settled him on the quilt to play with his favorite toys.

"Since we didn't get dessert and these needed taste testing anyway—" Brent shrugged.

"I'm in." Maggie took the plate from Brent's hand, placing it on the metal table. "I wanted to say I'm so sorry about today. I should've been paying more attention, and I should've never left the kitchen with something on the stove, but I could've sworn I'd lowered the flame."

Brent savored the tart flavor as it played on his tongue. "This is delicious." He mumbled around the bite in his mouth. "You'll need plenty of these for Crazy Pie Day."

"Really?" Her face beamed at his compliment. "Wait a minute. Are you changing the subject?"

"Yes, I am." Brent's eyebrows rose. "Don't apologize. You've been cooking for years. A stove fire was bound to happen."

"Thank you for letting me off the hook so easy, but in the future, I will be more careful. If you hadn't been here, I can't imagine what would've happened. The place would've gone up in flames. And Matt—" Her voice became a whisper as tears moistened the rims of her lashes. Brent wanted to pull her close and tell her he'd always be here for her, but that wasn't the nature of their relationship. Sure, she'd rushed into his arms earlier, but that was a thank-you from a grateful friend. Not wanting to overthink it, he put his arm around her shoulders. She laid her head against his chest, and his heart melted like the plastic spoon in the pie filling.

Chapter Ten

Maggie dragged her arm across her forehead, trying to wipe away the sweat with her sleeve. Even in late November, the kitchen felt like a sauna. She slid another batch of sweet potato pies into the bottom oven and checked on the pecan pies in the middle compartment. The pecan pies looked perfect. The Apple Blossom Tarts were a huge success. They sold out of them within the first hour of being open for Crazy Pie Day, so she'd pulled dough from the refrigerator to make more. Five o'clock couldn't get here soon enough.

She and Kristen spent Monday afternoon and evening baking a vast variety of pies, trying to meet their standing orders for Thanksgiving, while trying to calculate what might be needed for the big event.

No way could she have anticipated the overwhelming response to Crazy Pie Day. People walked through the bakery door from all over Reseda County. Even her cousin twice removed had come in—the cousin she'd thought had moved to Houston.

Maggie pushed through the swinging doors and placed a pan of her all-American apple pies on the counter next to a pile of white dessert boxes.

"Do you have any more pecan pies?" Freida asked as she studied the chalk board behind the counter where the specialty items and prices stood on display.

Millie Guthery, the youngest member of the team, manned the electronic pad, taking payments while Brent hustled back and forth between boxing pies and handing them out to customers who had already paid.

"We have some in the oven if you can wait about thirty minutes," Millie said.

Freida turned and surveyed the shop. "This is worse than a doctor's office. There's not even an empty spot to stand in, much less a chair for sitting."

"If you'd like to go ahead and pay for the pie, then you won't have to stand in line again, and you can ask Brent for it when it comes out."

Freida dug in her purse, producing a credit card. "Sounds good to me. I might walk over to the grocery store and pick up a baking bag for the turkey. Will you hold my pie?"

Maggie glanced over her shoulder at Freida, a smile tugging at her lips. There was no mistaking Freida's stern look.

"Yes, ma'am. We won't give your pecan pie to anyone else," Millie promised, taking the plastic card from the older woman.

Brent brushed past Maggie. "Can you believe this?" He grabbed a white box, placing one of the pies inside. Folding the lid, he creased the sides and closed it securely.

"No, it truly is Crazy Pie Day. You nailed the name." She laughed. "I couldn't imagine this many people coming."

"They do get the pies at a small discount." Brent

looked over his shoulder at the collection of people.

"Yeah, but ten percent off isn't that much," Maggie whispered close to him. "But who am I to argue with success."

When Freida moved away from the counter, Harry Branson stepped forward. "I'll take one of those delicious-looking apple pies and a sweet potato one, too."

Maggie moved toward Millie. "Oh, Harry, I'm sorry. The sweet potato pies won't be out for another hour at least. Can I interest you in a pecan pie? They should be done in a few more minutes."

"Remember, I get one of those," Freida called before pushing open the glass door and letting four more people enter the already crowded front area. "Don't be giving mine away." She stepped across the threshold and let the door slip shut.

Harry chuckled. "She's something else."

"Definitely," Maggie said "So, pecan pie?"

"No, I'll take the apple now and come back later. I've got my heart set on a good sweet potato pie for our Thanksgiving meal."

"Tell you what," Brent said from behind Maggie. "When the sweet potato pies come out, I'll set one aside for you."

"Sounds perfect." Harry moved further down the counter to wait for Brent to box up his apple pie.

"Here you go, Harry."

"Thanks, and like Freida said, 'Don't give mine away.' I'll be back for it this afternoon."

Mille spoke with Mr. Gibson off to the side by the third display case where they kept the gluten-free items. "Do we have any gluten-free pies?" She called above the noise of the customers.

"Yes, we do." Maggie pointed to a box in the display case closest to her. "Put it aside. Special for you, Mr. Gibson."

"Thanks, girlie."

Brent grabbed a pad of sticky notes and jotted down both Frieda and Harry's orders, then stuck the pieces of paper to the wall beside the chalkboard along with a growing number of other names. The wall resembled a small patchwork quilt with the various colors of sticky notes, handwriting flares, and names.

Maggie pulled her phone from her back pocket to check the time. Ten o'clock. She fought a groan and adjusted her attitude. The bakery could use the business. So what if her feet ached. She could rest tonight. With that thought in mind, she pushed through the doors into the kitchen to check on the pecan pies.

Kristen held open the door to the middle oven, while she waved a mitten in front of the sheet of pies. A puff of smoke dissipated as she stirred the air with the cloth. "These almost burned."

"Oh, goodness. Thank you." Maggie rushed over to take the tray from Kristen, picking up potholders as she passed the metal table. "We can't afford another fire. We were lucky the damage from the one Sunday was minimal." Maggie took the sheet of pies from Kristen and transported them to the middle metal table to cool. "Nor can we afford to lose any pies. We're barely keeping up now."

"I know." Kristen closed the middle compartment. Squatting, she checked the bottom oven then set the timer for ten more minutes. "If you'd told me we'd have half the county here, I'd called you a dreamer. A big dreamer, but here they are, all wanting our pies and treats."

"When I found out about Brent's grand idea and that Tyler approved it, I wanted to throttle them both, but now…"

"You want to hug him? Give him a big fat thank-you kiss?" Mischief played in Kristen's eyes as she waggled her eyebrows. "Come on. Tell me how it's going with the two of you." She threw down the oven mitt and leaned her hip against the table, placing her full attention on Maggie.

Maggie glanced up from the pie she inspected. "There's nothing to tell, really. We've come to a place of cooperative understanding."

"Hmm, I see." Kristen lifted the Apple Blossom Tarts from the table into the top oven and slid them onto the rack. "What does that look like, exactly?"

Maggie picked at a dark spot on one of the pecan pies, making sure none were too far gone to serve. She needed all her customers to be one hundred percent satisfied. According to Brent, the bakery's good reputation would go a long way to helping her secure financing. "Look, Brent doesn't seem interested in me that way. I've come to the place where I don't want to do him bodily harm for not telling me about being a partner in the first place." Picking up the tray of pies, Maggie shrugged. "So, I'd call that cooperative understanding."

Before Maggie could slip through the swinging doors to deliver the pecan pies to be boxed, Brent jogged into the kitchen. "We've received ten more orders for pumpkin pies and a dozen more for your All-American Apple."

"We're never going to keep up," Kristen huffed, marching to the commercial refrigerator to pull out more dough. "I'm glad we thought ahead and prepped as much dough as we did." Swinging the gray metal door wide, she stepped inside, allowing the cool air to stream into the hot kitchen.

"We only need to make it to five." Maggie encouraged her.

"Speaking of five, are we still on for tonight?" Brent asked.

Kristen's head popped back out of the refrigerator entrance. She nailed Maggie with a glare. "Nothing to tell? Right."

"What?" Confusion showed in the lines on Brent's face.

"Nothing. Ignore her." Maggie's feet ached already, and she'd worn her most comfortable shoes in anticipation of a busy day. But she had no idea it would be so… crazy.

The thought of having to do more than survive the day made her want to throw in the dish towel. "I forgot we were supposed to finish the proposal tonight."

"Well, will you be up for it?" Brent took the tray of pies from Maggie's hands, his own brushing against hers.

A quick tingle raced up her arm. "I'll have to be. If I want the financing, I need to have a business proposal, and I'm running out of time."

His face softened. "If you're not up to it, we can do it some other time. Maybe this weekend after Thanksgiving."

"No," she met his gaze. "I appreciate the offer, but it needs to be done. Simply because I had hoped to binge-watch *All Creatures Great and Small,* season two, while eating chocolate and cuddling up next to Matt, doesn't mean I can put it off."

A grin weaved across Brent's full lips. "*All Creatures Great and Small,* got it. We'll have to fit it all in." Brent pushed through the two kitchen doors into the front with the pecan pies.

Turning, Maggie found Kristen standing outside the refrigerator with her arms wrapped around a large bowl of dough. "You may want to be careful tonight, or it might be Brent and not your little man you'll be cuddling with on your sofa."

Maggie dismissed the insinuation with a wave of her hand, but the image it created lingered and refused to be so easily pushed aside.

~

Brent rolled his shoulders, trying to stretch out the kinks in his muscles. Between boxing pies, toting purchases to the cars of their older customers, and hauling trays of baked goods between the kitchen and the long counter, his arms ached. Of course, he'd never let on to Maggie or his coworkers. They all thought he'd returned to top-notch condition after his rehab, and for the most part, he had.

In truth, even he didn't know the full extent that his injuries played on his mental and physical well-being. That is, not until Sunday. He replayed the scene in his mind. Fear had crept into his heart for a split second, leaving him paralyzed, endangering Maggie and her son. In essence, he froze. Brent thanked the Lord again that his training kicked into gear before the fire got out of hand, but the frustration at his reaction time still lingered.

The fire at Fort Sam Houston, as well as the arsonist who set it, had stolen enough of his life— a full year and a half to be exact. He didn't want to give that snapshot from his past any more of his time or energy. The bakery and his family lay before him. A new beginning. He only wished the authorities could have proven their prime suspect, Sergeant First Class Cyrus Carver, set the fire. Going through the story with Maggie had prompted a flood of memories.

Months after the blaze, Brent had run into the guy at the base hospital. His cool steel gaze bore into Brent when they neared one another in the hallway. With curled lips, the dark-haired man slowed, leaning close to Brent as they passed and murmured, "You still smell like smoke, Lieutenant. It's a hard stench to get out of your skin."

Fury rose in Brent's chest. He balled his fists to keep from taking a swing at the enlisted man, refusing to take the bait. Brent had met other men of Carver's caliber.

"I'd be careful, Sergeant. From what I hear, you're not smelling like roses either."

With a grunt, Carver bumped into Brent's shoulder and sneered. Brent caught a glance of his front teeth. One gleamed with a gold cap. With a shove, Carver stepped around him and disappeared down the corridor, but Carver's calculated words left no doubt in Brent's mind he had set the fire.

Brent filed a complaint about the man's behavior, but he didn't know if it had led to his discharge or not. Carver was a troublemaker with a bad temper. Good riddance to him.

The ache in his calves from being on his feet all

day brought his mind back to the present. Brent rounded the counter and moved to the front door of the bakery, pushing the thoughts of the past from his mind. He exhaled a sigh, blowing away the picture of Cyrus Carver from his mind.

Instead, he shifted his focus to all the good that would come from the event today. They'd survived Crazy Pie Day. A sense of satisfaction grew in him. His ads had worked their magic, and half the county would now be serving a Sweet Things pie with their Thanksgiving banquet. He hoped this would become an annual affair, widening their exposure across nearby communities.

Grabbing the sign hanging on the front door, he flipped it to close, but before he could turn the lock, he caught sight of John McAllister and Marilyn Kemp sprinting hand in hand toward the shop. For a professional relationship, they sure looked cozy, keeping in step with one another as they held hands and jogged along the sidewalk.

A rumble of laughter stirred in Brent's chest. His friend had found more than a home during his search, just as he suspected. He'd been right about that list.

John waved when he spotted him through the glass.

Brent opened the door to let the couple inside. "Hey, you two. You almost missed the whole thing."

"We were sidetracked looking at a home near the river. I think I might have found a winner for John, though." Marilyn puffed, placing one hand over her heart to catch her breath, but Brent noticed she kept hold of John's hand with the other. "I couldn't miss one of the biggest events in the county. Everyone's been talking about this for days. Well, ever since the ads appeared in *The Daily Blossom*."

"Marilyn does like being in on the buzz of anything going on in the community."

"It's part of the job." A warm smile lifted the corners of her red lips as she turned her gaze on John. Then with a slight shift of her body, she nudged his shoulder.

You'd have thought she'd kissed him on the lips in full view of the preacher the way he blushed— a silly schoolboy grin blooming on his face. He cut his eyes toward Brent before meeting Marilyn's gaze. "And you are good at your job."

The way their eyes shimmered as they stared at one another made Brent feel like a third wheel. "Fortunately for you, I didn't lock the door yet." Brent turned, pointing to the depleted display cases. "We have been busy. Not much left."

"That's all right. I'm not picky." John headed across the tile floor to inspect the few items on the shelves in the display counters. "I don't want to show up at the Kemp's empty handed."

Within the cases sat a few blueberry muffins from the morning's offerings, a single sweet potato pie that had not been claimed by its owner, and three Apple Blossom Tarts Maggie wanted to set aside to take to her mom and dad's house for the Thanksgiving festivities. At the last minute, she scooted them into the case, afraid they wouldn't make it to five o'clock without running out of pies.

Brent hated to tell them the apple tarts were off limits. "See anything you'd like?"

Marilyn looked over John's shoulder at the meager offering. "Oh John, let's buy all of them. There are only four left. Then Maggie and Brent can say Crazy Pie Day was a total sellout." She bounced on her toes, her three-inch heels clacking against the hard ceramic tiles.

Brent couldn't recall Marilyn Kemp ever bouncing at least not in his lifetime. Flirting, yes; flouncing, often. But bouncing? That was new. Brent studied her with fresh eyes, pressing his lips together to keep the question burning in his mind from slipping onto his lips. *What happened to you?*

"Great idea." John beamed. "Kill two birds with one stone."

"Plus, they could have JoJo do a story about the event. They could talk about who came and what pies they bought. Like the mayor and maybe the principal of the high school—leaders in our community." Marilyn oozed enthusiasm. "It'd be a perfect piece for after Thanksgiving."

Brent crossed his arms waiting for the fallout he expected would come. Surely, she had some snarky remark or tidbit of gossip up her sleeve, but none came. "That's actually not a bad idea."

"Don't sound so surprised, Brent. I do have a few of those from time to time."

"Yes, you do," John slipped his arm around her waist. "You're a creative thinker."

Brent expected Marilyn to bask in John's compliment, but to Brent's amazement, she lowered her lashes, hooding her eyes.

Brent leaned his hand on the counter near the keypad to keep from toppling over in sheer astonishment.

The kitchen doors swung open, and Maggie sailed through with her clothe purse on her shoulder. "Hey, I thought I heard voices." She tossed her purse under the counter.

"Yes, we were running late, but Brent let us into the shop out of the kindness of his heart." John grinned.

"We were discussing the great success you had today," Marilyn said. "We're going to buy the last four pies, so you can say it was a total sellout." Her voice rose with excitement. "Then you and Brent can have JoJo come and do a follow-up story on the wonderful support the town showed one of its favorite small businesses."

"What a great idea, Aunt Marilyn, but I kind of wanted at least one of the apple tarts to take to Mom's house."

"Well, how 'bout John buys them and brings them with him when he comes." Marilyn turned her smile on John who squeezed her a little closer. "Libby invited us both for dinner."

Maggie's eyes widened. "Then, have at it. Purchase all of them."

Brent retrieved the remaining pies from the display case while Maggie keyed the purchase into the pad. "That'll be thirty-five dollars."

John fished out his wallet and presented a credit card to her. "I suppose you and Brent will both be at Libby's tomorrow."

Brent glanced over his shoulder as he folded down the sides of the white box, covering the first of the three Apple Blossom Tarts. "I have dinner at the Silver Spur Ranch. Nikki will kill me if I miss my first Thanksgiving home in so long." Brent slid the full box onto the counter beside the register then turned back to box the others.

"Then perhaps you can come for dessert." Marilyn picked up the box. "Since it will be your establishment providing most of the goodies."

Brent's hands fumbled with the cardboard, tearing an edge. *Your establishment*? How did she know he was a partner in the bakery? Did Tyler or Maggie spill the beans to their family? He glanced at Maggie and caught her gaze. The surprise in her eyes confirmed she hadn't been the one to tell her aunt.

"Now, Marilyn, you know I told you that in strictest of confidence," John said.

Brent turned to face them with another pie, boxed and ready to go. He handed the box to Marilyn.

"What did I say?" She dropped John's hand to take the offered white parcel, her tone dripping with innocence.

John scowled at Marilyn. "About Brent being a silent partner in the bakery. That's not common knowledge." He dipped his chin letting his gaze fall on his boots. "Sorry, man."

"Me, too." Marilyn hugged the two boxes to her chest. "I didn't mean to speak out of turn. It's so wonderful you've supported Tyler and your community in such a concrete way."

"It's all right." Brent tamped down his irritation, in order to assure the two everything would be fine. "I don't expect it to be a secret much longer. Not with Tyler selling his portion of the business. By Christmas everyone will know who the owners are."

"So will you come have a slice of pie with us Thursday?" Marilyn asked, bringing the topic back to her suggestion.

Brent shrugged. "I don't know. I hate to intrude."

Maggie leaned her hip against the counter and crossed her arms. "You should come. I know my mom would love to have you. She invites several of her friends who don't have family in town. Mom hates the idea of any one being alone over the holidays."

"That's sweet, but with the boys from the bunkhouse, Wade and Bernadette and their crew, and the chatty twins, I'll be anything but alone."

Maggie giggled. "No, you'll be lucky to have a quiet thought in your own head with that round-up."

"I know, right?" Turning his back to them, Brent stepped to the counter where the last two pies waited to be boxed. Folding the sides up, he placed a pie in each of the cardboard containers.

"You should come," Maggie said. "It'll give us a chance to discuss the proposal and make a plan to finish it over the long holiday weekend instead of trying to work on them tonight."

"I figured you'd be too tired. Honestly, I'm not sure I could concentrate on numbers tonight either."

"Right? So, why don't you plan on coming? I'm sure my parents would love to see you."

"Proposal? Are you considering purchasing Tyler's half of the bakery?" Marilyn placed the two boxes she held in her hands back on the counter by the keypad and leaned in closer.

Brent shot a glance in Maggie's direction. The look in her eyes when their gazes met tugged at his heart. A rabbit caught by a fox.

"Oh, Maggie, how wonderful." Marilyn clucked her tongue. "Of course, it only makes sense after all the energy and time you've put into this place. Why wouldn't you be the one to buy out your brother?"

"I hope to buy it," Maggie said.

"So, you and Brent would be partners." Marilyn pursed her lips. "But if you're writing a proposal, that must mean you don't have the needed funds."

"I have some of the money, but I'm short of Tyler's asking price, and he wants to close the deal before the wedding."

"I understand," Marilyn said. "So, where are you going to get the needed funds?"

Brent closed the tops of the two boxes, stacking one on top of the other. Turning, he found Marilyn's attention resting on him.

"You do have a few influential friends." Marilyn tilted her head in his direction.

Brent stepped to Maggie's side, a wave of protection rushing through him. Placing the last two boxes on top of the other two, he rested his arm across Maggie's shoulders.

Maggie glanced up at him, raising an eyebrow. He saw the question in her expression, but she didn't move away. He figured he'd hear about it when the other couple left.

"With Maggie's talent, energy, and kind heart, she doesn't need me to find her funding, though I do have four prospects in mind. I'm helping with the proposal since I have experience with the terms that need to be in the paperwork to satisfy an investor's questions and concerns."

"I'm a little surprised you're not buying Tyler out, yourself." Marilyn's brows furrowed.

John placed his hand on her back. "I don't think that's any of our concern."

His gentle tone drew her gaze. "Oh, you're right, of

course. I've done it again, overstepping the lines. None of my business." She waved her hand in the air, shooing the statement away.

Her words compelled Brent to give her an answer. "I'll be honest. I thought about it, but this shop wouldn't be Sweet Things without Maggie. It's her passion for encouraging people with her sweet treats that draws customers back. She cares about the people, and she cares about her pastries. Maggie *is* Sweet Things." He smiled down at the woman by his side. "It's where she belongs."

Maggie lifted her chin and wrapped her arms around his middle. "Thank you." A smile lit her eyes. If they had been alone, Brent would've been tempted to taste those pink lips.

With effort, Brent broke the connection with Maggie and faced the pair standing in front of them. "That's what the proposal is for. We're working on getting her the financing she needs, so she can stay right here."

Maggie dropped her arms but didn't move from his side.

"That's so romantic," Marilyn cooed, slipping into John's arms.

Brent pushed the boxes toward them, forcing a smile to his lips.

Scurrying out of Brent's reach, Maggie moved around the counter and headed toward the door. "Thank you, guys, so much for purchasing the last of the pies. I'll be sure to call JoJo and see if they would be interested in doing a follow-up piece. Great idea, Aunt Marilyn."

Marilyn followed Maggie to the door, her heels

clacking against the tile. "Happy to help."

John picked up the four pie boxes. "So, are you coming to the Kemps for dessert or not?" His friend leaned across the counter, drawing closer to him and lowered his voice. "I could use the extra support. First time I'm meeting the whole family." His eyes grew wide. "A little back up might be a good thing."

Brent couldn't let his friend go into enemy territory without him. It'd be unthinkable to let down a fellow soldier. Besides, now, he needed to be there for Maggie, so they could work on the proposal. His gaze drifted toward Maggie standing by the door, and he made his decision. "I'll be there." Not simply because his buddy needed him, but also because the dark-haired girl with ringlets, who gave away free cupcakes to kids, wanted him to come.

Chapter Eleven

Brent moaned and leaned back in the Queen Anne chair that sat cattycornered to the couch, wishing he could loosen his belt a notch. Between Nikki and Bernadette, they managed to make every single one of his favorite dishes, right down to the pumpkin pie with whipped cream. How was he ever going to eat another round of dessert at Maggie's parents? Checking his phone, he noted the time. He needed to leave in another forty-five minutes. That is if he could get out of this chair.

Maggie had sent him a text earlier, wishing him a Happy Thanksgiving and letting him know when everyone planned to gather for dessert. She included a lot of emojis of pies, a tom turkey in a pilgrim's hat, and something resembling a bear in a rocking chair. Not up on emoji lingo, he went the safe route and replied, "See ya then."

He pushed his phone back into his pocket and slouched a little lower in the chair, feeling like a stuffed turkey.

Spotting Nikki from the couch, Dan said, "You two out did yourselves." He patted his stomach as he assumed the after-Thanksgiving position. Reaching for the remote, he flipped channels and landed on an SEC football game. Blue, the old mutt, entered the living room, made a few circles, then plopped down at the corner of the couch near Dan.

Nikki chuckled. "I'm just glad I made two turkeys, or there wouldn't be enough for leftovers. And I know how you feel about leftovers."

"They're the best part of Thanksgiving." Dan heaved a sigh and untucked his shirt. Sliding the remote back onto the coffee table, he propped his socked feet up on the wooden structure.

"We have cookies in the oven, so I hope you still have a little room." A sly grin pushed up the corners of her lips before she disappeared back into the kitchen. The sounds of clanking dishes and female chatter floated into the room above the hum of the football announcers discussing the last play.

Wade hobbled into the living room from the entryway, carrying Lani, the blond-haired cutie, in his arms and Duncan, the six-year-old, on his back. How he handled all five kids, their property, and the sheriff's office, Brent had no clue. He struggled to keep up with the bakery and the few other investments he maintained.

"All right, tiger, off the dad express."

"Aw," The little boy moaned.

Wade handed Lani to Brent before flipping Duncan over his shoulder and plopping him onto the opposite end of the couch from Dan. The little boy giggled, pushing up to a sitting position on the middle seat. Wade reclaimed Lani with a few raspberries to her tummy as he strolled back to the couch, then checked for the little boy before relaxing into the cushions.

The sweet girl laid her head on Wade's chest, sucking her thumb. Her eye lids drooped, growing heavier with each tiny circle Wade traced on her back.

Brent missed John's presence today since he'd spent the holiday over at the Kemps, but he'd enjoyed having time with his brothers and their families. The conversation at the table reminded him how much he enjoyed the connection with them.

"You know," Wade's low timbre cut into Brent's thoughts. "The only thing missing today is Maggie. You should've invited her to come to dinner since she invited you to her parents' house for dessert. After all, she's going to be your partner." Dan waggled his eyebrows.

Brent ignored his brother's lame insinuation that more existed between him and Maggie than business. The picture of her upturned face, his arm around her, and her full lips flashed into his mind, making his pulse race. "She's not my partner yet." Brent fumbled. "We hope she'll get the backing, but she's short the asking price."

"Why doesn't she ask her brother to let her make payments? You know, keep it in the family?" Dan asked.

"She doesn't think it's fair to make him wait. Besides, he and Nadine need the money for their start in Atlanta."

"I heard they're opening a graphics design business." Wade placed an arm around Duncan and drew the boy closer to his side.

"That's the rumor. Tyler's pretty pumped about it. Of course, he'd be pumped about anything involving

Nadine." Brent chuckled, aware of the twinge of envy rising in him. He'd never deny his friend the happiness he deserved, but over the last few weeks working in the bakery with Maggie, he'd begun to wonder if he'd have his own 'forever.' It never failed when he thought of the future that a certain brunette with hazel eyes stood front and center.

"Speaking of rumors, I heard there was a kitchen fire at the bakery the other day. Anything we should be worried about?" Dan leaned forward, resting his elbows on his knees.

Brent shook his head, trying to mask the fear that crept over him at the mention of the incident. "Nope, I put it out, and the damaged hood can be replaced. It still functions, but before the next health inspection, I'll have to hire a guy to put in a new one."

"So, how are you?" Wade met his gaze over the top of a patch of wayward blond curls. The little girl snuggled close. "I mean, after what happened to you at Fort Sam Houston. I figured this might put a bad taste in your mouth."

"I won't lie. It shook me up. But I handled the situation, and everyone came out of it safe." Brent let his gaze move to the floor. His heart pounded like a rock band in his ear. He pushed the panic deeper, refusing to give in to the ridiculous rush.

"I know whenever we have a shooting in the department, it affects everyone. The fact that any one of us can be called on to put our lives on the line that gets driven home, hard." Wade laid his head on top of Lani's. Soft snores flittered into the air like specks of fairy dust. "We always have our guys talk to someone to insure they're coping well. Did you have a chance to talk to anyone about what happened to you?"

"Yeah, the commander made sure to include a few sessions of therapy as part of my rehab. Body, soul, mind." Brent rambled off the commander's motto. "Since they thought the motor pool fire was arson, he wanted to make sure I was in the right headspace to help with the investigation as much as I could, as a witness."

"Arson?" Dan grabbed the remote and muted the game. "You didn't tell us it was a crime."

Wade scowled. "You should've told us. Did they catch the perp?"

"No." Brent swallowed hard, fighting to keep his voice calm and even. "They had a few suspects, but nothing the authorities could prove. The primary suspect was discharged but not in connection with the fire. Since there was a man in the motor pool, whoever did it, is facing attempted murder charges along with the arson."

"There was a man inside the burning building?" Dan asked.

"Could the man identify the perp?" Wade asked, sounding every inch a sheriff.

"No, he couldn't identify the guy." Brent gave them one of his lop-sided grins, wanting to downplay the incident.

"Cookies are ready," Nikki called from the kitchen.

Brent let out a sigh, saved by the oven timer.

Wade released the little boy, who slipped off the couch and hurried toward the other room. Standing, Wade placed Lani on the couch without disturbing her. "I knew you'd been injured during the motor pool fire, but you never mentioned there was someone inside."

"There's more to it." Brent shrugged.

"You've kept us in the dark long enough. Spill it." Impatience colored Dan's tone.

"I spotted the man through a window and called in the fire, but I wasn't exactly on duty when I entered the building."

"So, you went in without your gear," Dan said.

"And without backup." Wade widened his stance, crossing his arms, looking for all the world like an immovable mountain. "That was a foolhardy thing to do."

Brent grabbed the arms of the chair, clinching them tight. This was the reason he'd avoided telling his family the details. He didn't need his older brothers second-guessing his decisions in the name of protecting him.

"You should've waited," Dan said. "It could've been a lot worse."

Brent vaulted from his seat. "You don't have to tell me. I've paid the price for my decision with a year and half of my life, relearning to use my arm and shoulder again. But I had to do something I couldn't leave him to die. I had to see if he was alive. I had to save him if I could. It was my job."

"What happened?" Wade moved toward him, placing his hand on his shoulder, compassion filling his eyes. "It's all right. You can tell us."

The last of the anger drained from him. "When I reached the man, he was unconscious but alive. The flames were all around us, but I thought I could get him out. Then an explosion went off near the back where the fluids were kept. I tried to foist him over my shoulder."

Wade dropped his hand but didn't step away.

"Then the man regained consciousness. In a split second, he'd pushed me away, assuming I was his attacker. He sent me into the flames. I recovered quickly and rolled to put out the flames, but the damage was done. If I'd had on my gear, I'd been fine."

Dan nodded. "But if you'd waited, the man would've been dead."

"More than likely. We'll never know." Brent slipped back into his seat, leaning his forearms on his knees. "I made a stupid choice."

"No, you made the hard choice. The one you swore to make when you chose to join the fire brigade." Dan rose and tousled Brent's hair as if he were still twelve.

Brent swatted at his hand but couldn't keep the grin off his face.

"And I'm nothing but proud of you."

"You're a hero, little brother. No denying it." Wade thumped his back twice. "I'd expect nothing less from a Thibodeaux. Pops would be so proud of you."

"Maybe." Brent let the image of his grandfather fill his mind. He missed him, and it pained him that he'd been unable to make the funeral. His brothers, however, sent him their grandfather's well-worn Bible. Having it through those long months of surgery and rehab had given Brent a sense of peace, a closeness to the man he loved.

"No, he'd be crowing like a rooster," Wade said. "But he would've agreed with us about Maggie and Matt. You should've invited them over for Thanksgiving dinner."

Nikki popped back into the doorway. "If you want any cookies, you'd better hustle up. The kids have almost polished them off." Meeting Dan's gaze, she added, "The twins need a bath. Chocolate from head to toe."

~

Maggie paced back and forth in her mom's kitchen, checking her phone for a text message every few minutes. Throughout the day, she and Brent had exchanged messages. His last text made it sound as if he were walking out the door headed her way. So where was he?

Her pulse strummed. She'd gone out on a limb inviting him to come for dessert. They had so much fun with Crazy Pie Day, even with the extra work. She longed to spend more time with him to the point of using the proposal as an excuse to persuade him to come over to her mom's. What had she been thinking?

Then the image of his strong, chiseled jawline sporting a five o'clock shadow and those stormy green eyes popped into her brain. His warm touch when he pulled her close to protect her from her aunt's probing questions had sent prickles dancing across her body. Even now, her mouth was as dry as a Texas summer thinking about it.

Matt sat in his highchair eating bits of turkey and the last dregs of his cornbread dressing. The meal ended an hour ago, but her son ate at a slower pace. Okay, so he played a lot with his food and then ate it, but she didn't have the energy to battle with him today.

She paused next to his chair to remove a piece of sweet potatoes from his curls. Maggie would be so grateful whenever he outgrew this stage of discovery.

Her mother glanced over her shoulder toward her before she plunged her hands into the soapy dishwater.

"Relax. He'll be here."

"I am relaxed." Maggie tried to play it off, but her nerves were on edge. She pivoted and headed back around the table. The more time she spent with Brent, the more he invaded her thoughts. At first, she'd chalked it up to her old crush. Now, though, she couldn't ignore the feelings that plagued her every time he came near.

"You're pacing like a caged lion." Libby rinsed a dish under the warm water. "You'd think you hadn't known Brent for most of your life the way you're acting. It's Brent."

"I know." She caught the sharpness in her tone and softened her words. "It's been different though since I found out he's a partner in the business. I'm not sure how to treat him."

"Treat him like you've been treating him."

"I can't. He's not just Tyler's friend who needed something to occupy his time until he got bored and moved on." Maggie frowned. "He's an ex-fireman, ex-soldier, billionaire, who owns half the bakery I love." *And who turns my insides mushy like warm, gooey dough.* "What am I supposed to do?"

"Hmm, when you say it like that, it does sound complicated." Her mom rinsed the soap from the sponge and moved around the kitchen wiping the counters. The food had been put away, but the desserts remained out, displayed on the kitchen island along with a stack of paper plates decorated with cartoon turkeys. "Can you make the coffee?"

"Sure." Maggie wiped her hands on a napkin to remove the sweet potato chunks, then grabbed the carafe. She waited as it filled with water. "Complicated is a good word for my relationship with Brent."

"Ooh, I like the word relationship, too." Her mother grinned as she dumped the crumbs from her hand into the trash can.

"Mom, we're business partners, nothing else. Okay, almost business partners if I can get this proposal ready in time."

"One can hope for more," her mother said in a singsong fashion.

Ignoring the not-so-subtle hint, Maggie placed the carafe on the hot plate and opened the top of the coffee maker to add the grounds. "Brent has a few prospective investors lined up for me to meet with next week."

"Oh, then you do have to finish your proposal." Her mom rinsed the sponge, pushing it onto the ledge of the sink by the faucet. "It's a good thing the bakery is closed over the long weekend. It gives you a couple of days to get everything ready. You should invite Brent over to your place Friday to work on it."

"I don't know. We're supposed to work on it tonight. That's why he's coming over."

"I doubt that." Her mom shot her a knowing glance then she strolled toward Matt. "He's coming over because you invited him, and he enjoys your company. Besides, after all the food we've consumed, who can think clear enough to work on business?"

"Now, it's my turn to have doubts. There's no way he's coming over because he loves my company. He should be sick of it after all the time we spend together at the bakery." Maggie hadn't made it easy on Brent. From the moment he started working at the shop, she'd been suspicious, hard to work with, and at times downright hostile. The fact he had offered to help her and wanted her to succeed made him a saint in her book. A dark-haired, broad-shouldered saint who looked good even in a lime green apron.

Leaning over the highchair, Maggie's mom unsnapped the bib from around Matt's neck and picked up the toddler. "I'll keep Little Man for you, so you can give Brent … I mean, the proposal your full attention."

Maggie pushed the button on the coffee maker then leaned her hip against the counter facing her mom. She struggled to remove the image of Brent and his knee-wobbling half grin out of her mind.

"It would be nice to knock it out and not have to worry about the details anymore. Then I could spend Saturday working on the presentation for the investors."

A roar rose from the living room. "Sounds like Texas scored again." Maggie's mom pressed a kiss to the sticky cheek of her grandson. "You, young man, need a bath." Meeting Maggie's gaze, she asked, "Do you mind handling dessert?"

"Not if you're going to bathe that messy monster." Maggie swung her son from her mother's arms and tickled his tummy. Handing him back, she said, "thank you. And don't forget behind the ears." Wiggling her fingers, she tickled his midsection. The boy squealed when she tweaked his tummy.

A clamor rose from the living room, and a few minutes later, Tyler shuffled into the kitchen in his sock feet, holding Nadine's hand. Brent followed. "Hey, Mom, look who finally showed up. I guess we can have dessert now."

Nadine nudged Tyler with her shoulder. "Be nice to your friend, or he might not want to be your best man at the wedding."

"I am being nice, but I've been waiting to sample those Apple Blossom Tarts all day. It's been pure torture. Aunt Marilyn said we had to wait until our honored guest arrived." Tyler bowed in Brent's direction. "Now he's here, so let's have pie."

"Don't pay any attention to Tyler. I'm glad you're here." Maggie's mom sidled up to the six-foot-three man and hugged him with her free arm.

Matt clambered toward Brent, leaping from her grasp. "Bwent"

Without hesitation, he took the little boy into his arms. Matt's face lit up. "Gand-gand, me pie too." Pointing to the desserts, Matt's eyes widened. "Pie. Me, pie."

Brent laughed and tickled Matt under his chin. The little boy hunched his shoulders, burying his chin against his chest. "Pie, you say? What do you think, Mrs. Kemp? Can this young man have pie?" Brent's words were meant for Maggie's mom, but his eyes lingered on her.

The twinge of pleasure pulsing through her made the corners of her lips rise.

"I suppose if he's going to eat dessert, before bath time is better than after." Her mom chuckled, taking Matt from Brent's arms. "Back into your chair you go."

Maggie picked up the pie server and cut the Apple Blossom Tart into eight slices. Then she used the cake server and a knife to slice the red velvet cake she'd made special for today while she and Kristen were baking in preparation for Crazy Pie Day.

Tyler strolled to the kitchen doorway. Poking his head around the door jamb, he hollered down the hall to the occupants of the living room. "Come and get it."

The way the entire group stampeded across the wooden floor to the kitchen, Maggie would've thought no one had eaten a crumb in days. They nearly knocked over her dad in the process.

The smell of the brewing coffee filled the room. Maggie dished the pie slices onto the paper plates while her mother pulled down ten mugs from the cabinet above the coffee maker.

John and Marilyn both grabbed a slice of pie before taking a seat at the table, and Tyler snatched one for Matt who had turned in his highchair to watch the action. "Here you go, buddy."

Nadine balanced a plate with a slice of pie and two plates with cake on her arm. "You know he's going to want one of each. Plus, when you slice the pumpkin pie, he'll be back."

"He's not going to fit into his tux if he keeps eating like this." Maggie grinned.

Nadine nodded. "Try and tell him that." Her eyes glowed as her gaze landed on her future groom.

"So, how are the wedding plans going?" Brent grabbed one of the plates with the apple tart on it, along with a cup of coffee before joining the others at the table.

Maggie couldn't help feeling a pinch of jealousy. Nadine and her brother had found what she'd found with Ted, a love that would go the distance. For a long time, she didn't dare dream of finding anything close to what she'd lost, but the way she felt proound Brent made her ... She let her gaze drift to him seated next to her brother at the dinner table. A pang pulled at her heart, what was it? Perhaps, hope. Could she find that kind of love again?

His eyes locked on hers. The intensity of the storm in their depth pulled at her. Startled, she dragged her gaze from his and turned her focus back to slicing the pumpkin pie. Sliding a piece onto a plate, she strolled to the table and deposited the wedge in front of her brother.

"So far, we have the venue, the rings, the license." Nadine nodded toward Maggie. "And the cake. Now, all I need is a dress."

"Oh, I thought you got your dress ages ago." Maggie poured a cup of coffee, stirring in a dribble of creamer. "I mean you couldn't have made it any easier for the bridesmaids by giving us a color and letting us pick our own style." An errand she still hadn't accomplished.

"It's so hard to fit all body types into the same style dress."

"Amen, sister." Maggie's curvy hips looked better in jeans than in a swath of clingy dress material.

Libby leaned her chin on her fist, tucking her foot under her in her chair. "Have you looked at Edwards? They have a great selection. Or maybe Gayfers?"

"Ouch, talk about pricey." Maggie cut into her slice of pumpkin pie and took a bite.

"I've been to every store in Reseda County, but nothing seems right," Nadine said.

"Maybe, you should think outside the box. Who says your wedding dress has to be a wedding dress. You should wear what makes you feel beautiful."

Maggie's mom nodded. "She's right. Maybe a flowy pants suit. Or instead of a long dress with a train, go for a short cute one with a wide bow."

"Okay, if this is going to devolve into a lengthy discussion on wedding fashion, I'm out of here." Tyler lifted the plate with the pumpkin pie on it.

"All right, instead let's talk about the bachelor camping trip." Brent scrapped his fork across the paper plate in front of him then licked the prongs clean. "Are we still on for the weekend before Christmas eve? That's not too far away."

"A couple of weeks should be enough time for you to gather the snacks and beverages." Tyler chuckled. "Remember, no tools." He winked. "I wouldn't want to have to bail you out of jail."

All eyes turned toward Brent. He froze with his cup of coffee in midair.

"This sounds promising." John scooted forward in his chair.

Marilyn grinned. "It sure does."

Letting out a deep sigh, Brent put down his cup. "It was a dumb dare I shouldn't have accepted. Teenager stuff. Sheriff McCain, who was sheriff at the time, almost caught me." Brent nailed Tyler with a glare. "That's all."

"Hmm, sounds like there's more to the story, but I'll weasel it out of you later," Maggie said. "When we're alone." The words slipped out before she thought them through.

A cat-that-ate-the-canary grin pulled across her brother's lips as the others oohed and aahed at the remark. John chuckled. "You should see your face." He pointed to Brent.

Brent shrugged. "All right, everybody's had their fun."

Heat worked its way up Maggie's neck. If she

didn't escape soon, everybody would see the embarrassment painted on her cheeks.

Brent glanced her way. "So, are you ready to get to work on the proposal?"

Sliding her chair back, she stood. "Yes, I am." She turned to her mom. "Are you still up for bathing Matt?"

"Of course." Her mother shooed her away with a wave of her hand. "You two go on into the office. I'm sure no one will bother you in there."

"Thanks, Mom," Maggie leaned over and kissed her mother's cheek. "You da bomb."

"No, I'm the Gand-Gand."

Chapter Twelve

Brent stretched his aching shoulders, pulling his elbows together behind him to release the tension he felt across his back. They'd been at it all afternoon, hovering over their computers at Maggie's kitchen table.

Thanksgiving evening had proven to be a bust. They managed to work for about two hours, not adding much to what they had accomplished the Sunday before Crazy Pie Day. They'd agreed to meet today for lunch at her house to see if they couldn't finish the proposal. He wanted to give her time to practice the presentation before having to do it live on Monday afternoon for Mrs. Thornton, one of the four investors he'd lined up for her.

Libby and Nadine had taken Matt with them Black Friday shopping, giving him and Maggie the needed time to focus. Brent had written enough proposals that he knew the components needed from memory, but for Maggie, he wanted the document to hit all the high notes, showcasing the unique qualities of the bakery.

Tilting his head to one side and then to the other, Brent heard a slight crack as his neck loosened. He glanced at the time on the microwave display, but the red numbers blurred together. He rubbed his eyes with his forefinger and thumb, but it didn't help. "I think I have information blindness."

Maggie looked over her laptop. "I know what you mean." She leaned back and picked up her phone from beside the computer. "Its five-thirty. We've been working on this since noon." She raised her arms above her head and stretched like a cat in a warm ray of sunshine. "I guess we need to wrap it up soon. Mom will be bringing Matt home around six for dinner and bath time. What's left?"

Brent tapped the keys of his computer to bring up the list of the items for the proposal. "Okay, we've done the target customer description, the mission and goal statement, and the financials for the business. The return on investment looks pretty solid, barring any major catastrophes."

"Like a hurricane? Or a fire?" She grinned as a piece of her brunette hair fell from her ponytail, drifting down to her shoulders.

"Exactly." Brent's hands itched to push the stray hair that framed her face so perfectly behind her ear.

"I've worked on the hole in the market that the bakery addresses, along with a description of our current bake staff and counter help as well as our long-term goals."

"I guess that leaves us with the historical performance of the company. I brought the books, so we'd have the full picture." Brent stood and headed into the living room to retrieve the records from his backpack.

"Don't forget, the benefits gained by the investors for trusting me with their money."

"The first item mentioned should be that they get free cupcakes for life." Brent pulled out his chair and dropped back into the seat.

Maggie laid her hand on his arm. "I appreciate this so much. I know I gave you a hard time when I thought you were my competition." She winced. "Sorry, but I don't know what I would've done without you. Lining up potential investors, helping gather all the information. You've saved me."

Brent placed his hand over hers and let the warmth of her touch soak into his skin. It'd been a long time since he'd fought his feelings for anyone. With the scars, he'd accepted his days of dating were over. "It's my pleasure. Besides, it's a bit selfish. I don't want to have to train a new partner."

Her hazel eyes glowed. "Me, either."

The air zipped around him. Brent swore he could hear pops and snaps as her hand lingered in his, the gentleness of her touch, the smoothness of her skin. Then she lifted her hand. "I don't know about you, but I could use a break from all this information overload. How about I make some dinner? Then after Matt goes to bed, we can finish up. Will that work?"

"Sounds good. I'll need to let Nikki know I won't be there for supper. She likes to have a head count, since the ranch hands come in to eat with them." Brent grabbed his phone from the table and stepped outside the back door to make the call.

"How's it going over there?" Nikki's voice held a hint of teasing. "Getting any work done?"

The muffled sounds of a struggle on the other end of the phone caught Brent's attention. "Go ahead, poke fun. But we're making progress."

"Good for you." A banging sound erupted over the line, causing Brent to hold the phone away from his ear until the noise stopped. "No, don't do that, sweetie."

"Am I interrupting something?"

"No, I'm rounding up the twins to get them to the table." Nikki sighed. "Some days that's easier than others. Today, your nephew decided he wanted to learn to play drums on my pots with a spoon while I cooked dinner."

Brent chuckled. "David has always shown great musical talent like when he sings in his car seat to the 'Wheels on the Bus.'"

"Laugh now, buddy, but one day it's going to be you chasing after a kid or two."

"Are you threatening me? You know I'm a confirmed bachelor. Besides, what woman would want to look at my ugly mug every day?" He couldn't fight the compulsion to touch his left jaw.

"Oh, I could name twenty or more without breaking a sweat who would love to have the opportunity. Don't kid yourself, Brent. Your bachelorhood is a ticking time bomb about to be blown away."

"Apparently, all the beating and banging David subjected you to has affected your brain." Brent laughed. "You've gone balmy." Before Nikki could answer, he redirected the conversation back to his original intent. "Look, I'm calling to let you know I'm eating over at Maggie's place, so we can finish up after Matt goes to bed."

"Umm, a woman and a child. I can hear that clock ticking. Tick, tock. Tick, tock."

"I'm hanging up now, Sis."

"Tick, tick, tick."

"Not listening. Bye." Brent ended the call, smiling from ear to ear. His ego needed that boost. He could always count on his sister-in-law Nikki to be his number one cheerleader when it came to his love life. As he was the last unattached Thibodeaux brother, she held out high hopes for him.

Turning, he stuffed his phone into his front pocket before spotting Maggie through the window standing in the kitchen. Maggie's face lit up as Matt and her mother, Libby, appeared from the living room. Wrapping her arms around the two-year-old, Maggie snuggled him close to her, covering his cheeks with kisses. Without putting him down, she stretched her empty arm around her mother, pulling her in for a quick hug.

Brent's chest swelled with pride. He loved the way Maggie acted with her son. Matt's presence made her beam like sunshine in July. She was a natural beauty, but at times like these, she stole his breath away.

She must've sensed him staring because she flashed him a devastating smile. He swallowed the lump in his throat. Maybe Nikki wasn't far off the mark. Maybe his days as a bachelor were numbered.

Who was he kidding? Maggie could have her choice of men. Why in the world would she pick a man with so much baggage? A man who came with his own set of fears.

~

Matt's head rested on his arm on the highchair tray. Maggie stroked his blond hair, pushing a small strand out of his closed eyes. "I figured the day with Mom and Nadine would wear him out."

"Did he get enough to eat?" The brows above Brent's dark green eyes crinkled in concern. "I'm no expert, but doesn't he need more than a spoonful of spaghetti since he's a growing boy?"

Maggie nodded. "Usually, I try to get at least two or three spoonsful into him, but tonight I couldn't have kept him awake if I'd tried." Maggie stood and collected the dirty plates from off the table. "Trust me, he eats very well."

Brent rubbed the little boy's chubby arm. "I can see that. He's a stout little man."

"He takes after his father. Ted was big and fierce when necessary, but once people got to know him, they found him to be a big teddy bear. That's why I took to calling him Ted instead of Theo like his mother." She shrugged and placed the plates on the counter next to the sink. "He seemed more like a Ted to me."

"It's good you have such wonderful memories of him." Brent rose, pushing his chair back with his legs. Crossing the floor, he stopped beside Maggie, who stood scraping the food from the plates with a fork. His nearness made her antsy, causing her to clank the plates together.

Moving around her, he opened the dishwasher. "Hand them to me, and I'll load."

"Thanks." She tried to remember the last time someone had helped her with the after-dinner dishes. Maggie tended to wait until Matt went down for the evening before tackling the dishes or the laundry or the other hundred little tasks that fell to her since she'd been widowed. How had three years slipped by so fast? Some days, it seemed so fresh.

She glanced toward her sleeping son. Ted

would've loved being a father, but the helicopter accident took him before she'd even realized they were expecting. Her heart ached, not like it did at first when she discovered she was carrying his child, but rather, the ache had shifted to a dull pang.

Glancing at Brent, she watched as he rearranged a few of the items already in the rack. The simple act brought back the memory of dozens of evenings spent with her husband, eating dinner together, doing dishes, and watching TV while holding hands on the couch. Within those five years of marriage, they'd lived a lifetime— a beautiful, wonderful lifetime that she missed every day.

When Brent looked up, he met her gaze. A quizzical look crossed his face. "Are you all right?"

She nodded, afraid to say anything, not sure she could keep the tears at bay. Blinking, she willed them to stay away then turned to pick up another dish.

He straightened, touching her shoulder.

She stilled but refused to meet his gaze. The sadness lingered too close to the surface.

"Maggie, is there anything I can do? What happened?" He dropped his hand but stayed close.

She pressed her lips together, trying to regain control. "It's silly." She shrugged, keeping her gaze on the running water.

"Tell me please. Did I do something to upset you?"

Giggling, she wiped a stray tear from her cheek with the back of her hand. "Only if helping with the dishes is a crime."

His face scrunched into a cobweb of lines. "I don't follow."

"It's not you or anything you've done. I'm not sure

why I'm feeling so sappy. Guess I'm tired. We've used up a lot of my brain power." Sniffling, she picked up the scrub brush and swished it around inside the dinosaur bowl before handing it to Brent. "It's … been a long time since I've had help with the after-dinner dishes." Glancing at him, she found his dark green eyes shining at her, full of compassion.

With a mischievous grin, he added, "Glad to be of service, ma'am." He drew his shoulders back and stood at attention, giving her a quick salute.

A giggle bubbled up inside her. Leave it to Brent to lighten things up. "Stop it, soldier. Before I report you to your commanding officer."

His eyes widened. "In this situation, I believe that might be you." A grin swung across his lips.

Her heart melted. She'd always adored Brent and thought he was hot stuff when he was in high school, but now she admired him for the compassionate man he'd become. "Well, in that case, soldier, I'm recruiting you for toddler duty."

"My pleasure, ma'am." Reaching over, Brent snagged the last of the glasses from the sink and placed them on the top rack.

Maggie opened the cabinet door beneath the sink and pulled out the dishwasher detergent. Filling the compartment with one of the new pods, she shut the door and pushed the start button. Leaning against the counter, she faced the table where her son sat still sleeping with spaghetti sauce ringing his lips. "Are you ready for your next assignment?"

"As ready as I'll ever be." Brent nudged her with his hip like he used to do when they were teens. Then he wrapped his arm around her shoulders and pulled her to him. "Thanks for dinner, Magnolia."

She hated her name, but when he said it, it sounded sweeter somehow like a warm, gooey chocolate chip cookie.

A woodsy scent swirled around her as she felt his lips touch her temple. She closed her eyes and let her head lean against his shoulder. He tightened his grip and rested his cheek on the crown of her head. This was the second time she'd found herself in his arms, and she liked it.

"Momma," a croaky voice called out.

Maggie jumped, almost knocking Brent's chin with her head. She'd been snuggling with a man who owned part of the bakery where she worked as the manager, an employee. Talk about playing with fire. She pulled away from his arms.

He wore a sheepish grin, but not one shred of remorse shown on his face. *Surely, he thinks of me as a friend.* But the gleam in his eye didn't fit with that scenario. The heat she saw made her pulse race, sending nervous energy crackling through her. *He's a friend, just a friend.* She repeated this mantra in her head as she marched across the tile to the highchair to retrieve Matt.

Brent followed her. "Here, let me get him."

Maggie loosened the tray, and Brent pulled the little man out of his seat into his arms.

"I guess we'd better wash his face," Brent said. Matt laid his head on Brent's shoulder and threw his pudgy arms around his neck.

Maggie pulled a paper towel from the holder and wet it under the kitchen faucet. Retracing her steps, she wiped his face. The spaghetti sauce clung to the toddler's cheeks, but Maggie gave the stubborn spots an extra swipe. "Let's see if we can put some pajamas on him."

"Lead the way, ma'am." Brent lifted the two-year-old back onto his shoulder.

Maggie walked through the living room, down a short hall, to Matt's bedroom, becoming very conscious of the small size and state of her home. Brent made it easy to forget he came from money. "It's not much, but it's cozy." She kicked a pile of dirty clothes out of the doorway as she entered the small bedroom.

"It suits you. Warm and homey."

Maggie reached for Matt and placed him on the changing table. "Can you hand me those PJs on top of his dresser?"

Brent grabbed the shirt and pants covered in cars and handed them to Maggie. "Here you go."

Matt stretched his arms above his head, never opening his eyes. Sliding off his stained shirt, Maggie took the opportunity to slip the sleeves of the PJs onto his arms and wiggle the collar over his head.

Brent moved to the other end of the changing table to help slide off Matt's pants. They worked together to get the little boy into his sleepwear. Matt rolled to his side when they finished.

"We'd better put him into his bed before he rolls off this table," Brent said.

"Yeah, you're right. Mom and Nadine must've run him ragged. He never sleeps through being moved around like this." Maggie glanced over at Matt's toddler's bed, looking for his favorite plush toy. "I thought I left Dino beside his pillow." She moved around the room lifting discarded clothes from the floor and tossing them into a laundry basket that sat inside the closet, but no dino appeared. "Let me go check the living room. Maybe it's still in his diaper bag. He'll need it if he wakes up in the night."

"Sure, go ahead. I'll stand watch. Come on buddy. Let's get comfortable while we wait."

Maggie scanned the floor in the living room but didn't see the toy. Sitting on the couch, she dug into the diaper bag, hoping her mom hadn't left it in her car. After pulling out three pull ups, a sticky sippy cup, and a bag of cheerios, she found the green plush animal. "There you are."

Not wanting to leave Brent stranded, she hurried to Matt's room but paused at the door. Brent's deep voice rumbled out the words to "Amazing Grace." The tune floated out soft and sweet. She peeked around the half-closed door and found the six-three man folded up in her antique lady-size rocking chair, holding Matt on his shoulder, singing with his eyes closed.

When he'd finished the chorus, she meant to enter but his words stopped her. "You know you are one lucky little boy. You have a great mom. She's out there right now hunting for your favorite toy."

Maggie squeezed the dino to her chest. She shouldn't be eavesdropping, even if the conversation was between a man and a two-year-old toddler, but she stayed glued to the spot.

"Yes, sir, she is something else. She's pretty and talented and smart. Boy, can she cook too. But most of all, you're lucky because she loves you so much. She has a big heart and most of it is full of loving you."

His words caught her off guard. He thought of her as pretty and smart? Looking down at the smudges on her shirt, she wondered how in the world he ever thought of her as pretty. Most days, she wore a bright green apron with flour and chocolate smeared across the front with her hair pulled back in a ponytail to keep it out of the way. She rarely wore make-up. She didn't know if he'd ever seen her without food or spit-up on her clothing.

The man had to be blind. How could he think she was smart? They'd plowed through numbers for the last several hours. He had to know her shortcomings with figures. Sure, she wasn't a dunce, but she wasn't a business genius like him either.

The soft words of another hymn drew her from her thoughts. Placing her hand on the doorknob, she pushed it open.

Brent looked up at her, smiling. "He's snoring." Slowly, he rose from the chair. He leaned over the small bed and deposited the little boy onto the mattress.

Maggie gathered the blankets at the foot of the bed and pulled them over the sleeping child.

"How can they do that?" Brent knelt on one knee beside the boy.

"Do what?"

"Sleep like that. Without any care in the world. Trusting you will look after him."

"I don't know but isn't it wonderful? What I wouldn't give to be so carefree. Ever since Ted passed, I've been working hard to make ends meet. To make sure I can take care of Matt without leaving him to be raised by others. The doubts and worries keep me up some nights."

"I can't imagine the sacrifices you've made." Brent stood and met her gaze.

Feeling uncomfortable with the conversation, Maggie moved the topic to him. "Look who's talking about sacrifices." She nudged his shoulder with hers. "Brent, you've given the ultimate price. You've put your life on the line for others by being a fireman and a soldier. You've served your country and your community."

Brent hung his head.

"I don't feel like a hero. I feel like a coward." He straightened. "I still have nightmares about the fire that caused my injuries. They don't happen as often since I left the Army, but I still have them." His expression grew serious. Maggie could tell this admission had cost him a part of his pride. "The other day, I hesitated. The fire at the bakery shouldn't have gotten as bad as it did. I should've reacted quicker, but I froze."

Maggie moved toward him and took his hand in both of her hands. "You did what needed to be done. We lost a stove hood. So what? You rescued me and Matt and saved the shop."

"Maggie, if anything ever happened to you …" He shook his head, not meeting her gaze.

"But it didn't." She squeezed his hand. "Because of you."

Chapter Thirteen

Brent rounded Deadman's Curve, heading back to Silver Spur Ranch, driving Dan's truck. He'd left his motorcycle at home, knowing he'd be tired when he and Maggie finished. He hadn't expected it to be this late. It was close to midnight, and the road was deserted. He and Maggie had worked until they finished the proposal with all the figures and future forecasts in place. They'd even sketched out a two-year marketing plan hoping to entice her prospective investors with a promise of a quick return on their investment.

As Brent watched his headlights push across the pavement, Dan's question from yesterday drifted into his mind. Why couldn't he be Maggie's investor or a silent partner, like he had been for Tyler? Of course, he knew the answer.

However, he had no intention of losing Maggie as part of the business over money either, so he needed the proposal to hit its mark. He'd lined up four promising perspective investors that he felt certain would be interested in keeping the bakery up and running and keeping Maggie right where she belonged at Sweet Things.

Turning onto Deadwood Drive, Brent slowed his

speed. When he passed the empty parking lot of Harry's Hardware, he noted how the outside security lights flooded the gravel parking lot, giving it an eerie yellow glow. For some reason, a sense of uneasiness washed over him. Brent adjusted his position. To fend off his concerns, he reached for the radio.

Headlights washed past him going the other direction as he headed towards Pope Bridge. The truck rumbled over the uneven road before he entered the long stretch of bridge. The railing gleamed in the beam of his own headlights. He shifted in his seat, trying to stay awake.

Glancing at his side mirror, he spotted another truck coming onto the bridge, a few car lengths behind him. He settled in his seat and adjusted the radio to a new station, one with livelier music to keep him focused.

Landing on a country station, he drummed his fingers on the steering wheel in time with the beat. His truck bounced when he exited the bridge and hit smooth pavement again.

Another thirty minutes and he'd be home in his warm bed. He stretched his neck and shoulders, relishing the thought of sleeping past ten. Maybe something to eat before hitting the sack wouldn't hurt either. There were plenty of leftovers from yesterday's banquet for a late-night snack.

As he'd settled on a slice of pumpkin pie for his treat, a bright light flooded the cab of his truck. It reflected off his rearview mirror, momentarily blinding him. His right hand shot up to cover the mirror, while he tried to keep the wheels in the correct lane.

With the brilliant lights keeping pace with him,

Brent swiveled in his seat to look behind him.

Another truck hugged his bumper. He couldn't make out the color or the model of the vehicle.

In an instant, the driver gunned his engine and rammed Brent's bumper. The force of the impact pushed Brent forward in his seat. His restraints pulled tight around his middle and across his shoulder, keeping him from going through the windshield. "What in heaven's name?"

Before Brent could react, the other truck hit his bumper a second time. Brent floored the gas pedal, the motor roaring into action.

Flying down the two-lane highway, he considered his options. He knew this stretch of road better than he knew his own name. He could see the other truck in his rearview mirror, making up ground. Old Thompson Road popped into his mind.

Just as the headlights neared, Brent swerved into the old dirt road, etched out between two stands of trees. At one time, the local mill had used the dirt road for hauling lumber. He pulled further in, hoping the trees would give him coverage. He cut his engine and waited.

Within minutes, the other truck zipped by.

Brent exhaled and let the stillness of the night calm his thrumming nerves He leaned his head back on the seat. Who would want to hurt him? What was wrong with them? Then, he remembered he was in Dan's truck. Could they have been after Dan?

It didn't matter who the target was he needed to see the damage to the vehicle.

Releasing his seat belt, Brent jumped from the cab of the Chevrolet Trail Boss. He reached back into the cab to grab his phone from the middle console. Rounding the back end, he clicked the flashlight app on his phone. The beam bounced against the black of the truck. Squatting, Brent inspected the cracked fender. A piece hung near the ground, so he snapped it off, figuring it wouldn't make the trip home anyway.

As he rose with the piece of plastic in hand, he heard the motor of a vehicle not too far away, the low rumble vibrating across the night air. It was moving slowly, probably the same vehicle tracking him. Clicking off the light, he inched his way along the side of the truck to the front end, putting him further away from the road. He crouched low, keeping his eyes focused on the asphalt in the distance.

The other truck crept along the highway. Whoever was behind the wheel had figured out he was hiding. It stopped a few yards past his position on the other side of the trees.

Brent slipped from the front and crept alongside the truck to the driver's door for a quick getaway in case they found him. He dialed 9-1-1 on his phone and pushed send. Holding the phone close to his ear to diminish the light, he listened as the line on the other end rang.

The other truck idled where it stopped for what seemed like an eternity.

"What is the nature of your emergency?"

Ducking down, Brent asked, "Hey, is this Penny?"

"Yes, who is this? You know you can't use this line for personal calls."

"This is Brent Thibodeaux. Look, someone is following me. I'm out on State Highway 62 near the old lumber mill, and I need you to send a unit. The driver rammed me twice with his truck." Brent looked over the bed of his truck to see if the other vehicle had moved. It sat in the same spot.

"I'll send Deputy Adams your direction. He's close. Should be there within minutes."

"Tell him I'm parked on Old Thompson Road."

"I'll radio him, hold the line. Don't hang up."

"Trust me. I'm not planning on it."

~

Sadly, Brent found himself Saturday morning in Wade's office around ten instead of his nice warm bed as he'd hoped. The force of the two impacts had left him sore and if he were honest, cranky. He stood in the doorway of the Sheriff's office nursing a hot cup of coffee, Deputy Perez had given him, while he waited for Wade to finish a phone call.

"Yeah, I know." Wade nodded to Brent, then swiveled his chair turning his back to him. "I sent the information over to City Council Tuesday before everything shut down for the Thanksgiving holiday."

There was silence in the room as Wade listened. Finally, he huffed and stood. "I'm not even supposed to be in today. Look Jasper, you're going to have to wait until next week. I have a bit of an emergency. Some hot head letting his road rage get the best of him." Wade chuckled. "Sure, sure. A season of gratitude, not attitude. Funny, but you're right. I'll call you Monday." Placing the phone back on its base, Wade turned to face Brent. "Sorry about that. It never fails if I step foot in the office the phone rings."

"It's the curse of a small town. Everybody knows when you're here." Brent ambled to the chairs in front of Wade's desk. Taking a seat, he lifted the picture sitting on the corner of the wooden structure. Bernadette and several of their current foster children stared back at him. "You have a good-looking group."

Wade plopped into the leather chair. "Thanks. If you'd told me when I was in the FBI that I'd be married and caring for foster kids, I would've called you a liar. The FBI feels like a lifetime ago."

Brent replaced the picture. "I know what you mean. Working at the bakery is a far cry from rushing into fires or running the obstacle course in the military."

"But you wouldn't have it any other way, would you?" Wade shot him a knowing glance. "I've seen how you are with Maggie."

Brent thought of denying the accusation but decided not to. "Yeah, I do care for her. I've always had a soft spot for her. She's Tyler's little sister. Guess I sort of adopted her the way you and Bernadette have taken on these kids." He pointed to the picture.

"You can't pull the wool over these old eyes bud. I see how you look at her. How you act when you talk about her. It's more than fondness." Wade straightened in his seat and leaned his elbows on the wooden surface. "You're falling in love with her."

Brent shook his head but couldn't deny it. He'd been fighting his feelings for the woman from the moment he'd caught her in his arms that first day in the bakery.

"Admit it." Wade prodded.

Brent chuckled. "I'm sure you didn't come in on your day off to ask me about my love life." Brent drew out the last two words to make his point. "How about we get down to business, so we can both go home."

Wade shrugged, leaning back in his seat. "Fine, but

no amount of dodging the question will keep you safe. It's written all over your face every time somebody mentions her name." Opening a drawer, he pulled out an electronic notepad. "Okay, tell me again what happened for the record."

Brent related the story to Wade, trying to remember every detail. He told him about the truck, describing it to the best of his ability, noted when and where the incident happened, and reminded Wade he'd been driving Dan's truck.

"Do you think the target could've been Dan?" Brent asked.

"Whoa now, I'm not sure it's anything more than someone with road rage. Maybe they thought you'd cut them off, or they drank one too many beers and went looking for trouble." Wade tapped the keys of the notepad before looking back at Brent.

"Maybe, but the road was empty. I know I didn't cut anyone off." Brent scowled. "And the way he came back looking for me. It seemed targeted."

"Well, it is a holiday weekend. Lots of people celebrate non-stop and don't know when to quit." Wade steepled his fingers. "But I'll be sure to have the deputies keep an eye out for any trucks with damage to the front bumper, and we'll check the body shops."

"Good. I want to make sure Dan's not in any danger."

"Do you know of anyone who might want to hurt him?" Wade asked. "Or has he mentioned having any trouble with anyone?"

"No, has he mentioned anyone to you?" Brent rubbed his chin, the bristles of his unshaven face prickling against his hand.

Wade shook his head. "I'll call him. I'm like you, I want both of you to be safe."

"So, are we done here?" Brent asked.

"Yeah, and if anything comes up, I'll keep you posted." Wade slid the electronic notepad to the side of his desk and picked up the top file folder on the stack. "I guess I'll see you tomorrow at church."

Brent headed to the door, but before he passed through the threshold, Wade called to him. "Hey, Brent, is there anyone who'd want to see you hurt?"

Hesitating, Brent considered the question. "Maybe a handful of arsonists, but most of them are still in prison."

"No one springs to mind?" Wade's brows furrowed.

"There are a few, but not many people know I've moved back home. I doubt anyone could find me." Just as he turned to leave, the image of Cyrus Carver raced into his thoughts. Impossible. The man had no way of knowing he was in Orange Blossom, or did he?

"Did you think of someone?" Wade's voice held a tinge of concern.

"No," Brent smiled, dismissing what seemed to be too far-fetched.

"Okay, but if you do, don't hesitate to let me know. I don't care if it was or wasn't a targeted assault; no one threatens my brothers and gets away with it."

"I have no doubt, Sheriff Thibodeaux, you'll find our culprit and bring him to justice." Brent closed the door behind him. He hoped Wade was right that it was a random act of violence rather than someone after Dan. But he couldn't get the image of the truck idling on the road, waiting for him, out of his head.

Chapter Fourteen

Maggie stood next to the large refrigerator door, reading over the inventory list on a clipboard. The bakery was running low on several key ingredients. All the time she'd spent hunting for an investor. What a waste. Precious time, she could've been spending at the bakery. A lot of good it had done, running all over town in pursuit of her dreams. She pressed her lips together and batted her lashes to keep the tears at bay.

With a quick swipe under her eyes, Maggie placed the clipboard on the metal table so she could mark the items needed. After calling in the order this morning, she could start on the petit fours for the Baptists Women's Christmas Fellowship. She hoped her suppliers could get to her before closing or she'd never have the pastries ready by Saturday, the first weekend in December.

Her vision blurred as she marked item after item. How had she let things get so out of hand? Why had she wasted so much time at the banks? Then there was the four so-called interested investors Brent had set up for her. Mr. Walter, Mrs. Thornton, and the others. She should've been here running the business she wanted to buy, not running after money. Now, she'd be playing catch-up all next week.

Money. It always came back to money. Sniffling, she flipped the page and continued checking the list.

It wasn't like I needed millions. Thirty thousand was all. Is it asking too much for a little help? For someone to believe in me? All the banks refused to lend me the money, and don't even get me started on the investors. What a bust.

On top of that, she'd been so overwhelmed with being everywhere on time, looking professional, and making her presentation to one bunch of suits after another, she hadn't had time to decorate the bakery for Christmas.

A wave of self-pity washed over her. "What did you expect?" She mumbled to herself, forgetting Kristen stood a few feet away at one of the metal tables, stirring cake batter with the last of their flour. She swiped at the tears daring to fall.

"What did you say?" Kristen looked up from the bowl.

"Nothing." Maggie released a sigh.

"Now, don't be a Gloomy Gus. So, the banks weren't willing to loan you the money. They aren't the only source of funding in this community." Kristen circled the metal table toward the stacked ovens. The timer blared, letting everyone in the kitchen know the cupcakes were done. She picked up the oven mitts and stuffed her hands inside them. "Didn't you tell me Brent has a few people set up to meet with you?"

"Yes, and I did meet with them yesterday." Maggie frowned.

"So, how did it go?"

"I spent the whole day hopping from one meeting

to another." She shook her head. "Nothing came of it. No one seemed impressed with a lifetime supply of free cupcakes."

Kristen feigned horror. "Imagine that. How heartless?" She sobered. "Does Brent have any other contacts who could help?"

"He does, but I'm afraid it'll be his family, and one Thibodeaux to deal with is enough for me. Besides, I'd feel funny asking them to bankroll my dream. I mean I'm part of the Bible Babes with Nikki, and Bernadette is in here all the time with the kids." Maggie put the clipboard on the table and placed her chin in her hand. "I wanted to get the backing without having to ask Brent or his family for the funds."

Kristen pulled two of the cupcake pans from the oven. Turning, she placed them on the table. "You know Brent would give you the money in a heartbeat, and then you'd still only be dealing with one Thibodeaux. One handsome, funny, great-with-kids, Thibodeaux." She grinned at Maggie over her shoulder as she pulled the other two cupcake pans from the oven. "Or so I've been told."

"He is great with Matt, no doubt, and with his own niece and nephew, but that doesn't mean I want to be in his debt." Maggie straightened. "No, I want to find the funding myself. It's one thing for him to help me write the proposal and point me to some contacts. It's another thing for him or his family to provide the actual cash."

"Don't be stubborn. Hear him out. If he wants to help you secure the funding, let him." Kristen waved the oven mittens over the pans of steaming cupcakes. "Besides, you're assuming his contacts are family members. He knows people in the business world.

Maybe he has more potential investors, and the four you met were his top choices. Why not ask him? You might be surprised."

Brent pushed through the kitchen doors. "Why not ask him what?"

"Nothing. We were talking about the proposal." Maggie scooped up the clipboard with the inventory list on it. "I'm going to use the office for a minute to place a couple of orders. We are seriously low on supplies."

"Yeah, no problem." Brent gave her one of his half-grins. "*Mi casa es su casa.*"

Kristen frowned. "That's house."

"I don't know the word for office."

A smile crossed Maggie's lips as she opened the door and stepped onto the brown carpet. Rolling the leather chair out from under the desk, she took a seat.

Brent appeared in the doorway. "I know you're busy, but could I talk to you for a minute?"

"Sure, what do you need?"

"Well, I was going to ask you that same question." Brent slid into one of the metal folding chairs. "You've been down this week, and I wondered if there was anything I could do to cheer you up."

"That's sweet of you, but there's nothing anyone can do. I mean besides giving me the thirty thousand." She shrugged.

"Done." Brent grinned. "Glad to help."

"You know how I feel about the idea. I don't want your money." Maggie nailed him with a glare before turning on the computer screen.

They'd been over this several times. She'd come to terms with the fact he'd been a silent partner since Tyler took over the bakery, but she didn't want Brent to sink any more money into the shop. She wanted to be equal partners with him, and that couldn't happen if he held the controlling interest.

Brent stood and rounded the desk. Leaning his back side against the edge, he faced her. "Why not? It's a simple solution to your problem. You need money. I have money."

His closeness sent flutters zipping through her stomach. "I don't want to rehash this. The thought of owing you or your family money makes me feel weird." Maggie wrinkled her nose as if she'd smelled something rotten. "I'm too close to all of you. It'd be like owing my parents money. I'd always be worried about it ruining our relationship."

"So…" Brent pursed his lips. "We have a relationship?"

Heat crept up her neck. Why did he have to be so charming? "You're such a flirt. You know what I mean. Our partnership."

"Fine. We don't have to go over this again but let me take you out to dinner. I can at least cheer you up with a good meal and maybe some flying pigs." Brent waggled his eyebrows.

She rolled her eyes and suppressed the giggles forming like bubbles in her chest. "You're a nut."

"But am I a nut with a date?"

Maggie met his gaze. His dark green eyes held a hint of seriousness in them. A date with Brent Thibodeaux, the man, not her teen crush.

"Well?" He took her hand. "Will you, Maggie Kemp Bishop, go out with me tonight?"

Her heart leaped into her throat. "Yes," she squeaked. Clearing her throat, she tried again. "Yes, it sounds wonderful. I'll call Mom and see if she can keep Matt a little longer."

"No need. I'm fully aware you and Matt are a package deal. I always did like a good BOGO."

~

"Piggy," Matt shouted. "Pink piggy."

Maggie moved closer to the mural that stretched the length of the back wall of The Flying Pig Barbeque. The five little piggies in the painting danced and somersaulted with their wings spread wide in a crisp blue Texas sky filled with fluffy white clouds. To Maggie, they appeared so lighthearted.

Matt reached his chubby hand out to touch the piggy peeking down at him from one of the clouds.

She caught his hand, pulling it to her lips and kissed his plump fingers. "No touching, sweetie." Stepping back, she studied the mural. The whimsy of the painting gave the restaurant a fun, festive feel. Too bad her heart felt like lead.

Glancing over her shoulder, she found Brent watching them from the table. Though he'd said he wanted to cheer her up, she feared his true reason for bringing her and Matt to The Flying Pig was to discuss other options for her funding. After bombing out with the investors, she'd tried all the local banks and came up empty. So, if he wanted to talk about money, her heart wasn't in it. Not tonight. A girl could only take so much rejection in a single week.

Maneuvering through the restaurant, she slid into the seat across from Brent at a table for four and placed her purse and Matt's diaper bag in one of the empty seats. Frieda, the waitress, appeared with a highchair before she had a chance to settle the toddler on her lap.

"Here ya go." Frieda pushed the other chair closer to Brent, setting the highchair near Maggie.

"Thanks, Frieda." Maggie stood and deposited Matt into the seat.

Freida gave each of them a plastic-covered menu then set three crayons on the red checkered tablecloth along with a kid's menu with a picture of the mural from the wall in front of Matt.

Smiling, she pulled a pen from the bun on the back of her head and an order pad from the pocket of her apron. "What can I get you two to drink?"

"I'll take a sweet tea." Brent looked over his menu at Maggie

"Me, too."

Freida pointed her pen in Matt's direction. "What can I get for the little guy?"

Matt picked up the blue crayon and scribbled a few marks on the paper.

"Oh, I have his sippy cup." Maggie turned and dug in the diaper bag to produce the mentioned item. She set it on the table within Matt's reach.

"Will this be on one ticket or two?" Freida asked.

Maggie paused and met Brent's gaze. After all the stink she'd made about not wanting to take his money, maybe she should pay for her own dinner. But he'd called it a date. Confused, Maggie sat tongue-tied.

Brent laughed. "I can't believe it. You've left Maggie speechless."

Freida glanced between them. "I'm not sure what's going on, but do you need a minute to decide about the check?"

Maggie had lifted her hand to tell Freida she'd pay for her own meal when Brent pulled her hand back down to the tabletop. "One check, please, and bring it to me."

Brent never let go of her hand, but instead, he intertwined his fingers with hers. The sensation of his touch sent little delightful prickles racing up her arms.

"Got it." Freida grinned then hustled around the crowded tables toward the drink station.

When Maggie met Brent's gaze, she found tenderness in his eyes. "I meant it when I said this was a date. One that is long overdue. Don't you?"

Maggie's heart flip-flopped at the warmth of his touch. Of course, nothing could come of a date with Brent. Business partners shouldn't date. They had to keep things at a professional level. Nothing more than friendship could exist between them, ever, but even as she focused her mind on the sheer impossibility of a relationship with him, her heart reacted to the touch of his hand, the sound of his voice as he spoke, and his stupid half grin. Boy, she was in trouble. If she didn't know any better, she'd say she was falling in love with him.

Brent leaned in closer, shortening the distance between them across the table. "Uh-oh, here comes trouble."

"You can say that again." Maggie shook her head still deep in her own thoughts.

Nodding, Brent glanced over Maggie's shoulder. She followed his gaze to find Aunt Marilyn and Brent's friend, John McAllister, weaving their way toward them. Maggie pulled her hand away from Brent's just in time.

"What a wonderful surprise to see you here." Marilyn planted a kiss on top of Matt's head. He didn't look up from his scribbling. "We were just discussing the bakery and the super success of the Crazy Pie Day."

"Hey, John," Brent stood and shook his hand. "Why don't you have a seat."

Maggie grabbed her purse and the diaper bag and stuffed them both under the highchair.

"Are you sure we're not intruding?" Marilyn asked.

"Not at all." Brent peered at Maggie, his eyebrows raised.

She read the question in his look. "Please, join us. We haven't ordered yet."

"Oh, that'd be nice," John said. "We've been out house hunting. I think we've found our winner."

"It's a lovely place with five acres, a barn, and the cutest man-made pond filled with fish," Marilyn gushed.

"There is a house on the property, right?" Maggie teased.

"Of course, don't be silly." Marilyn beamed as she glanced over at John. "It's lovely. A single story with lots of potential."

"I thought you'd found a property out by the river." Brent leaned back in his chair. He seemed so at ease with John. Brent had told her they'd met about a year and a half ago in rehab when Brent was learning how to use his left arm and shoulder again. John used the same physical therapy wing in the hospital during his rehab on his knee.

"I looked at a house out there, but I wanted something closer to town." John grinned and his eyes lingered in Marilyn's direction.

Maggie could've cut the chemistry between the

two of them with a knife. She hadn't seen her aunt this happy in a long time. "So, are you here to celebrate?"

"John needs to make an offer, so I can send it over to the sellers before anyone else gets a look at the property, but I'm confident, he'll be moving in sometime soon. Then we can celebrate."

"I wanted to thank Marilyn with a proper meal for all the hard work she's put in for me. She hunted through a lot of frogs to find this beauty."

Brent raised an eyebrow. "So, this is a thank you dinner, not a date?"

Quashing a giggle, Maggie worked to keep a straight face. After the way they acted on Thanksgiving Day, there had been no doubt in anyone's mind they were dating.

Marilyn blushed and played with the rolled silverware sitting on the table. "Well..." She glanced up at John. "I guess the cat's out of the bag, so to speak."

John lit up like a strand of Christmas lights. "I suppose we'd better tell them before they hear it from someone else. We've been seeing each other for a few weeks now, but we wanted to keep it quiet while we were getting to know each other."

"No kidding." A light chuckle rumbled from his chest. "Good for you, John. You deserve some happiness in your life." He thumped his friend on the back.

Maggie squeezed her aunt's hand. "I'm so pleased for both of you."

Freida approached their table with the drinks. Tucking the empty tray under her arm, she pulled out her order pad. "What can I get you to drink, Marilyn?"

"Let me have a Diet Coke."

"I'll take an unsweet tea," John said.

She turned to Brent. "Should I add this to your check?" Then she cut her eyes toward Maggie with a look, daring her to say anything.

Maggie laughed. Poor Freida, the woman had no idea she'd stepped into a land mine of romantic hearts and hope-filled dreams.

After dinner, John took Matt to look at the mural while Brent stood in line to pay the bill. Maggie lingered at the table with Marilyn enjoying a moment of simple conversation. Worn out from heralding the wonders of the bakery to complete strangers, she welcomed this small respite.

"I'm so glad you've found a place for John." Maggie sipped her iced tea.

"Me too. It fits him so well." Marilyn sighed, a smile of contentment crossing her bright red lips.

Maggie loved her Aunt Marilyn even though in the past she'd been a bit of a gossip, but to her credit, she'd changed. When Maggie moved back from California, she'd been pleased to find that her aunt had joined the Community Cowboy Church and participated in the Bible Babes group. She'd invited Maggie to attend, then the women had adopted her, giving her a baby shower. She quickly became friends with the core group.

Marilyn cocked her head to one side and studied her. "Are you all right? Did you and Brent finish the proposal? You were working on it last time I saw you."

"Please, don't ask." Maggie groaned, flopping back in her chair. "I've spent the last three days making pitches to more people than I care to mention."

"Any takers?"

Maggie wagged her head. She tried to keep that sinking feeling from washing over her, but the waves of disappointment rushed in without any regard for her wishes. "Unfortunately, no. It seems no one is interested in helping a poor but humble baker." She made light of the situation because she couldn't bear the thought of her aunt taking pity on her.

"Oh, sweetie, I'm so sorry." Marilyn touched her hand resting on top of the checkered tablecloth. "Is there anything I can do?"

Maggie swallowed the lump that formed in her throat. "Thanks for the offer, but I don't think there's anything you can do for me, unless you have thirty thousand dollars lying around collecting dust." She chortled.

Marilyn's eyes widened. "Is that all you need?"

"Yep, but it might as well be a million. The banks are unwilling to loan me the money since it would have to be an unsecured loan. Apparently, you have to have money to borrow money."

"So, is that Tyler's asking price? It seems rather low."

Maggie shook her head as she twirled the straw in her glass of melting ice. "The asking price is more, but I have some of the insurance money from Ted's policy payout. Not tons obviously, but enough to cover a large portion of what's needed. Still, I'm shy thirty thousand." Maggie bit her lip. It made her nervous, talking so candidly with her aunt about money.

"When would you need it in case I come up with someone who might be able to help?"

Maggie shot her a quizzical look.

"Hey, I've been networking in this town for years. Realtors hobnob with all kinds."

Shrugging, she said, "Tyler would like to have his half of the bakery sold by Christmas. No later than New Years for sure, since they plan to move to Atlanta right after the holidays." Maggie drank the last of her watered-down tea. "Which gives me about three weeks."

"Well, I'll see what I can do." Marilyn's lips pulled into a tight bow as she tapped her finger against their red hue. "I might have an idea."

"An idea is good, but what I need is nothing short of a Christmas miracle."

Chapter Fifteen

Brent wiggled the long, fat box from under the pile of seasonal decorations filling the shelves of the storage room. Easter rabbits, colored eggs, and golden pots with plastic coins in them littered the floor of the tiny space, making it difficult for him to maneuver the awkwardly shaped box holding the bakery's Christmas tree.

He stepped back to avoid the plastic storage bins standing near him. Moving the bins out of the way with his foot, he gave the long box another yank. A stack of friendly-faced Halloween pumpkins sitting close to the edge of the third shelf shook each time he tugged.

Stopping, he let go of the box. "This isn't going to work."

"What's not working?" Maggie appeared in the doorway, wiping her hands on her apron.

The aroma of sweet sugar and cinnamon wreathed its way around him. He grinned. She wore as many spices on her clothing as she used in her baking. A white streak of flour dusted her cheek. His fingers itched to wipe it away.

"You have ..." He tapped his cheek.

She swiped at the other side.

"No, more here." He motioned again to the spot on his face as he moved closer to her.

"Here?" She used the edge of her apron to remove the spot, adding to the powder on her skin.

"Wait. It's …" Brent ran his thumb across her cheek, swiping away the flour, then letting his hand rest along her jawline. His gaze moved from her hazel eyes, landing on her pink, full lips. What he wouldn't give to kiss her right now. It's all he'd thought about since their date at The Flying Pig.

Sure, they'd been interrupted by Marilyn and John, but that night when he'd taken her home, he'd carried the sleeping toddler inside for her and helped her tuck him in for the night. In the quiet, standing in Matt's room in the glow of the nightlight, he'd struggled with the idea of kissing her goodnight.

She looked so beautiful as she tended to her son, placing his favorite toy in his arms and stroking his hair out of his eyes. Her warmth drew him to her like Santa to a Christmas cookie. The more time they spent together, the harder it became for him to remember she was his best friend's little sister. To him, she'd grown into an exquisite, loving, compassionate woman. One, no man could ignore.

Maggie touched his hand and smiled.

Heat rose within him. As the urge to kiss her grew, he leaned toward her, but before his lips covered hers, someone cleared their throat.

"Sorry for interrupting."

Brent pulled his gaze from Maggie. Glancing over her shoulder, he found Kristen standing behind her. He let his hand drop to his side and frowned.

"I really, really hate to interrupt, but the fruit

vendor is here, and he's going on about dates and whether we're making fruitcakes again this year. I didn't know what to tell him. We haven't discussed the holiday specialties yet. So, I thought it would be better if you talked with him."

Maggie's eyes widened. "With all the fuss about the proposal, I forgot to make up the Holiday Specialty Menu. It's like I've completely lost sight of Christmas. I mean no menu, no decorations. Who am I?"

"That's understandable." Kristen shrugged. "Anyone would, with all you have on your plate. The finances, your brother's wedding, and then Crazy Pie Day."

Maggie and Kristen both turned their gaze toward Brent. Would he ever live that down? Even though it was a huge success, the staff had paid for it in time and energy. He'd pledged to be better prepared next year.

Next year. A nagging feeling crept over him. If Maggie didn't get the funding, there would be no next year with her.

"Besides your usual duties of mom, daughter, and top bakery chef, I imagine one or two smaller things might get overlooked," Kristen said.

"Maybe, but there's no excuse for overlooking Christmas. Brent and I are staying after closing tonight to remedy the decoration issue. How about after I talk with the fruit vendor, we sit down and make up our Holiday Specialty Menu. That way, we'll have a plan. We can make it simple but elegant."

"Good, because after the desserts you served at the Baptist Women's Christmas Fellowship, we've received four more requests for us to cater events. Not to mention all the exposure from Crazy Pie Day."

"Making a specialty menu is a good idea," Brent said. "When you get finished, I'd like to look over it, so I'll be familiar with the items and the pricing. Then I'll spruce it up a bit with a design tool and make copies. Maybe, I can do another ad for our services."

Maggie sighed. "I can't keep my head above water now. I don't know if I can churn out the baked goods and act as a caterer."

"Of course not, we'd hire extra help for any events that needed us to provide servers. Otherwise, it'll be baked goods."

The look on Maggie's face told him she wasn't overjoyed by the thought of them offering catering help. "We can work out a schedule that can benefit everyone. If we offer extra hours, I'm sure a few of our bakers will take us up on it. Who can't use a little extra cash in their pockets during the holidays?"

"You're trying to kill me, aren't you? Your plan is to work me to death and become king of Sweet Things." Maggie rolled her eyes. "Come on, Kristen. Let's talk with the fruit vendor. I have a feeling I'm about to order a lot more apples, dates, and cherries. I wonder if he sells candied fruits?" Maggie and Kristen disappeared from the doorway.

Brent squatted to pick up the Christmas tree box, but before he could get a good grip on it, he heard Maggie behind him.

"Oh, don't forget to dig out the bins with the lights and tinsel. There should be two plastic containers with ornaments in them. Last year, we put a train around the bottom of the tree, but this year, we should keep it simple and use the red quilted tree skirt. It'll make the bakery feel more festive."

~

Maggie pushed play on her favorite music app. and positioned the Bluetooth speaker, so it faced out toward the dining area of Sweet Things. The soft strands of "White Christmas" floated into the air, filling the bakery to her delight. "I love this song," she said to no one in particular.

Kristen and Millie, a part-time employee, spent the late afternoon putting together the artificial Christmas tree while Maggie worked on filling a last-minute order for an office party. The women placed the tree near the long glass window so it could be seen from the sidewalk. They stood fluffing the bottom branches, prepping them for the ornaments.

"I love this song, too." Brent hummed along with the tune as he plugged one strand of lights into another. The multicolored bulbs burst on, giving the bakery a cheery Christmasy feel.

"That's more like it." Maggie scooted around the counter, grabbing the plastic bin sitting on the first table. "A little music, some lights, and we're halfway there."

"Halfway where?" Brent met her gaze. His dark green eyes filled with mischief.

"Halfway to being done and ready for the next three weeks. I can't believe I let all this slip up on me."

"I don't know." Brent unraveled the silver tinsel from around the third strand of lights. "It sneaks up on me every year. Thanksgiving comes and I figure I have loads of time and then boom. It's like Christmas in two days."

Maggie shook her head. The man was incorrigible. "Well, wait until you have kids. There's no getting around Christmas. Even though Matt is still young, everybody starts asking for gift ideas sometime around mid-October. They want to know what I've bought for him already, so they won't duplicate any items. So normally, I've been thinking about Christmas for several months before it's upon us."

"Man, it must be rough having so many people care about your little guy." Kristen placed her hand over her heart while making a sad face. "So tough."

Millie giggled.

Grabbing a stuffed candy cane from her stash of ornaments, Maggie lobbed it at her friend who ducked. "One day you'll have your own important little people, then we'll talk about holiday expectations."

With the stray tinsel picked from the strand of lights, Brent plugged it into the other ones and looped the lights around the tree. Maggie set the bin on the floor and followed him around the tree, poking the lights into place on the branches.

Brent gave her a quizzical look. "Picky?"

"No, but we have a reputation to uphold. We don't want our customers to think we don't care about the details, do we?"

"No, I guess we don't." He beamed and continued his trek around the tree.

Maggie relished the thought of Sweet Things becoming hers and being able to serve the customers she'd come to know. Plus, with the way things were going between her and Brent, she kind of liked the idea of being his partner. In fact, she rather looked forward to it.

She glanced over at him as he reached above his head to hide the end of the strand within the top of the branches. His shirttail lifted, and she could see the scars on the left side of his back. Funny, she'd grown so accustomed to the scars on his left cheek she didn't notice them anymore. He was handsome and well-built even with the added markings. Any woman would agree.

He caught her staring, so she busied herself tucking the light in front of her further into the branches. "There. Perfect." She stepped back from the tree to examine their progress.

"What do you think?" Kristen asked.

Maggie tilted her head, taking in the glow of the lights. "Umm, it needs ornaments and maybe some tinsel."

"I love tinsel," Millie said. "Do we have any red?"

"Maybe, Tyler has collected several different colors over the years." Maggie pointed to the biggest bin. "Look in there. If we have any, that's where it would be."

The four of them worked together with the Christmas music spurring them on until all the branches were exploding with color. As Kristen tried to place the last ornament in an open spot near the top of the tree, she lost her balance and bumped into the lower branches.

A few of the glass ornaments jarred loose and dropped to the floor, smashing into pieces.

"Are you all right?" Brent grabbed Kristen around the waist and helped her back onto her feet.

"I'm fine, but look at this mess." Kristen glanced at Maggie. "I hope these weren't family heirlooms."

Maggie waved her hand. "Noo, they're old but not valuable."

"Okay, good." Relief flooded Kristen's face.

"I'll go get the broom and sweep it up. You guys put on the tinsel, and we'll call it a night." Maggie moved through the swinging doors and into the kitchen. Ten minutes later, the broken glass lay in her dustpan.

Hitting the swinging doors with her hip, she hustled into the kitchen to the trash can, anxious to be done for the evening, so she could head home to Matt. She still had a load of laundry to do and a few gifts to order online before she crawled into bed.

She lifted the lid to the trash. Full. She scowled and blew out her breath. "Better now than later." Dumping the dustpan on top, she pulled the large plastic bag out of the can, tied the drawstrings tight, and headed to the back door of the bakery.

Stepping out into the alley, Maggie left the door open, letting the light from inside stream into the darkness. She hurried to the dumpster that sat between her bakery and the shop next door. She didn't like coming out into the alley alone at night. Sliding the handle on the metal door up, she released the portal and swung the bag into the large blue container before relatching the handle.

"Don't you have some fellow who could take care of that for you?"

Maggie jumped, her heart in her throat, every nerve in her body thrumming with the sudden jolt of adrenaline. Turning, she found a middle-aged man dressed in jeans and a black T-shirt, standing at the entrance to the alleyway.

"Sorry, if I scared you." He chuckled and took a few steps in her direction.

All her internal alarm bells clanged out a warning,

and she stepped back. "As a matter of fact, I do have a couple of friends who could help me. I was just about to join them." She poked her hands in her apron pockets and marched toward the open door, determined not to let this guy shake her nerves.

The man strolled toward her, his boots clicking against the asphalt. He held his hands up in front of him. "No need to be concerned about me. I was passing by and remembered a guy I knew from the military who said he owned a bakery back in his hometown. I think it was this bakery, Sweet Things."

Maggie stopped a few feet from the doorway. She studied his body language. Was he a threat? His words sounded harmless enough. They even bordered on friendly, but the tone gave her pause. Not wanting to seem afraid, she said, "You must mean Brent Thibodeaux."

"Yeah, that's the guy."

"Did you two serve together? Were you in the fire brigade as well?" Maggie edged toward the door and stepped onto the threshold. She had no intention of hanging around a dark alley talking to a stranger.

"Not exactly, but we did have one topic in common." He advanced a few more steps close enough for Maggie to see the anger in his eyes "But I see you need to go, so I won't keep you."

For some reason, she blurted out, "Do you want me to give Brent a message?"

"No, I've already taken care of that." The man spun around and walked away.

Maggie slipped into the safety of the kitchen and slammed the door shut, turning the locks. Leaning against the hard wood, she prayed, "Father, thank you for your protection, tonight. I know we are to love our fellow man, but this one—" A verse from the last Bible Babes meeting popped into her mind, and she recited it. "When I am afraid, I will trust in you."

Chapter Sixteen

"**Did I hear** you talking to someone?" Brent strolled through the double doors of the kitchen. His brown hair was mussed and sticking out in odd places, looking like he'd wrestled the Christmas tree instead of decorating it.

Maggie smiled, even though her encounter with the guy in the alley had left her feeling vulnerable. "Yeah, I met one of your old Army buddies, or at least he said he knew you from your military days. He came into the alley when I was throwing the trash into the dumpster."

"An old Army buddy? Here in Orange Blossom?" Brent scowled and hurried toward the back door. Turning the bolt, he stepped out into the alley then came back in and reset the locks. "Well, he seems to be gone now."

"Yeah, he left once I stepped into the kitchen," Maggie said. "To be honest, he gave me the creeps."

Concern flashed across Brent's face. "Did you get a good look at him?"

"Yeah, he came close enough to me when I stood in the kitchen doorway that I could see his face." Maggie tilted her head, trying to remember as much about the man as she could. "I'd say he was average height, dark hair, middle-aged, and his eyes were set close together. He smelled funny, like grease."

"Did you notice any gold caps on his front teeth?"

"Yeah, I did. So, you do know him." Maggie crossed her arms over her middle to stop the trembling in her stomach. The guy's tone and the look in his eyes left her uneasy.

Brent shook his head, moving toward her. "I wouldn't say I know him, but I had a few run-ins with him. His name is Cyrus Carver, and he's bad news." He touched her shoulder. "Are you okay?"

Maggie nodded and leaned into his chest, letting the warmth of his touch seep into her, calming her frayed nerves.

After a few moments, Brent asked, "What did he say to you exactly?"

"He said he remembered an army buddy who told him he owned a bakery called Sweet Things and then he gave me the oddest look. Like he was a cat and I was the mouse he planned to have for dinner." Maggie shivered again. "Super creepy. Then I don't know why, but I asked him if he wanted me to give you a message."

"What did he say?" Brent met her gaze as she lifted her chin to look him in the eye.

"No, that he already had."

Brent's jaw tightened, the nerve pulsing under his skin. "What did he mean by that?"

"You were the message. He wanted me to know he could get to you." Brent pulled her closer, his arms tightening around her. "I can't believe he's here in town. My town. With my people." Letting go of her, he paced.

"You're scaring me, Brent. Who is this guy exactly? How do you know him?" She'd never seen him so conflicted. Her easy going, flirty friend had turned into the serious military man he was trained to be, right before her eyes.

"He's someone who ought to be in jail but isn't. He's the guy from the motor pool fire at Fort Sam Houston."

"The one who put you into rehab for a year and a half?" Maggie's heart melted. She couldn't imagine the pain and agony he'd gone through during those long months of recovery.

"Yeah, but neither the military police nor the fire brigade could charge him with the crime. He got off, but not long after, they discharged him for other incidents, or so I was told by my captain." He stopped pacing, taking her by the shoulders. "Maggie, I want you to promise me that while this guy is in town, you will take extra precautions. Don't leave your car unlocked. Don't go anywhere alone if it's not a highly populated area, and whatever you do, don't get caught with him by yourself again."

"I can't stop taking out the trash because some crazy guy might be in the alley. I can't live in fear."

"I'm not asking you to be fearful. I'm asking you to be careful."

Maggie studied his face. "This isn't about tonight, is it? Something else has happened." She gripped his hand. "Tell me what's going on. I need to know what we're dealing with here. I have a son and a business to protect."

"You're right. I should've told you sooner. On the way home from your house Friday night, a truck followed me across the bridge and tried to ram me off the road. I lost him by hiding on the old mill road. I called the sheriff's department, and they dispatched a unit.

"I reported it to Wade, and he's been looking for the vehicle. But so far, no luck. He thinks it's probably a rental from another town or one he stole. We may not ever locate it."

"Why didn't you tell me sooner?" Maggie tamped down the anxiety building in her.

"Because I wasn't sure who we were dealing with. Wade thought it might have been an angry drunk. You know, too much holiday celebration." Brent's gaze went to the floor. "I didn't know it was him until now. That's why I need you to promise to be careful. This guy is dangerous, and for some reason, I'm in his crosshairs."

~

"Lock the door and wait for me," Brent repeated to Maggie as he let Millie and Kristen exit the shop. The heavy front door swished shut, and the lock turned with a click.

Brent walked the ladies to their cars parked a few feet down the sidewalk, not too far from the front of the shop. He could've watched them from inside with the streetlights on, but he didn't want to take any chances. Carver was dangerous, and he didn't want anyone he knew to be hurt because of his association with the man. Anger coursed through him at the thought of Carver approaching Maggie. The gall of the man.

Kristen and Millie slipped into their driver's seats and took turns pulling away from the curb. Kristen waved as she passed him standing on the sidewalk, her car headed down Main Street.

Returning to the bakery, he used his key to let himself inside. The overhead lights were off, and the only glow came from the multicolored lights on the Christmas tree. The glimmer bounced off the gold and red decorations, bathing the tables and chairs in an enchanted explosion of hues. It reminded him of the Christmas trees from his childhood before his parents' accident. He and his brothers always looked through the store catalogues and made a long list of toys they wanted from Santa, but his parents somehow managed to keep the focus of the season on Jesus. A longing grew in his heart. Boy, how he missed them and Pops Harris.

Maggie bustled into the room from the kitchen. "I thought I heard you come in. Did Kristen and Millie reach their cars safely?"

"Yes, and I warned them to be vigilant when they arrived home. I told them to look all around the area before getting out of their cars and to be sure to lock their front doors the instant they enter their home."

"What a contrast to consider someone wanting to hurt others while everyone else is celebrating this season of peace and love and goodwill toward man. It seems wrong." Maggie picked up her purse from off the table and slid it over her head, letting it hang across her body. Turning, she sighed. "Christmas should focus on the good of God, not the evil of man."

"I agree wholeheartedly, but we live in a fallen world." Not wanting to dwell on the harsh realities he'd seen working as a fireman, he gestured toward the tree. "Will Matt approve?"

Maggie moved toward him. A soft sigh slipped

from her lips. "He's going to love it. Matt's at that stage where he wants to touch anything bright and blingy. I'm going to have my work cut out for me, if I bring him to the shop. He'll have all the lower branches bare in minutes."

Brent laughed and inhaled the sweet scent of cinnamon that she wore from the day's baking.

"The tree did turn out lovely, didn't it?"

"Yeah, lovely," Brent let his gaze rest squarely on Maggie while she watched the lights flicker.

Maggie leaned her head against his chest and without a second thought, he wrapped his arm around her as they stood admiring the beauty of the tree. "There is so much up in the air this season. The bakery, Tyler and Nadine's wedding, and now this Carver guy. Peace seems to have leaked out of the season altogether."

Brent pulled her closer to his side. "It's all going to work out about the bakery."

"Why? Because you're going to force me to take your money?" She glanced at him, mischief playing in her eyes.

"No, I would never do that. I've learned my lesson about that solution. But I have been praying about it for you. I don't think the Lord intends to remove the bakery from your life or you from the bakery. You're the heart and soul of this business. It's where you belong. Here. With me."

Maggie turned in his arms to face him. Lifting her chin, she said, "Do I belong here with you?"

He stroked her cheek and let his fingers drift toward the dark curls framing her face. "Definitely."

She tilted her head to one side, as if inviting him to

kiss her. His heart drummed within his chest. He'd waited for this moment for weeks, thought about it daily, even dreamed of it in his sleep.

He lowered his lips to hers. A simple gentle brush of his against hers, but the warmth of her skin against his hand and the sweet taste of her pink lips made him hunger for more. His heart raced as he deepened the kiss.

Running her arms around his neck, she rose onto her tiptoes, pressing her lips to his. She matched his urgency until she pulled away, breathless.

Brent leaned his forehead against hers, not wanting to let her go. He was falling in love with her. Shoot, who was he kidding? He wasn't falling in love; he'd already tripped, tumbled down the hill and landed with a thud. Who knew when it had happened? He only knew if heaven could be on earth, then kissing Maggie Kemp Bishop was heaven.

Chapter Seventeen

Maggie stepped back. Her heart pounded like horse hoofs in a stampede. What had she done?

Answer: She'd kissed Brent. And not any ole kiss. Oh no, it had been a knee-weakening, belly-quivering, my-whole-life-changed-in-an-instant kind of kiss. Unsure what to say or do next, Maggie fumbled in her purse for her keys. "I-I-I'd better go. I still need to pick up Matt from Mom's house. She's been so great about picking him up from day care and watching him for me. I don't want to keep her waiting."

Brent pressed his lips together, his dark green eyes stormy in the wake of their kiss. "No, of course not."

The strength of the temptation to rush back into his arms and claim his lips again unnerved her. She'd known what it was like to love and be loved because of her husband Ted. Then he'd been taken from her, and she'd been left on her own to figure out the world for both her and Matt.

"Let me grab my things, and I'll be glad to walk you out." Brent ducked behind the counter. When he emerged, he held his electronic pad and a pile of paperwork. Patting the loose sheets, he said, "I thought of a few more people to contact about the rare opportunity to invest in a community bakery." His half-grin sprang to life and the storm that had been present in his eyes earlier dissipated, replaced by a teasing glint.

"Oh, I like the sound of that, a community bakery, but you've already done so much. I hate for you to keep putting your neck on the line for me."

"It's okay, Magpie. I can handle it." Brent rounded the counter and took Maggie by the elbow, leading her toward the front door. "I'll follow you to your mom's house and then to your home."

"If it's necessary." Maggie didn't want to argue. She trusted Brent's instincts about Cyrus Carver. Though she hated to inconvenience him, running him all over town.

"It is necessary." His jaw set firm. "I don't like the fact he could get to you so easily tonight. He was sending me a message, and I for one am going to heed it." Brent stopped outside the heavy glass door and pushed his key into the lock. The click sounded like a clap of thunder in the quiet of the empty street. "I'll walk you to your car, then you drive me down to my truck. Once you and Matt are home, I'm going to stop by Wade's to let him know Carver is in town."

"Okay." Maggie tightened her grip on her purse strap. They walked in silence to her car. Her mind swirled with the events of the evening. One minute, her lips tingled at the thought of the kiss. The next minute, she jumped at the noises behind her. Every creek magnified ten times louder than on any other night.

She slipped behind the steering wheel. Brent shut the door for her and waited until she'd pushed the power locks, cranked the car, and waved. He jogged down the sidewalk to the other end of the parking lot, then stood outside his vehicle, patting his jeans pockets. He must be looking for his keys. Gazing down, she grabbed her seat belt and pulled it across her, clicking the buckle into place.

The roar of an engine filled her ears. Maggie glanced up in time to see a truck come barreling around the corner of Main Street and Pine. The truck was headed straight for Brent who'd bent over his rear tire, as if he were looking for a leak.

"Brent!" She slammed her car into reverse. Pulling out of the parking space, she aimed for the truck and jammed the gas pedal to the floorboard. Her engine picked up speed, but not fast enough to satisfy her. "Come on, come on," she willed for the older car to fly.

As the truck reached Brent, its engine to revved to a deafening pitch. Brent straightened, saw the truck, and jumped to the curb.

Maggie jerked the steering wheel to the left, squeezing between Brent's truck and the oncoming vehicle. It swerved to miss her and zipped past, but the tinted windows made it impossible for her to see the driver's face. As fast as the truck appeared, it vanished around the next corner, the echoes of the engine the only remaining evidence it had been there at all.

Slamming the gearshift into park, she ran from the car to Brent. "Are you all right? Did he hit you?" She knelt beside Brent on the sidewalk.

Brent moaned. "I'm fine." Sitting up, he brushed the dirt from his shoulders and arms. "Just my pride is bruised. I should've expected him to take some kind of action after his appearance in the alley. He wants to make sure I know he has me in his sights."

"Well, we know." She stood, brushing off the knees of her jeans. "We'd better go see Wade right now. He needs to know what level of crazy we're dealing with here." Maggie extended her hand to Brent, who took it and pushed up to his knees before standing.

"I think you're right. We need to go see Wade. Can your mom watch Matt a little longer?"

"For this, I don't think she'll mind." Brent took a few steps toward the back of his truck, favoring his left hip when he walked. "You might need a doctor to take a look at you."

~

Maggie waited for Brent in her car while he changed the tire on his truck. Apparently, the lunatic driver had ensured Brent would be in position for his attempted hit and run by driving a nail through the rubber into one of his back tires.

While Brent loosened the lug nuts, she called Wade to let him know they'd be running by his ranch, Home-4-Us. But when he picked up, he'd told her to meet him at the sheriff's office.

When Brent finished and put the damaged tire into the bed of his truck, Maggie followed him to the parking lot of the sheriff's office. Wade waited for them at the front desk and buzzed them back into the bullpen.

"Okay, so let me get this straight, Cyrus Carver is here in Orange Blossom," Wade repeated what Brent had told him so far.

"Right, he approached Maggie tonight in the alley behind the bakery." Brent plopped back against the chair sitting across from Wade's desk.

Wade scratched down the details as Maggie and Brent gave them to him.

"Are you sure it's Carver?" Wade asked.

Maggie checked the time on her phone and straightened in her chair. A sudden wave of exhaustion washed over her. She turned her phone face down in her lap.

"Yes, from Maggie's description of the man in the alley, it's him. You can't miss those gold front teeth."

"He said he knew Brent and that they had served together," Maggie added.

"You were in the alley behind the bakery alone."

Maggie nodded. "I took out the trash since it was full. He came out of nowhere. I turned my back to the street, and when I turned around, he was standing there. He said he knew Brent, and I asked him if he wanted me to give him a message. By this time, I'd moved back to the kitchen door. The man gave off a vibe that put me on my guard."

"Did he give Brent a message?" Wade scowled.

"No, he said he already had."

"The minute Maggie told me, I knew he meant *she* was the message. He was saying he could get to her."

Maggie scooted to the edge of her chair. "When the truck came around the corner heading for Brent, I thought for sure the guy was going to kill him."

"And he might have if it wasn't for your quick thinking. Cutting him off like that." Brent reached over and laid his hand on her arm. "I'm grateful you had my back."

Maggie lowered her eyes at the compliment. "Well, I can't lose you now. There's no way I can afford both halves of the bakery." She shrugged and squeezed his hand before removing hers. He lifted his away, and the air against her skin felt cool.

"Maggie, could you see the driver of the truck?" Wade asked.

"No, I couldn't, but with the way everything played out tonight, it had to be Carver."

"I agree, but it would go a long way if you could have identified him as the driver. As it is, all we have is conjecture." Wade huffed, tapping his pen against the desk. "Did he threaten you or Brent when he spoke with you?"

Maggie wagged her head, biting her bottom lip. The guy's actions seemed menacing, appearing at night, moving close, but he'd never said anything threatening.

"So, we got Cyrus Carver in town. He spoke to Maggie in a dark alley but didn't say anything that could be construed as a threat, and then we have the speeding truck that tried to take you out, but neither one of you saw the driver." Wade dropped the pen to the wooden surface. "There's not much I can do."

Maggie popped out of her chair. "What do you mean? The guy obviously came here for Brent. He's not going to be satisfied until he's hurt him or worse."

"Don't worry. I can take care of myself," Brent said.

"Like tonight?" Maggie pushed back the fear rising in her. She'd let her guard down and allowed Brent into her world. Now, he stood in harm's way. She clutched the neck of her shirt. Losing him was out of the question. She couldn't go through grief like that again.

Brent stood, placing his hands on her shoulders. "Nothing is going to happen to me, Maggie." He glanced at Wade. "My brother, the sheriff, will make sure of it. Won't you, Wade?"

"You'd better believe it. Just because all the

evidence is circumstantial doesn't mean I won't watch this Carver like a hawk. Plus, I'm going to put someone on Brent. Maybe, we can catch him the next time he tries something."

Maggie blew out a breath. "Thanks. I know you'll keep him safe."

"Speaking of keeping people safe, can you have a unit follow Maggie home tonight? She needs to pick up Matt from her mom's. I don't want her driving around alone."

"Sure, I'll have Deputy Perez to follow you and make sure you get home safe." Wade stepped out of the office to make the arrangements, leaving Maggie and Brent alone.

"You should head home. Matt needs his mom. Make sure to lock all the doors and windows tonight. Call me once you get home, if you don't mind." Brent's half grin inched across his lips.

"I'll do that, and thanks for looking out for me. I'll feel better with an escort at least for tonight." The concern that warred in her settled with the thought of Regan Perez looking out for her. She was a fellow Bible Babe and close friend.

"Yeah, I'll be less worried knowing you have a trained deputy on your six."

"What about you? Are you going to get an escort home?"

"Probably not. I've been in the military for over a decade. I can handle myself if necessary. Besides, I'm going to stay here and see if Wade and I can find a way to draw out Carver. I don't want to spend the rest of the Christmas season looking over my shoulder and worrying about you and Matt."

"What are you thinking?" Maggie asked.

Brent leaned his backside against the desk, the muscles in his jaw tightening. "I'm thinking we may need to set a trap. Let word get around town about Tyler's bachelor campout and see if he doesn't show."

"That sounds risky."

Brent stood and settled his hands on her arms. "It might be, but it's better than being tied up in knots, waiting for his next move." He pulled her to him, and she buried her face in his chest. The woodsy scent of his cologne wrapped around her. "I need to know you and Matt are safe, and that's not going to happen as long as this lunatic is loose."

Chapter Eighteen

The line for morning coffee and pastries ran out the door and down the sidewalk past the large window where the Christmas tree blinked its colored lights. Maggie pinched her arm to make sure she wasn't dreaming as she slid a pan of cream-filled Danishes into the case. Ever since Crazy Pie Day, Sweet Things had been hopping. She hated to admit the extra advertisements had garnered the shop a slew of new customers, but it seemed like the only explanation for their newfound fame.

It didn't hurt either that Brent had taken Marilyn's advice and contacted JoJo Meyers for a follow-up story on the success of the day. Apparently, who had come in and what type of pies they had purchased was big news in the Orange Blossom community. Who would've guessed?

Aunt Marilyn, that's who. The thought lingered when Maggie noticed her aunt standing in line outside the front door. Maggie remembered the days when her aunt would've pushed her way into the busy shop, expecting special privileges since she was family, but today she stood in line and waited her turn. Boy, how things had changed over the last three years.

Maggie stepped behind Millie, who stood taking orders at the electronic pad. Brent dashed between the pastry cases and the coffee dispensers, filling the orders as they popped up on the screen. Even Tyler appeared this morning to lend a hand. He scooted around the tables, clearing dishes and keeping the coffee counter stocked.

Ever since Brent's confession about being a silent partner in the bakery, Tyler had spent less time in the shop. Maggie figured he wanted to let Brent find his footing. Plus, he and Nadine were preparing for the wedding and their big move to Atlanta.

She snuck a glance at Brent as she dodged between the moving crew members and made a beeline for the kitchen. "Have you seen how crazy it is out there?"

"I know, right?" Kristen juggled a hot tray of cannoli, slipping it onto the metal table in front of the ovens before she dropped it. "I cannot believe what a difference advertising has made already." She met Maggie's gaze. "We might break the record from last December."

"December is one of our more profitable months with all the church luncheons and Christmas parties and club events, but you could be right. It's been a steady stream of customers all week." Maggie pulled a big bowl out from under the table and placed it on the shiny surface. Walking to the refrigerator, she grabbed the dough she'd been chilling since yesterday. The Children's Benefit at the Senior Citizen's Center took place this evening. "Can you handle the cases while I start the cookies for the benefit?"

"On it," Kristen said.

Maggie sprinkled a dusting of flour on the wooden

board she used to roll out dough.

"Hey, Maggie," Tyler stuck his head and shoulders inside the door. "Aunt Marilyn is here and wants to see you."

"Me? What does she want?"

"I don't know. She said it was important, and you'd want to hear what she has to say." Tyler shrugged. "What do you want me to tell her?"

Looking at the dough then back at Tyler, she huffed. "Fine. Give me a minute, and I'll be right there."

Kristen chuckled. "The best laid plans."

"Right. I'll try to keep it short, so I can get these cookies underway. I don't want to run out of time and be rushed getting them to the center." Maggie placed the wrapped dough back in the refrigerator and tried to dust the flour from her hands. "They will need to cool before we can decorate them."

"The kids always love the Rudolph and Grinch ones." Kristen stirred the cream then folded in some sugar. "Be sure to make plenty of those."

Maggie hustled through the kitchen doors and spied her aunt sitting near the Christmas tree at one of the back tables. Tyler lifted plates from its surface and gave the table a needed swipe.

"Hey, Aunt Marilyn, what can I do for you?" Maggie used the hem of her apron to wipe the flour from her hands.

"I wanted to discuss some business with you. Why don't you sit down for a minute? I promise I won't keep you long."

Maggie glanced around the bakery. The line had dwindled, and all the customers fit inside the shop.

Taking a deep breath, Maggie squelched her impulse to turn and head back to the kitchen. Instead, she pulled out the chair opposite her aunt and slid into the seat. "What can I do for you?"

"That's the million-dollar question. Or should I say the thirty-thousand-dollar question."

Maggie scowled, already lost in the conversation. "I'm sorry. What are we talking about?"

"You, dear. We are talking about you, and me, and Sweet Things."

Maggie tilted her head, giving her aunt her full attention. "Okay, I'm listening."

"Good." Marilyn beamed, leaning closer to Maggie. "So, I contacted my investment agent."

"Wait. You have an investment agent?" Maggie couldn't believe what she was hearing. She hadn't pictured her aunt as being savvy with money.

"Yes, I have an investment agent. When you work on commission, you have to make sure you can meet your month-to-month bills."

"That makes sense," Maggie said. "But what does that have to do with Sweet Things?"

"I'm getting to that." Marilyn tsked. "I chatted with my investment agent about your situation and told him you want to purchase Tyler's half of the bakery. He thought my investing in you would be a good move for my portfolio."

"Wait. What?" Maggie popped up straight in her chair. "You want to invest thirty thousand dollars with me in Sweet Things?" Maggie clutched the bib of her apron. "You want to be my backer?"

"Yes, I believe every community needs a bakery. A place where people can gather, eat and connect, and

Brent was right. You are Sweet Things. You've turned this place into a wonderful haven of solace and sweet delights."

"You…you want to back me?" Maggie repeated the words but couldn't quite wrap her brain around their meaning. Pointing, she said, "You."

Marilyn frowned. "If you keep saying it like that, I might have second thoughts."

Pursing her lips, Maggie leaned her elbows on the table. "Okay, so you want to back me in my purchase of Sweet Things. What's in it for you?"

"Well, didn't you tell me you and Brent worked up a business proposal? What did you offer your other potential investors?"

Maggie pushed down the excitement bursting inside her. Was she hearing right? Her Aunt Marilyn wanted to fund her. Her dreams were about to come true, and she didn't need to go much further than her own front door to find the person who could help her. "We had mapped out a payment plan to reimburse my investor over the next three years with interest. Plus, free perks here in the bakery as well as free cupcakes for life."

"If that plan suits you, then I'm good with it, but I will hold you to the lifetime free cupcakes." Marilyn stuck out her hand, a grin rising to her eyes. "So, do we have a deal? If so, I can have the check to you by next Friday which should give you plenty of time for you and Tyler to get the paperwork in order before his Christmas eve nuptials."

"It sounds perfect." Maggie shook Marilyn's hand, then pulled her aunt out of her chair and threw her arms around her. "Thank you, Aunt Marilyn. You don't know what this means to me."

"My dear Maggie, I might have a small idea. You're not the only one in our family who's started over after losing their dream." Marilyn squeezed her tight. "My marriage had been so bad I didn't even want to keep the man's last name. I changed it back legally to wash away all it represented." Pushing Maggie back, Marilyn met her gaze. A tear lingered in her eye. "So, I know a little about rebuilding a life. You've done such a wonderful job for you and Matt."

Gulping down the emotion threatening to clog her throat, Maggie said, "Thank you so much."

Then, to her surprise, her aunt kissed her cheek and whispered near her ear, "I'm so proud of you."

~

The afternoon sun streamed in through the large plate-glass window, showing every bent branch and gnarled limb on the artificial tree. Maggie straightened one of the ornaments near the top before turning toward the table next to her. Picking up the plates and cups, she carried them to the gray tub, depositing them on top of the pile.

The morning rush had been insane, but after eleven, the madness dwindled to a steady drizzle of customers, giving her time to work on the cookies for the Senior Citizen's Center Benefit. Kristen suggested she make more Grinch and Rudolph cookies, so she did, but she also made plenty of angels and snowmen to complete the order with a few extras for good measure.

Now at three in the afternoon, only one group of elderly women lingered over coffee and cream puffs. Maggie scooted around the counter to fish out the packets of sweeteners to replenish the supply on the coffee bar.

The door opened with a swoosh, and boots clacked on the tile floor before she glanced over her shoulder. For a moment, she feared she'd find Cyrus Carver when she turned, but Wade Thibodeaux stood in front of the register, grinning at her in his full sheriff's uniform.

Relief flooded through her. "Well, hello there. What can I get for you?" She left the box of sweeteners on the counter and joined him. "Need a jolt of java to keep you on your toes?"

"Sounds good." Wade removed his hat and placed it on the counter.

"For here or to go?"

"To go, please."

She poured the coffee then asked, "two creamers, right?"

"Right. I'm surprised you remembered. It's been a while since you've been out front. You're usually stuck in the back, baking for the whole town." Wade's smile wreathed its way up to his eyes, causing crinkles to form.

Maggie slid the hot cup with the holder on it across the counter to Wade.

"How much do I owe you?" He reached for his wallet.

"It's on the house for your help the other night."

"Have you had any more trouble? My patrol units haven't reported anything suspicious in your neighborhood or near the Silver Spur Ranch." Wade lifted the cup of coffee to his lips.

"No, it's been quiet. Thank goodness." Maggie shifted her weight from one foot to the other. She'd been running all day, and like the old saying, her dogs were barking. When Wade stayed glued to the spot where he was standing, she asked, "Is there anything else I can do for you?"

"I had hoped to speak to you alone for a moment. Do you have a sec?"

"Sure, let's grab a seat." Maggie headed to the first table in the cafe section. Sliding into the seat, she waited for Wade to settle in the chair next to her and find a place to drop his hat. "So, what is this about?"

"I wanted to talk to you about the bakery. It's come to my attention that you are still looking for funding, so you can buy out Tyler's portion. I think I can help."

Maggie shook her head, laughing. "Of all things."

A frown pulled at the corners of his lips. "What's so funny?"

"You are the second person to come in today and offer their financial backing."

"Really?" Wade offered a half grin reminding her of Brent. Wade and Brent did favor each other quite a bit, but Brent had more muscle.

"Yeah, can you believe it? I've been all over town searching for an investor, begging the banks to take a chance on me, and today, I've had two very different individuals waltz in off the street and offer their help."

"So, did you take the other person's offer?"

"Yes, I did. It came from a source I never would have ever thought to ask. A complete surprise, but it made perfect sense."

"Can I ask who's the lucky person receiving a lifetime of free cupcakes?" Wade held his coffee between his hands. "The kids are going to hate I missed out on that opportunity."

"Sure, but I'm pretty certain you'll be as surprised

as I was." Maggie beamed. "My Aunt Marilyn."

Wade shook his head. "No way. Not our Marilyn, the realtor?"

Maggie laughed. "Yep, the one and the same. She asked about it the other night when Brent took Matt and me out for dinner. We ran into her and John at The Flying Pig. She asked how my hunt for an investor was going, but I didn't know she was interested."

"Wow, that's wonderful," Wade said. "But you'd better let …" Wade's words fell away as the front door swung open, and Brent entered the bakery. The instant he spotted Wade and Maggie sitting together, he headed to their table.

"Am I interrupting anything?"

His acting skills needed a lot of work in Maggie's opinion. "Don't give me that innocent look. You knew your brother planned on chatting with me today about investing in Sweet Things."

"Maybe, I knew a little something about it." Brent's six-foot-three frame hovered over them. "So, do you have any good news to share?"

"Possibly."

Wade leaned back, seemingly content to watch.

"So, did you accept Wade's offer?" Brent held up his hands. "I know you didn't want to take my family's money, but I can't imagine running this place without you. Besides, Wade needs those free cupcakes."

"Sorry, brother. She did not accept my offer."

"Look, Maggie, don't let the fact it's my brother stand in your way of accepting his help. You'd still be an equal partner."

"That's not the reason I declined his offer." Maggie stood and pushed her chair back under the table, trying to contain her excitement.

"Then why?" Brent asked, a mixture of concern and confusion dancing across his face.

"Because I already have an investor." Maggie squealed, throwing her arms into the air.

Brent's eyes widened and his smile engulfed his whole face. "What are you talking about? When did this happen?"

"This morning. Aunt Marilyn came in and offered to be my investor. We went over the proposal, and she said I'd have the money by next Friday right before the bachelor's campout."

"Oh, Maggie. That's great news." He lifted her and swung her around in a full circle. "Who would've thought Marilyn would have been the answer?"

"I know. She surprised everyone."

Chapter Nineteen

Brent waited until Maggie was out of earshot. "Thanks, Wade, for trying to help."

"No problem. I'm glad she found her backing." Shaking his head, Wade chuckled. "Marilyn. I'd call that a minor miracle."

"I know, right?" Brent pulled out the chair Maggie had vacated. Looking over his shoulder, he found Millie preoccupied, restocking the display case with fresh baked goodies. "So, have you heard anything back from the military police at Fort Sam Houston?"

"As a matter of fact, I have. Seems our guy received an other-than-honorable discharge six months after the fire."

"It must've happened right after I saw him at the hospital. I knew he'd been discharged, but I didn't know the circumstances surrounding the decision. My captain kept me in the loop about the investigation during my recovery and rehab." Brent shrugged. "They wound up closing it after all the leads dried up. We both thought Carver was our arsonist, but nothing tied him to the fire except for the fact that he worked at the motor pool."

"Right, but they did have their suspicions. His

direct supervisor filed a report about supplies missing from the motor pool, pointing to him as the thief."

"I didn't know about that," Brent said.

"You'll never guess who made those allegations."

"The man I found unconscious in the motor pool fire?"

"On the nose." Wade rolled his coffee cup between the palms of his hands. "According to the investigators, the fire was an attempt at revenge. They also think Cyrus Carver is after you because you interfered with his plan. In his own twisted way, he blames you for his discharge from the Army."

"Well, whatever his thinking, I don't want him coming after Maggie or Matt."

"Yeah, I don't like the fact he's here in our little town. He's dangerous and willing to resort to any means to exact his revenge. I brought all my deputies up to speed this morning."

"Any luck finding the truck from the other night?"

"No. We've tried all the car rentals. Now, we're going through the recent auto thefts. It makes sense if he's a known thief he'd steal the vehicle."

"True and since we know he's a firebug, he might have burned the vehicle to get rid of any evidence."

Wade snapped his fingers. "I'll have Deputy Adams look into any abandoned vehicles the county might have towed to the impound." Taking out his phone, he sent a text message then slid the device onto the table in front of him. "So, are you ready for the bachelor campout next weekend? You do know as the best man you're responsible for all the food and drinks." Wade shot him a look. "And entertainment."

"I know. I know." Brent ran his hand along his

jawline. "I made a list, and I think I have everything down. I bought firewood for the campfire and propane gas for the grill. I have a list of snack foods, the length of my arm and a variety of sodas to pick up including the groom's favorite. Plus, I spoke with Nikki and she's letting me go through her meat freezer to choose the best ribeye steaks this side of the Mississippi. I'm talking two inches thick easy."

"Oh, the guys are gonna love that." Wade grabbed his phone when it vibrated against the plexiglass of the tabletop. "Looks like Adams is going to the impound as we speak."

"Great. I hope he finds the truck."

Wade shut off the phone. "What's on the menu for entertainment?"

"How about loud music and some tall tales from our exploits as youths? Then maybe some early morning fishing in the Sine River, like we used to do in high school."

Chuckling, Wade stood and poked his phone in his back pocket. "Sounds good, bro."

Not wanting to put a damper on the plans for Tyler, Brent hesitated before he asked, "Should we tell the other guys about the stakeout? For their safety?"

"No, the plan will go smoother if we keep it to those who need to know. Otherwise, word could get out that it's a setup." Wade shrugged. "You know how small towns work. The grapevine runs at full speed, and we want the grapevine working for us in this case."

"Definitely. I've chatted up the campout with as many of our customers as I could."

"Keep up the good work. We need this guy to show, and this plan is our best means of flushing him out."

"So, what do you have in place?" Brent checked to see if Millie was still busy. A twenty-something entered the front door and walked to the counter.

Wade lowered his voice. "I'm stationing units around the camping area, especially along the two roads that lead into the park. I've instructed the deputies to stay out of sight. Plus, we'll have several men on foot planted around the location."

Leaning closer to his brother, Brent said, "I'll be glad when this is over. I'm a little tired of having to look over my shoulder. It seems everyone here thinks I've turned into the safety police. No offense."

"None taken." Wade grabbed his empty coffee cup and walked toward the coffee station.

Brent followed. "All that sounds good. Now, if he'll cooperate."

Lifting the lid off his go cup, Wade pulled the lever on the urn to refill it. "If Carver catches wind that you're camping out, he won't be able to resist going to find you. He'll think you're vulnerable."

The young woman slung her yoga mat over her shoulder before picking up her go mug.

Shoving his hands in his apron pockets, Brent glanced at his boots and waited for the woman to leave. "I know this was my idea to use the campout as a trap, but I don't want anyone to get hurt."

"Of course not, but think of it this way, Carver's going to show up whether we have a plan in place or not. So, I'd much rather have my deputies watching your backs than for you to be out there without any preparation." Wade squeezed Brent's shoulder. "Don't worry. This will work."

The kitchen doors swung out as Maggie headed behind the counter carrying a tray in each hand. "Hot stuff coming through." She placed the trays on the counter for Millie to stock the cases. Glancing over her shoulder, she said, "Oh Wade, you're still here."

"Brent's been going on and on about the campout." Wade slapped Brent on the back.

"What? Wait a minute. He's the one asking all these questions about the big night," Brent countered.

Turning, she gave them a give-me-a-break look that set both men to chuckling. "I'm sure you two will make Tyler's bachelor party very memorable. But not too memorable."

"Got it," Brent said.

Wade traced the edges of the lid to seal it. "I'd better head out or Deputy Perez will think I got lost."

"Hey, before you go, I wanted to box up a few cupcakes for you, to ease the disappointment with the kids about losing out on the lifetime supply." She moved into action before Wade could refuse her offer.

He grabbed his hat. "Thanks, I appreciate the help. I need all I can get with our crew."

Maggie pulled a box from the shelf and filled it with a variety of cupcakes from the display case. "Plus, I wanted to talk to you about Cyrus Carver. I keep going over the afternoon of our fire."

Brent frowned at the concern in her eyes. Had Cyrus gotten to her again? He hated that this man occupied so much of their time.

Closing the lid, she handed the box to Wade. "When it happened, I told Brent I could have sworn I had lowered the flame under the pot before I went to his office. But I figured I was mistaken. I must've left the flame on high. Now, though, I recall not only lowering the flame, but I also remember that the back door was unlocked."

"Is the back door normally secured?" Wade asked.

"Oh, yeah, we keep it locked even during the day. It keeps people from wandering in from the alley. Plus, I don't have to remember to lock it each evening before I leave."

Wade scowled.

"I mean I check it, but rarely is it unlocked." Maggie licked her lips, shifting her weight from one foot to the other. "But on that afternoon, when Brent directed us out of the kitchen, it was already open. In fact, the door wasn't closed all the way."

"Are you saying Carver is responsible for the kitchen fire?"

"I'm saying I remember lowering the flame, I remember the door being open, and I remember a black truck passing by the alleyway along the side street."

~

Brent hummed as he finished working on the advertisements for the new Christmas holiday menu. He planned to contact Curtis at *The Daily Blossom* on Monday, so the ads would be up and running as soon as possible. With all the time spent looking for investors, Maggie was right. Christmas had snuck up on them both.

His chest expanded a good six inches with pride every time he thought about her obtaining the funding on her own. Sure, he'd helped with the proposal, but Maggie was the one to sell her aunt on the idea.

He rolled the leather chair out from under the desk, facing away from the door, and stretched his long legs out in front of him, causing the chair to squeak. The clinking of pots and pans drifted into his office. No, his and Maggie's office. A smile threaded its way across his lips. He liked the sound of that.

Being her partner, he'd be the one she tossed ideas around with, the one whom she'd count on, the one she'd look to for input and encouragement. Yes, he liked the sound of all of that, but his heart wanted more. He'd fallen for the brown haired, hazel eyed beauty.

The image of Tyler scowling his disapproval emerged. They weren't teens anymore. The "hands off my sister" rule worked great when she was a wee babe of fourteen, but the wee babe had grown into a hot babe and neither one of them would be going into this relationship blind.

He needed to tell her how he felt, but when? Life for him swept along at a raging pace. He'd thought once the funding was settled, he'd have the opportunity. Then Cyrus Carver showed up, causing trouble. Add in the holidays, a wedding, a bachelor campout, and life spiraled from one day to the next at the speed of galloping horses.

A soft knock drew his attention. "Hey, we're finished for the evening. Do you want to walk us to our cars? I made Kristen wait like you asked." Maggie stepped out of the doorway and pulled her apron over her head, hanging it on a hook outside the office door. The bakery closed daily at five, but with cleaning up and prep for the next day, it tended to be closer to seven before the bakery chefs were ready to go.

"Yeah, I'll be right there." Brent saved the images and text on his computer screen to a file. "You know we ought to go celebrate. Live it up big."

Yawning, Maggie peeked around the doorframe. "I need to go pick up Matt. After this week of unusual hours and meetings, we need a night in."

Brent stood, sliding the chair back into place. "How would you feel about company?"

~

With the lights low, the television screen exploded with action when the final scene of *Toy Story* played out. The movie was one of Matt's favorites since it spotlighted a loveable dinosaur. Maggie knew sections of the movie by heart. Matt snuggled up beside Brent. She savored the sight. The broad-chested man had his arm draped over the little boy. Both had their eyes closed, and Matt made little sniffling noises as he inhaled. Congestion left over from his most recent ear infection.

The empty pizza box from their dinner lay sprawled open on the coffee table, right next to Brent's socked feet that poked out from under the fuzzy blanket covering him.

Maggie smothered a giggle. Brent looked adorable wrapped in Matt's fuzzy lamb blanket. This big, six-three man huddled next to her three-foot Mini-Me.

Brent had been a good sport when Matt wanted to sit next to him and share his blanket to watch the movie. He'd drawn the little boy to him and made sure he was comfortable. Then, whenever the dinosaur, Rex, made an appearance, they both pointed and yelled, "Dino." Until Matt drifted off during one of the longer scenes.

She studied Brent's features. His well-formed jaw gave him a striking appearance, and his full lips begged to be kissed. She licked her lips and pressed them together to resist the pull. Her glance landed on the scars he worried over. For her, they faded away. The scars were just another piece of who he was, a kind man who took care of those he loved.

Loved. Now, that was a risky word. Every time she stood close to Brent her heart melted into a gooey mush, like soft bread dough. She cared for him, always had, and in truth, always would. But the more they worked together, the more aware of her feelings she became. On numerous occasions, their eyes connected across the seating area of Sweet Things. Her heart never failed to flutter like a cage full of butterflies wanting to be released. That kiss they share, the memory never failed to bring warmth to her cheeks. Oh boy, she was in trouble.

Brent stirred, and she gave in to the temptation. Leaning over, she placed her lips atop his full mouth. He met her kiss, then his lips pulled into a smile, and he opened his eyes. "That's nice. Can we do it again now that I'm awake?"

She planted a quick kiss on his lips, then pointed at Matt, who squirmed between them. "We'd better put him to bed. He has a big day tomorrow with Grandpa."

"Right. You and your mom are going shopping, so you won't be at the shop in the morning." Brent scooped the boy into his arms and held him against his chest.

Maggie loved how at ease he acted with Matt. How he jumped in to help as if he'd been doing it forever. "Yeah, Kristen and I made a deal. I'll go this Saturday, and she'll go the next one, so we can finish up our Christmas shopping. Plus, I need to find a dress for Tyler's wedding." Maggie scooted off the couch, giving

Brent enough room to get to his feet.

"Wait. Aren't you a bridesmaid? I thought you already had that covered." Brent gathered the blanket that had fallen to the cushion and draped it over the sleeping toddler.

"Again, everything was put on the back burner until I could find the financing. Livelihood took precedence. What can I say?"

Maggie led Brent down the hall to Matt's room. The night light glowed softly, creating shadows in the nooks and crannies of the small space. He sat in the rocking chair holding Matt while she pulled out a clean pair of pajamas from the top drawer of the dresser. Without waking him, she laid him on the changing table and undressed him, then changed his pull-ups.

"Boy, he's zonked." Brent came alongside her as she slid the boy's arm into his sleeves and pulled the top over his head. "Being in the military and part of the fire brigade, I learned to sleep wherever I found myself, typically in the barracks or the firehouse sleeping quarters with a bunch of other guys who snored and talked in their sleep. But he's got it nailed already."

Maggie glanced at him, giving him a smile. "Yeah, he's turning into a kid right before my eyes."

"I know. He's grown even in the last few weeks since I've been home." Brent caressed the tyke's blond hair. "You've done such a good job with him."

Tears prickled her eyes at his compliment. How she longed to be a good mother to Matt, but so many things were beyond her control. The words from her scripture reading for Bible Babes popped into her mind. "Come to me, all who are weary and burdened, and I will give you rest."

Brent's arms slid around her, and his warm body pressed against her back. She leaned into him as he wrapped his arms around her. A sigh escaped her lips as she settled into his embrace.

"You know Nikki and Bernadette, both admire you. The way you've handled being a single mom on your own."

"Oh, I'm not kidding myself. Without my family and friends, I would've sunk like a rock a long time ago. I didn't do anything on my own. God provided a way for me and Matt." She turned in his arms. "Even you. He provided you to help me with the proposal."

"A fat lot of good that did you. Even the investors I handpicked turned you down."

"Yeah, but without the proposal I wouldn't have had all the facts ready for Aunt Marilyn, so maybe the proposal didn't generate the interest, but it did seal the deal." Maggie tucked her chin. "So, thank you."

"You've survived so much and are thriving." He crooked his finger, placing it under her chin and lifted her face. The love she discovered in his dark green eyes made her heart quiver.

"You know how I feel about you, don't you?" Brent ran his thumb over her cheek.

"I know," she whispered, letting herself relish the firmness of his arms around her. "But I come with a plus one. Every day, and I'm not sure you know what that takes."

"You're right. I don't know all the ins and outs of being a parent, but I've been watching Dan and Nikki with the twins, helping and learning." Brent kissed her forehead. "I'm willing to do what is necessary."

"But it's not only the doing. It's the feelings I'm

concerned about. Could you love him like your own?" Maggie stepped out of Brent's hold. Picking up her son from the changing table, she slid him into the toddler's bed, pulling the covers over him. The lamb blanket lay on the seat of the rocker.

Brent grabbed it and spread it over the sleeping child. "Maggie, I already care about Matt. I love that you have a plus one. He's part of you, of who you've become." He walked to her. "I'm not expecting that to change. I know he has to be first, but could there be room for me in your heart, too?"

Maggie pressed her lips together, shaking her head. "I don't know. Maybe."

"You don't know, or are you afraid of the answer?" Brent pulled her to him, and she let him.

Rolling onto her toes, she kissed his cheek, while her heart screamed the truth. Fear held her, kept her cautious, unwilling to take a chance. Meeting his gaze, she gave the only answer she could, an honest one. "I am afraid. My heart shattered when I lost Ted. It's taken a long time to glue all those pieces back together. Loving you is risky. What happens if I lose you?"

"I can't make you any guarantees because you're right, love is risky. And that goes for loving anyone— Parents, brothers, kids, but at least if you take a chance with me, then you could say you've been blessed with love twice. Because, Magpie, I do love you."

Chapter Twenty

Maggie twirled in front of the mirror, wearing the tea-length dress her mother had picked from the rack. "You look lovely," Libby commented. "It fits so well."

They'd traveled thirty minutes east to Lake Charles, Louisiana, to shop at some of the bigger stores in the mall in hopes of finding a suitable dress for Tyler and Nadine's wedding.

She and her mother tried Belk's first, then moved on to a formalwear store across from the food court, ending at the way-out-of-her-price-range boutique. Now, Maggie stood in Dillard's dressing room with a hook full of red dresses to work her way through.

"Oh, nice. This one is my favorite so far," Libby said.

"Me, too." Maggie touched the lace bodice with the soft lining underneath.

Her mother pulled a stray white thread from the neckline and tugged the sleeve to straighten it. "Marilyn tells me that she ran into you and Brent at The Flying Pig the other night having dinner." She looked over Maggie's shoulder and met her gaze in the mirror. "Is there anything your father and I should know? Are there sparks simmering?"

Maggie wanted to roll her eyes at her mother's attempt to pry, but she couldn't keep a smile from blooming on her face. "Perhaps." She shrugged.

"Perhaps? That's a yes or no question." Libby tsked.

"All right, yes, there are sparks. A tiny ember, but we're taking it slow. I have to consider Matt in all this, and he does too."

"What do you mean? He's great with Matt."

"I know, but being a full-time father is a lot different from helping occasionally when it's needed with your niece or nephew. Uncles get to hand the kids back. Dads don't. He should weigh the responsibility before he signs up for dating me."

Libby stepped back as Maggie turned to face her. "So, you think Brent's afraid of the challenge? I find that hard to believe. He doesn't strike me as the type to turn and run because something is hard. I mean, the guy has been in the military, and he's not only served his country, but by being part of the fire brigade, he served his military community as well."

"That's different." Maggie slipped the dress over her hips and took the next one off the hanger. "He had training. He was prepared."

Libby laughed as she placed the dress they both liked, back on the hanger. "You of all people should know nothing prepares you for parenthood. It's a learn-as-you-go proposition for everyone."

Maggie stepped into the next dress. She turned and her mother zipped it up for her. They both shook their heads. The color of red was too dark, and the floor-length gown didn't do anything for Maggie's figure.

"On to the next one."

"Can I give you a piece of advice about Brent?" Libby unzipped the dress.

Maggie stepped out of it. "Sure."

"You don't have to choose between Matt and Brent. It's not a choice. It's a blending, like it is in any family. They are all a blend of different personalities, different preferences. All families, whether by blood or by marriage, are blended."

Tossing the dress onto the pile on the chair, Maggie slipped the next one over her head, zipping it on the side. "A blending?" Maggie tried to keep the skepticism out of her tone as she examined her reflection.

"Yes, a blending. Look at Jesus. Joseph wasn't his father by birth, but he was his earthly father by God's design."

Maggie froze. She considered her mother to be wise, but her insight into this matter caught Maggie by surprise. "I never would have thought of that, but you're right."

"Of course, I'm right. Don't push Brent away because you think he's not ready. If he loves you, he'll love Matt." Maggie touched her tummy to still the butterflies rising in her.

After plowing through the mound of red dresses they had hauled into the dressing room, they both agreed the tea-length one with the lace bodice was the most flattering on Maggie by far.

~

At one, the aromas from the food court beckoned to them to stop for lunch. Maggie's mouth watered as she approached the counter to place her order. Her mom stood behind her, trying to decide what to get. "There's so much to choose from, "she said.

"You enjoy the kung pao chicken."

"I know, but I'm in the mood for something different." Libby squinted at the menu behind the counter.

"Well, I'm having the beef and broccoli with an egg roll and fried rice." Maggie glanced behind them. The line grew as her mother tried to decide. "Mom, people are waiting."

Libby spun around to see the crowd behind her. "Oh, sorry. I'll have the sweet and sour chicken with an egg roll." Libby pulled out her wallet from her purse. "My treat."

"I can pay for my own," Maggie said.

"Let me get it. After all, you need all your pennies if you're going to buy out Tyler." Her mom pulled a credit card from her wallet and slid it through the machine. "At least until you find your funding."

Maggie let out a sigh of relief. She'd been worried since her mother mentioned chatting with her Aunt Marilyn that her aunt might have spilled the beans about their new business arrangement.

"I thought you weren't in favor of my decision to buy out Tyler." Maggie picked up the black tray and moved toward an empty table.

"A woman can change her mind. Now that I know the whole story, I can see you and Brent doing well together."

"So, you've stated." Maggie placed her tray on the table and used a napkin to wipe away the crumbs. "Well, I have some good news on that front."

Libby slid into the chair across from her. "Did one

of the investors jump at the chance?"

"Not exactly, but I did find an investor."

"Who?" Maggie's mom opened the packaged chopsticks.

"You're never going to believe this."

Libby paused, holding the chopsticks in mid-air. "Okay, now my curiosity is running wild."

"Aunt Marilyn."

Her mom's mouth dropped open. "Marilyn is your investor?"

"I know, right?" Maggie broke her chopsticks apart. "She asked me some questions the night at The Flying Pig, and I answered them not knowing she'd even consider becoming my backer. Then she stopped by the bakery the other day to discuss the possibility. We went over the proposal, and she loved it."

"It's a Christmas miracle, if ever I've seen one." Libby shook her head. "She's another example of how people can change when they're growing in the Lord. She's so different from when I first married into the Kemp family. After her divorce, she held such bitterness in her heart against her ex-husband and his new wife. I can't blame her, but it was so bad for her. Marilyn changed her legal name back to Kemp because she didn't want any reminders of that time in her life. She wanted a clean start." Libby poked her chopsticks into the chicken and scooped up a bite.

"I can understand how it feels to start over. She mentioned it to me the other day when we met at the bakery. I guess she understands about rebuilding your life when things don't go according to your plan."

"She certainly does." Libby wiped her mouth with her napkin. "Speaking of plans, the Sunday school coordinator wanted me to thank you for stepping up to provide the desserts for the Sunday School Christmas Potluck. Your dad and I are so excited to see the nativity play. Nikki's little boy, David, will be one of the lambs and Danielle is playing the part of an angel. Of course, at their age, they won't have speaking parts."

The Sunday School Christmas Potluck. Maggie cringed. She'd forgotten all about volunteering to provide the desserts back in October when the chairwoman had contacted her. "Remind me again the date for the potluck."

"Pastor Connor wanted to have it before people started heading out of town for the holidays, so he thought Thursday night before Christmas would work best." Libby sipped her drink.

"Wow, that's going to make the weekend hectic. I mean the potluck on Thursday, then the wedding Saturday evening, and Christmas on Sunday."

"Yes, it's going to be a whirl wind for sure. But we've known about the Christmas Potluck since before Thanksgiving. Purdy's been putting it in the bulletin every week."

Maggie frowned. How was she going to get everything done? The minute she removed one item off her plate, something else fell onto it. "You're right, Mom. I'm sure I can manage some sugar cookies and a couple dozen cupcakes for the Sunday school gathering."

Grabbing her phone, Maggie texted Kristen to put the event on the calendar. She didn't need any more surprises before Christmas. It was bad enough she kept looking over her shoulder for Cyrus Carver.

She'd never been one to be afraid, but ever since

the man tried to harm Brent, she'd heeded Brent's advice about taking extra precautions. She scanned the area near her house before leaving and never stepped outside if there was an unfamiliar vehicle. She locked her doors and windows at the house. Plus, she'd taken to locking her car doors while driving.

Thanks to Carver's presence in Orange Blossom the whole staff at Sweet Things had become safety aware. Even today, here in Lake Charles, Maggie thought she'd caught a glimpse of the man from the alley, but when she did a double take, she couldn't find him. It was probably her imagination.

Chapter Twenty-one

The men lounged in the camping chairs around the fire that crackled in the center of their circle. The night air surrounded them, cool and crisp for a Texas December evening. Brent pulled his sweatshirt over his head, stuffing his arms into the sleeves as he settled next to Karl, Nadine's brother, who leaned against a log facing the fire. The others were in various stages of finishing their steak dinners.

Brent took in the scene, pleased that all the guys could make it. His old high school friends well received the idea of a camping trip for the bachelor party, and when he added the enticement of a steak dinner with all the trimmings, they'd agreed without hesitation.

Ryan Parker, who sat in one of the chairs, slid his paper plate to the ground, moaned, and rubbed his stomach. "Dee-licious. I haven't had a steak that good in ages."

"Homegrown beef and lots of marinade," Brent said. "Don't forget about the cookies and muffins I confiscated from the bakery."

"Oh, man. I don't know where I'm going to put it, but I'm sure there won't be any left come morning."

Brent grinned. "Probably not even a crumb." He

enjoyed being here with his old friends to reconnect, but he couldn't keep from wondering how things were going with his brother Wade and the sheriff units on stakeout in the area.

Brent had used his better judgment and discussed the situation with Tyler, who agreed to let Wade and his men stand watch. He knew he'd taken a chance, but he figured now that they were at the campsite, the risk was minimal, and Tyler needed to know.

Chuck Martin leaned forward, resting his forearms on his knees. "Do you guys remember when we moved that cow into Principal Grover's office after the lunchroom stopped serving chocolate milk?"

"Boy, do I. He was so mad, I thought for sure we were toast," Tyler said.

"I don't think it was the cow in his office that upset him, but the fact that the cow wore bottles of chocolate syrup around its neck like a Christmas wreath, and they had leaked all over his chair."

"His favorite chair." Ryan smirked. "Add the fact that we tied the cow to the bookshelf."

"Yeah, we didn't think that one through, did we?" Brent asked.

Tyler laughed, shaking his head. "I thought he was going *to have a cow* when he found his office trashed by Dairy Queen. She'd chewed through several of his books."

"We were lucky we weren't expelled," Brent said. "And that Pops didn't make us pay rent on Dairy Queen."

"Thank goodness for reasonable doubt," Ryan, the lawyer, said.

"You know Grover came in right before

Thanksgiving on Crazy Pie Day." Brent stretched his long legs out in front of him. "He's still the principal at the high school."

"No way. He was ancient when I was there," Karl said. "And I was four years behind you guys."

"Sometimes people get stuck." John McAllister leaned toward the fire, rubbing his hands together. "I should've brought a heavier jacket."

"The tents should keep us warm enough. The temperature is supposed to be in the mid-forties tonight, so it won't be too bad. Hope everyone brought a warm sleeping bag." Brent had checked the weather report every day for the last week, wanting everything to go well for his friend's last hurrah as a single man.

"I can't believe in one short week you will be a married." Chuck chortled. "Married. I thought you'd be the last one to get hitched. Always thought Thibodeaux here would be the first one to go down, not Ryan."

"Me? Why me?" Brent asked.

"Your family. They were so close, even after your parents passed. The way Pops stepped in and took care of you during your last year of high school. And all those summers before when you visited Orange Blossom, with you and your brothers. It was all about family for you."

"Guess my getting married five years ago messed with your plans," Ryan said to Chuck. "Sorrrry." He took a swig of his soft drink.

Chuck caught John's gaze. "What about you? Have you been married?"

"Nope, but I'm not opposed to the idea. In fact, I'm kind of fond of it." John's face glowed in the firelight.

"Okay, I know that look." Tyler teased. "Who is

she?"

Brent scowled, turning toward his friend. "Seriously, you don't know who he's talking about? Have you been living under a rock?"

"No, I've been living in wedding world. Which, by the way, takes up a lot of time and energy." Turning toward John, he asked, "So, who is she?"

Howling, Brent and John doubled over in laughter.

"Captain Observant, not." Brent wiped the tears from his eyes with the back of his hand. "You slay me."

"What?' Tyler scowled and waved off the insult.

"It's your Aunt Marilyn, "John answered.

"Aunt Marilyn. Wow."

"Didn't you think it was odd I was there for Thanksgiving?" John asked. "I mean if I were just a client."

"Not really. My family invites people over all the time for holiday events, so I didn't give it a second thought. Although Nadine did mention something about you two making a cute couple." Tyler sipped on his soda.

"I am so glad, after Saturday night Nadine will be in charge of your social life. Maybe she can keep you up to date on who is seeing who," Brent said.

"To be honest, it's a little more than seeing each other. I picked out a ring today." John's smile wreathed around his face.

Tyler's eyes widened, and he choked on his soda. "What? Are you kidding? That's great. Surprising, but great."

Brent rose from the ground to shake his friend's hand. "Congratulations, John. Now we have two things to celebrate." While up, Brent grabbed a trash bag and went around the circle gathering the empty plates and soda cans. Tyler crushed the can he held before tossing it into the bag.

Walking to the park trash, Brent pulled his phone out of his front pocket to make sure he hadn't missed any calls or texts from Wade. He'd left his phone on ring in case his brother tried to contact him. Nothing yet.

Brent also took a few precautions of his own. He'd packed his heavy-duty flashlight, a warning horn, and a fire extinguisher. This guy was a firebug, and if he struck out again, he'd use fire. That is, if he even showed tonight.

Brent threw the plastic black bag into the trash and replaced the lid. While returning to the group, he scanned the area. Nothing but trees in any direction. The small picnic area with the grill Brent had used to cook their meal stood empty and quiet.

It'd been more than a week since Brent had any contact with the man, so he hoped the guy had moved along, putting Orange Blossom in his rearview mirror, but he couldn't shake the feeling that Cyrus was close. The campout gave him too good of an opportunity to strike.

Joining the group, Brent took a seat on the ground and rested his back against the log once more. The fire danced and flitted as the soft night breeze blew against it, bringing the flames to life. Brent stretched his arms above his head and yawned. He rubbed his eyes. He wouldn't get much sleep tonight, even if he was exhausted. Catching Cyrus was his only goal.

~

Sometime close to half past two in the morning,

Brent's phone rang. He patted the ground next to his sleeping bag trying to locate the device. "Yeah?"

"Brent, this is Deputy Adams. I've been patrolling the river road and found a vehicle not far from your location. You'd better check the campsite. It could be nothing, but usually when I discover a truck parked out here at this time of night, it's a group of teens up to no good, but nobody's in the truck."

"Gotcha. I'll look around. Thanks for the heads-up."

"I'll stay in the area. Let me know what you find."

Brent ended the call and rolled out of his sleeping bag. Reaching for his shoes, he pushed his feet into them without untying them. Before opening the tent flap, he found his flashlight. He planned to make a thorough search of the area before returning to his tent. Hopefully Deputy Adams was right, and it was a bunch of teens up to mischief.

The cool night air greeted him as he stood. Clouds covered the moon, making the darkness around him seem like a heavy curtain. Clicking on the flashlight, he swept the immediate area near his tent. The group had spread out over two campsites to give everyone a bit of privacy. Tyler and John had set up their tents close to each other. Brent jogged the short distance, checking the tree line as he went. Nothing. Until he neared John's tent, a sharp clang rang out near the picnic area. His heart raced. Could it be Carver?

Heading in that direction, he turned off the flashlight hoping to surprise whoever it was. The rattle of metal grew louder the closer he came. He stopped by a tree on the perimeter to take a look. Someone was rummaging around in the trash can. Flipping on the light, Brent found two racoons looking for a midnight snack.

Relief flooded through him. He'd consider them cute if they hadn't nearly given him a heart attack. Remembering the truck spotted by Deputy Adams, he jogged back toward John and Tyler's tents then froze in place.

Someone stood a few feet outside of John's tent. Was it John? Brent swung the light over to him, expecting to see his friend. The figure whipped around as the beam hit him. Cyrus Carver.

"Stop." Brent yelled loud enough to wake the men in the tents.

Carver pulled a bottle from his pocket and lit the fuse.

John stepped out of his tent, pulling on his jacket. "What's going on?" He lifted his arm to block the beam of light.

"It's Carver." Brent rushed toward the man holding the burning bottle.

John lunged for him but missed.

Tyler emerged from his tent as Carver raced past. Turning, the arsonist tossed the bottle in Tyler's direction. He ducked as the flaming bottle streaked through the darkness and landed on the tent, igniting on impact.

Tyler pulled off his shirt and started to beat the flames with it.

Brent turned to run the other way. "John, wake the others. I've got a fire extinguisher in my truck." He took off toward the parking lot not far from the campsites. They needed to keep the fire from spreading.

His heart pumping, he pushed his legs to go faster.

Behind him, he could hear John rousing the other men. Reaching the truck, he punched in the code to unlock the door. He grabbed the extinguisher and raced back to their campsite.

Tyler pounded the ground where his tent had sat with his shirt, but the fire had a mind of its own and traveled to the dry grass. John, Ryan, and Chuck surrounded the blaze, slinging their jackets and other pieces of clothing at the growing red beast.

Brent ran to the circle of men, almost colliding with Ryan. "Stand back." Brent went through the motions he'd taught others, pulling the pin, aiming the nozzle, pressing the lever. The white foam spewed from the container, covering the grass like cold snowflakes on a winter's eve. The fire hissed and snarled, then with one last sputter died.

Exhausted from the adrenaline rush, the men collapsed in their chairs around the stones of the campfire.

Brent, still on high alert, fished his phone from his pocket and called Deputy Adams. "Did you catch him? He ran your way towards his truck."

"What? No, I haven't seen anyone."

"Are you still at his vehicle?" Brent asked.

"Sure am. What happened? Did you spot him?"

"Yeah, we spotted him, and he left us a little present. A Molotov cocktail."

"Is everyone okay?" Deputy Adams asked.

"We're all fine. Tyler's tent is toast, but he's okay. Can you send someone to take our statements? After all the excitement, we'd all like to go home."

"Certainly. I'll radio the Sheriff. He's on the road nearest to the park entrance. I'm sure he's going to want to check the scene himself and get the fire crew out here. I'll have a look around this area. Maybe Carver's waiting for me to leave. Might be in the tree line."

"Don't go alone." Brent couldn't stress enough the danger this guy posed. "Call for back up."

Deputy Adams chuckled. "You sound like the boss."

Chapter Twenty-two

The kitchen of Sweet Things bakery hummed with activity the Thursday before Christmas. Due to all of Brent's advertising efforts, the bakery received twice its usual holiday orders. If things stayed running at this pace, she'd be able to pay back her aunt's investment in no time. She couldn't wait to make her partnership with Brent official. She'd arranged for Tyler to come by after lunch when the crowd thinned to sign all the paperwork. A little thrill shot through her. She'd never be able to thank her aunt enough for believing in her.

"Again, you guys are the best for coming in today. I know, Ranita, you don't work on Thursdays, but I needed an all-hands-on-deck staff today." Maggie whisked the cake batter. "I forgot about my church's Sunday School Christmas Potluck. I'm so sorry, this one is on me. I must've blanked out whenever Pastor Connor made the announcements about this month's events. With the extra orders, I needed the help."

"Good thing your mother reminded you." Kristen squeezed the white icing onto the sugar cookies. She'd add the eyes and nose later, making them look like Rudolph, the red-nosed reindeer. "Or it wouldn't have made the calendar."

"Definitely. I'd been sunk for sure." Maggie placed the bowl onto the mixer and lowered the mixer head. With the push of a button, the machine whirred to life. All three bakers maneuvered around the kitchen, trying to stay out of each other's way. Ranita pulled cupcakes from the oven, then plucked them from the baking tins onto a cooling rack.

Maggie stopped the mixer and lifted the bowl from the platform. The batter looked light and fluffy. Perfect. Mr. Gibson would appreciate her efforts to accommodate his food allergies. He'd been one of the reasons she'd convinced Tyler to carry a few gluten-free items. Of course, other customers also enjoyed having the gluten-free choice.

"I couldn't imagine getting all these cookies and cupcakes ready for the potluck, along with the cakes for the Small Business Christmas Bash and finishing Nadine and Tyler's wedding cake." Maggie swiped at a strand of hair close to her eyes away from her face.

"Along with the usual fare we offer." Ranita spooned cupcake batter into the red paper linings.

The kitchen doors swung open, and Brent hustled through with both hands full. "Millie has everything under control out front. How's it going in here?" He set the bussing tub full of dirty dishes next to the dishwasher and pulled a rack from underneath to load.

"It's going," Kristen said without looking up.

When Maggie glanced up, he met her gaze and winked. Would the thrill of being in love with this man ever wear off? She hoped not.

Kristen put down the bag of white icing and picked up the one with black. "So, I hear you had some excitement the other night on your campout." She shot him a glance filled with mischief.

"Who told you about our night?" Brent asked over his shoulder.

"A little birdie who works for the fire department when he came in yesterday for a Danish." She mashed the icing in the bag, so it would be easier to use. "He said you guys almost burned down the woods."

"Remember the guy who showed up here in the alley?"

Ranita halted what she was doing. "Yeah, how could we forget? You've been warning us to be careful ever since he showed up. Don't tell me *he* had something to do with it."

"He started the fire."

"What? Are you kidding?" Kristen's eyes widened.

"Dead serious. He showed up in the middle of the night with a Molotov cocktail and a deep desire for revenge."

Kristen planted her fist on her hip. "Revenge? Why does he want revenge against you? Spill."

"Yeah, spill," Ranita said.

"You might as well tell them. It's a small town. They're bound to find out eventually." Maggie poured the batter into the cake pans and waited for Brent to tell his story, the story of how he got his scars. The story of how he came to be here with her.

Brent turned to face the three women. "There was a fire at the motor pool where I was based. I wasn't on duty, but I saw the smoke early one morning. I called it in to the fire station, but when I checked out the building, I found someone in the fire. So, I went in to get him."

"Oh man, what a brave thing to do." Ranita leaned

her forearms on the table still holding the ladle with batter on it.

"More stupid than brave. I didn't have any gear and no back up. There's a reason firemen work together." Brent's gaze drifted down to his boots. "Anyway, the guy lived but couldn't identify the culprit. The MPs believe the victim was Carver's target. I found out from Wade that the man I saved was Carver's motor pool supervisor. Some items had gone missing during a few of Carver's shifts and his supervisor reported the thefts, putting the spotlight on Carver."

"So, Carver wants revenge because you saved the guy in the motor pool," Ranita said.

"Partly, but I also reported him for a different incident that happened at the hospital after the motor pool fire."

"Why isn't this guy behind bars?" Kristen asked.

"We couldn't link him to the fire, but my report of insubordination was the last straw, and the Army discharged him."

"So, what's going to happen to him now? From what the fireman told me, he attacked Tyler. Threw the burning bottle straight at him." Kristen scowled. "Will he be locked up?"

"You bet your bottom dollar he will be. Once we catch him." Brent straightened to his full height. "I can't stress how important it is for everyone connected to me or the bakery to be careful. This man has it out for me."

Maggie met Brent's somber gaze. The fun, flirty man she'd come to love disappeared behind a stern expression. "Brent's right. We all need to be on alert, especially now that things have escalated."

"Because of his actions last Friday night, we have witnesses who can identify him. So, there's no getting out of this one," Brent said. "Wade has put out an APB on him, so, we have the whole state of Texas looking for Cyrus Carver."

"I hope Wade can find him." Ranita stood, pulling the tin of half-filled cupcake liners toward her.

Kristen picked up the bag with black icing and placed two dots on each cookie. "Well, I hope the guy has enough sense to leave while he still can. Surely, he knows any other attempts for revenge will put him at risk of being caught."

"You'd think." Ranita let the batter drizzle off the spoon into the liner.

Maggie pushed the cake pans into the oven. Pulling off her oven mitts, she helped Brent load the last of the dirty dishes. "Do you think Carver might have left town?" Her voice lowered to little more than a whisper, so the others wouldn't hear.

"Honestly, I don't know. It'd be the smart move, but from his actions, this guy doesn't seem to care if he gets caught. Which makes him twice as deadly."

She couldn't stand the thought of Brent being in harm's way. She'd nearly come unglued when he told her what happened to Tyler. So many things could've gone wrong. Anyone of the men could've been hurt including her brother and Brent.

A wave of panic washed over her. She'd survived Ted's sudden death but only because she was pregnant with Matt. Her baby needed her. She couldn't survive losing Brent. She'd fallen completely and utterly in love with the man, and she longed to have him forever, not a mere few months.

Selfishly, she prayed, *"Lord, please keep him safe. I don't have the strength to say goodbye now that I've found him."*

~

The noise level piqued at a decibel level close to deafening when the children ran through the fellowship hall of the Community Cowboy Church. Maggie dodged two boys who were playing tag, racing around the tables and chairs. Side-stepping them, she avoided a collision, saving the box of cookies from ending up on the floor.

Adults gathered in groups throughout the large room, chatting, trying to be heard above the squeals and laughter of the kids. The Sunday School Christmas Potluck was in full swing. Maggie scanned the crowd, looking for her parents. They were meeting her here with Matt. It took her a minute, but she found them.

Libby and Stuart Kemp lingered near the food tables loaded with crockpots, warming plates, and steaming hot pans, talking with a younger couple. Her father wore a tacky sweater with a huge Christmas tree on it, covered in colorful pom-poms as ornaments. He'd owned the thing for years. Her mother sported a beautiful red blouse with silver buttons and a pair of dark slacks.

Matt, who was snuggled in his grandmother's arms, watched a little girl hopping around while she held her dad's hand. Maggie waved at her mother who waved back without drawing Matt's attention. A smile crossed Maggie's lips when she saw Matt wearing his Christmas pajamas with the reindeer on them and a headband with reindeer antlers. When Matt moved, the antlers shook. Her mother must have bought those for him.

Maggie and Brent made several trips to her car to bring in the cookies and cupcakes for the event, then placed them on the table designated for the desserts. She fussed over the presentation to the amusement of Brent.

"I'm glad you find this so entertaining," she huffed.

"You know that's going to last for about ten seconds after the kids pounce on this table."

"I know, but I want it to look nice until then. As part-owner of Sweet Things, I have a reputation to uphold." She bumped his hip with hers. "So stop grinning, and help me, partner."

"*Partner*, I do like the sound of that."

How they filled all the orders she couldn't fathom. Her feet ached, and all she wanted to do was to grab Matt and head home, but she knew she needed to be present tonight to support her church and the Bible Babes, who were considered an honorary Sunday School group.

She and Brent worked together to put the doilies on the red and green trays, then they unboxed the cookies and placed them in columns on the doilies with reindeers on three trays and angels on the other three.

Brent insisted they ride together, so he could make sure she arrived safe. He'd been on high alert since Cyrus Carver appeared in the alley, but after Friday night's disaster, his alert level doubled. He'd taken to calling or texting several times a day to make sure she and Matt were okay.

She didn't mind the attention. In fact, it'd been

ages since she'd been treated with such care, but she had to admit she enjoyed the respite when he went to chat with his brothers, leaving her to display the cupcakes to her satisfaction.

"Hey there, girlie," Mr. Gibson called, approaching Maggie.

She turned from fiddling with the tiered cupcake holder to greet him. "Mr. Gibson, how are you tonight?"

"Splendid. I got word my son and his family will be here tomorrow to spend the Christmas weekend with me."

"How wonderful." Maggie frowned as she scanned the dessert table. Where had she put the gluten-free cake she'd made for him?

Mr. Gibson chuckled. "You don't look like it's wonderful."

"Oh, I'm sorry. I'm distracted. Overseeing the desserts for this group can be demanding." She pasted a big smile on her face to reassure the older gentleman she was in fact happy to hear his good news.

"Would you excuse me for a minute? I need to ask Brent a question about the dessert table."

"Certainly, girlie." Mr. Gibson clapped his hands together. "Are any of these cupcakes gluten-free, by chance?"

"No, but I do have something for you." Maggie patted the older man's arm and excused herself. Hurrying over to Brent, she took his hand, motioning with her head for him to follow her. When they were away from the group, Maggie asked, "Did you bring the cake I made for Mr. Gibson?"

"The cake for Mr. Gibson?" Brent's brow

furrowed. "I don't remember a cake."

"Shoot, I must've left it in the cooler when we were loading my car."

"Do you want me to go back and get it?" Brent asked.

"No, I'll go."

"I should go with you," Brent said.

"It's not far. It'll only take a few minutes. At most ten." Maggie squeezed his hand. "I'll be fine. Besides, it'll give me a minute alone with Matt."

"You're taking Matt?" Brent scowled. "Why not let me go? I can be there and back before you even miss me." That half-grin she loved appeared on his lips, making her want to kiss him. "Then you and Matt can enjoy the party."

"Thank you. I appreciate it, but I know which cake it is and where it's located. It'll be easier if I go."

"Are you sure?" Brent held her gaze.

"Yes," she said. "Don't worry. I'll be sure to lock the car doors. I'll take every precaution. Ten minutes— tops."

"All right, but if you're not back soon, I'll send out the cavalry." Brent leaned over and touched his lips to hers. She blushed, but her heart somersaulted with joy.

Chapter Twenty-three

Maggie pulled her car into the back alley, so they'd be closer to the kitchen. She didn't want to walk through the dark shop, and she didn't want to take the time for the fluorescence to warm up. She knew right where the cake was located, so she'd be in and out in no time.

For a second, she contemplated leaving Matt in the car since he looked so comfortable, snuggled into his car seat, but Brent's warning rang in her ears. Instead, she unbuckled him and grabbed his dinosaur and a few board books from off the seat. She'd put him in the office to play while she collected the cake from the refrigerator. *No sense in both of us being chilly.*

Maggie switched on the kitchen lights and waited for them to flicker to life. Then she checked the door. Locked. Passing the swinging kitchen doors, she hurried to the office and flipped on the overhead. "Okay, big man, I need you to stay here while I find the cake."

"Okay, Mommy."

Maggie placed Matt on the office carpet with his stuffed dinosaur and books. She hadn't taken the time to get Matt's diaper bag from her mom, so she didn't have his blanket or other necessities. It should be fine though. It wasn't like they were going to be here long.

"Dino." Matt squealed and hugged the stuffed animal tight to his chest. "I play roar." The toddler rolled to his hands and knees, bouncing his stuffed animal on the floor as he crawled.

"I'll be right back." She took one last glance over her shoulder, then headed to the refrigerator to get the cake, telling herself she'd be less than a minute.

Opening the heavy metal door, she flipped on the lights inside the unit and walked to the shelf where she thought she'd put the cake, but it wasn't there. "Rats." Someone must have moved it.

She scanned the contents and spotted the cake on one of the higher shelves covered with a plastic lid. She needed the step ladder to get it down. Hustling to the storage closet, she pulled it out from its place just inside the door.

Since the office sat right across the hall from the storage closet, Maggie peeked into the room. Matt knelt beside one of the metal chairs, playing with his dinosaur. Satisfied he was okay, she picked up the ladder.

Lugging it back to the walk-in refrigerator, she climbed the few steps, reaching upward to grab the cake, but she stopped midstream A noise caught her attention. She stopped and listened, but all she heard was the hum of the refrigerator. Pulling the cake toward her, she eased it from the shelf above her head. She hugged the cold cake to her chest as she reached the last step. There it went again—the noise—this time a crash, like glass breaking. Then another and another.

Matt! He must've gotten into something. She slid

the cake onto a shelf and raced out the door, but she stopped short the instant she cleared the refrigerator.

Flames roared throughout the kitchen, blocking the back door. The area near the window stood engulfed in fire. Pivoting, she found the way to the office littered with crackling, red blazes. She had to get to Matt. Why had she left him alone? Rushing toward the flames, she called for him.

"Momma," came the reply, then a scream.

Frantic, she tried to find a path through the flames, but the fire blazed everywhere. Smoke swirled around her, billowing from the red monster.

9-1-1. She stuck her hand in her back pocket and remembered she'd left her phone in the car. Coughing, she worked her way toward the kitchen doors, pushing one open, hoping to get to the phone behind the counter, but the fire raged in the front area as well.

Tears came to her eyes. The smoke stung, but her heart was the cause of her heated tear drops. She'd never forgive herself if something happened to Matt.

~

Brent checked his phone again. Twenty minutes had passed since Maggie left. He didn't want to be an overprotective boyfriend, but a bad feeling gnawed at his gut. Pulling his phone from his pocket, he pushed Maggie's number.

After a few rings, her phone went to voicemail. He couldn't shake the feeling that something was wrong.

Pastor Connor called for everyone's attention and asked one of the Sunday School teachers to say the blessing over the food. Brent bowed his head and sent up his own prayer. *Lord, please keep Maggie and Matt safe. I know I can trust you.*

Approaching the group where Dan stood, Brent pulled him aside. "Maggie left to go back to the bakery. She forgot the cake she'd made for Mr. Gibson, but she's been gone a while. I'm worried, so I'm going to check on her. See if she needs any help."

"Okay, but I can't guarantee there'll be any food left when you get back." Dan chuckled. "Nikki brought her famous chili."

Brent forced a smile. "I'll have to take my chances, but I need to borrow your truck."

"I thought you rode your motorcycle."

"No, Maggie and I rode together, and she took her car back to the bakery."

"Oh, I see." Dan dug his keys out and handed them to Brent. "Keep me posted."

"Thanks." Brent walked past the growing line at the food tables and headed for the door. Once he was in the truck, the urge to put the gas pedal to the floor overwhelmed him. He reached the bakery in record time, but the sight that met him caused his heart to stop.

A fire truck, along with an ambulance, sat outside the front of Sweet Things bakery. Blue lights flashed, lighting up the dark night sky. Flames flickered from the source of the blaze where the firemen attacked with high-pressure water.

His worst fears played out in front of him. He pulled the truck into a spot and jumped from the cab of the truck. Racing toward the barricades, he scanned the scene. He had to find Maggie. Surely, she and Matt had made it out to safety.

Spotting one of the deputies he knew, he rushed toward him. "Hey, Adams. Did you find anyone inside?"

"Not yet. But they're looking."

"Maggie and Matt might be in there." Brent flexed his fists to stay calm.

Two firemen emerged from the haze of smoke; one of them carried Maggie. He pushed past Adams and two other men to get to her.

"Maggie, Maggie." He reached her as they placed her on a stretcher. Leaning over her, he stroked her cheek. "You've got to be okay, darlin'. I need you too much."

She opened her eyes to his touch. "Matt's inside, in the office." She latched onto his shirt, keeping him close. "Please find him. Please."

The pleading in her voice tore his heart to shreds. He bent low and kissed her smudged cheek. Then he gave her hands a soft tug, forcing her to release him.

Matt needed him, and he could not fail. Burying the fear that rose in him, he scanned the scene.

When the EMT placed a blanket over Maggie, Brent grabbed one from the stack inside the ambulance. He found the nearest puddle of water from the streams being shot into the burning bakery and dunked the blanket into the cold water.

Calling out to the nearest fireman, he said, "There's a boy still in the building. He might be in the office." Without stopping to explain, Brent ran to the side street and straight to the back alley, the shortest route to the office. The back door had been reduced to charred planks. A swift kick with his foot laid the remains flat. Wrapping the water-soaked blanket around him, he entered the building.

Please Lord, let me get to him in time. Keep him safe. We need him.

The sounds of the firemen in the building drifted to him above the hissing noise of the fire. He knew if they spotted him, they'd make him leave. Covering his mouth and nose with his elbow, he pushed his way through flames to the storage room, the wet blanket keeping him untouched by the blaze.

"Matt." Why didn't he answer?

"Matt," He called again. This time he heard a squeal.

"Bwent," The toddler yelled, followed by a frightened cry.

Brent was never so relieved to hear a kid scream. It was one of the most beautiful sounds he'd ever heard.

Covering his face and head with the blanket, he dashed through the flames engulfing the kitchen into the office. The blaze had eaten up half of the carpet, and the flyers hanging on the walls were ashes on the floor. Following the cries of the child, he dropped to the ground and found Matt under the desk.

"Come on, Matt, my boy." Brent swooped the frightened child along with his dino into his arms and stood. "Let's get out of here."

"Mommy. I want Mommy." Matt sniffled.

"That's where we're going. Let's find Mommy."

Brent wrapped the blanket over Matt and maneuvered through the flames into the kitchen. The firemen had run several hoses to the back alley, and they were making progress on putting out the fire in the kitchen. He dodged the flames and headed toward the back door. Still alive.

"I have the boy." He called to one of the firemen as he stepped from the building.

The fireman's radio squawked to life. "The boy's

been found." Scowling, he turned to Brent. "You're lucky you made it out. You have no idea what an idiotic move that was."

"I couldn't let something happen to Matt. Not him." Brent held the boy tight to his chest, dropping the wet blanket to the ground.

When Brent rounded the corner of the bakery, or what was left of it, he spotted Maggie sitting on the stretcher in the ambulance.

The instant she saw him heading towards her with Matt, she jumped down from the back of the vehicle and ran to meet them. Grabbing Matt from Brent's arms, she smothered his face with kisses. "Oh Matt, my sweet boy." Tears rolled down her cheeks. "I thought I'd lost you." She gasped. "I thought ..." Hugging him, she glanced at Brent and mouthed, "Thank you."

Brent wrapped his arms around the two most important people in his world and held on for dear life. *Thank you, Lord Jesus, thank you.*

~

Wade's SUV pulled up while Brent waited with Maggie in the back of the ambulance. The EMT wanted to give Matt a once-over before sending them home for the evening. "This young man has been so brave," she said.

Wade approached the ambulance, his expression all business. "Hey, how is everyone?"

"We're okay." Maggie ruffled her son's blond hair. "Thanks to your brother again. He seems to swoop in and save the day. I might have to make him a cape if he keeps this up."

Wade chuckled. "He is pretty super, but I wouldn't make him a cape. It might give him a big head."

"Well, he's a hero in my book." She squeezed his hand and graced him with one of her dazzling smiles.

"I wanted to give you the news about Cyrus Carver in person." Wade met Brent's gaze. "The highway patrol caught him when he was leaving Reseda County about half an hour ago, thanks to that APB we put out and some quick thinking on my dispatcher's part. They're holding him until one of my deputies can pick him up."

"Fantastic." Gratitude flooded Brent's heart. Life would get back to normal. No more looking over his shoulder, no more worrying about Maggie and Matt. Brent glanced down at his finger's intertwined with hers. He'd come to depend on her.

"It gets better. The fool didn't even bother to get rid of the evidence from tonight's shenanigans. When the highway patrol pulled him over, they found rags, bottles, and paint thinner in his back seat. I'm sure when we match what's left from the bottles here to what we found in his vehicle, we'll be able to charge him with this arson too. Along with three counts of attempted murder."

"Oh man, you just made my year." Brent stepped down from the ambulance to shake his brother's hand. "I'm so glad this is over."

Wade pulled him in for a hug, thumping his back. "Me too, brother." Stepping away, he added, "You might want to go thank the assistant manager at Cantina Chillax. She called in the fire. Without her quick action, the whole block might have gone up in smoke, and my dispatcher wouldn't have alerted the other law enforcement agencies to be on the lookout for Carver. Maybe she needs a cape, too."

"I'll be sure to give her our thanks. Her quick action saved Maggie and Matt. For that, she's now a member of our free- -cupcakes-for-life program."

"She most certainly is." Maggie ran her arm around Matt.

The EMT straightened, hooking his stethoscope around his neck. "This little guy looks good to me. It should be safe to take him home."

Chapter Twenty-four

The doors to the fellowship hall flew open, and in stepped the newlyweds. The rest of the wedding party followed behind them. Brent and Maggie held hands as they entered the transformed hall.

The entire room was decked in Christmas fare. Whites, reds, and greens warmed the area, giving it an enchanted glow. All the round tables stood covered in white tablecloths with beautiful Christmas bouquets full of mistletoe and poinsettias in the center of them. Lighted wreaths hung at even intervals along the walls throughout the hall with a place to take pictures tucked into one of the corners. Evergreen branches hung from the latticework surrounding the cake and beverage tables, and a Christmas tree trimmed with white ornaments glowed on the edge of the dance floor near the DJ.

Maggie wore a tea-length red dress with lace on the bodice that made her hazel eyes shimmer.

Brent leaned close to her ear. "Save me a dance," he whispered.

"All of them," she said.

His heart stuttered. Her lashes hooded her eyes, so he couldn't read what she was thinking, but he hoped she meant what she said. They peeled off and headed in different directions. She followed the bridesmaids to the right, and he followed the groomsmen to the left.

They had one last duty to perform for the happy couple. The wedding party spread throughout the room waiting on the DJ.

The Doctor of Dance said into the mic, "May I present to you Mr. and Mrs. Tyler Kemp,"

The wedding party along with the entire room of guests erupted with applause. "It's about time." Somone called over the cheers, and "You go, Tyler," could be heard from several of the guys.

A few whistles pierced the air, then the DJ put on the first song of the night, the bride and groom's first dance together as man and wife. The lights lowered, and Tyler took Nadine's hand, leading her to the dance floor.

The other members of the wedding party dispersed some heading to the food tables, others joining family and friends.

Brent stood and soaked in the scene before him.

The look on Tyler's face told him all he needed to know. The man had fallen head-over-heels for the woman he held in his arms. With that thought, Brent scanned the fellowship hall for the woman who had captured his own heart completely.

She sat in the corner near the picture booth, next to her parents and Matt, chatting with the others at the table.

Brent moved through the room, dodging a few of the other guests who were moving toward the dance floor to join the newly married couple. When he reached the table, he held out his hand. "I believe this is my dance.'

She glanced at her mother. "Do you mind watching Matt?"

Libby met Brent's gaze, giving him a knowing look. "Not at all." She smiled.

She grasped his hand and allowed him to help her to her feet. As they turned to make their way to the dance floor, Brent caught sight of John and Marilyn by the photo booth. John knelt in front of Marilyn on one knee, holding a small black box.

Marilyn's eyes widened when he lifted the lid. She nodded profusely.

Maggie leaned close to Brent. "Am I seeing what I think I'm seeing?"

"Yes, another miracle." Brent chuckled, right before Maggie poked him in the ribs with her elbow. "What?"

"She's not who she used to be. That's what." Maggie hugged his arm. "John will be good for her."

"Yes, he will." Brent kissed the top of her head. "Now, let's go boogie."

She giggled. "That's another something I'd like to see."

Brent led them onto the dance floor when the song changed. The tempo slowed as a soft strum of a guitar floated out of the speakers. Pulling Maggie close, she laid her head on his shoulder, and he wrapped his arms around her. Every nerve in his body came to life. Having her near, set his heart to racing and calmed him, all at the same time.

"This is nice," she said, moving to the rhythm, relaxing into him.

Brent laid his cheek on the crown of her head. "It is

nice. We make good dance partners."

She lifted her head to meet his gaze. A twinkle of mischief played in her eyes. "We do? We've only made a few trips around the floor."

"We're doing all right, but I think we make pretty good business partners too" He gave her his signature half-grin.

"You would, but at present, we don't *have* a business. We have ashes."

"Only until the insurance comes through, then things will return to normal." Brent shrugged. "Unless you're not interested in the bakery anymore."

She stopped backing away from him with her fists on her hips. "You know good and well that I'm totally invested in the bakery."

"I know, I know." He wrapped his arm around her waist and pulled her to him. "I also think we make good partners in life." He glanced down at her to judge her reaction.

She scowled, "What do you mean?"

"We worked together well on the proposal, and we work together well when it comes to Matt. All in all, we make a great team."

"Is this a sales pitch?" Her eyebrows winged up.

"No, Maggie, this is a proposal, but not a business one." He stopped, right in the middle of the dance floor. "Maggie, I can't imagine my life without you. You know how much I care for you and Matt. I want to be there for both of you if you'll let me."

Tears glistened on her lashes. "Oh Brent, somewhere between the first day you walked into the bakery and you saving Matt, I fell in love with you. The man you've become. The other night at my house, you asked me if I didn't know or if I was afraid."

"I remember. You said you were afraid of losing me, but every relationship holds that risk."

Maggie reached up and placed her finger over his lips. "I know, and I'm not afraid anymore. I'd rather spend my days loving you and Matt than worrying about what might happen. So, with my whole heart, I accept your proposal."

Pulling her to him, he lowered his lips to hers. The kiss tasted so sweet. He framed her face with his hands and held her close, forgetting they were in a room full of people. To him, they were the only ones in the whole place.

When she responded to him in kind, his heart somersaulted. She kissed his lips, then his cheeks, then glided her hand over the scars that had changed the course of his life and brought him to her. "I love you, Brent Thibodeaux, and I will until the day I die."

The DJ broke into their moment. "Let's give it up for the kissing couple. Who needs mistletoe, right?" The crowd roared with cheers and laughter.

Brent waved at the guests before grabbing Maggie's hand and exiting the dance floor. He couldn't help grinning from ear to ear. She'd said yes to his most important proposal ever. Even with the bakery in shambles and with months of work ahead of them, all that mattered was she had said yes.

After the cake-cutting, they hustled back to the table near the photo booth to find Marilyn and John sitting across from Maggie's parents, beaming.

"Look." Marilyn wiggled the fingers on her left hand in Maggie's direction. "John proposed."

"Isn't it exciting?" Libby asked. "One wedding

down and another one to plan."

Maggie took her aunt's hand into hers and admired the beautiful pear-shaped diamond. "It's lovely." Leaning over, she hugged her aunt.

"You did a fine job picking out the ring," Stuart met John's gaze. "It's stunning."

"Congratulations, man." Brent stuck out his hand and shook John's. "If anyone deserves to be happy, it's the two of you."

"Thanks." John glowed. His chest puffed with pride. "I never thought I'd marry, much less meet a woman like Marilyn." He turned his gaze toward his fiancée, his eyes sparkling with pleasure.

Marilyn gushed, splaying her fingers on the tabletop to admire her ring. "I never expected to marry again either, but then I've never met anyone like John." She rested her head on his shoulder.

John took hold of her hand. "Let's go dance. I want to show you off a little bit."

Marilyn giggled. "I'm all yours."

Watching them thread their way to the dance floor, Brent's heart filled with joy for his friend. Who would've guessed when they rode into Orange Blossom in October what wonderful blessings the Lord had in store for them both.

Brent pulled out Maggie's chair then took the seat next to her. Libby sat holding Matt in her lap while Stuart cut into the slice of cake in front of him.

"Mommy." Matt launched himself at Maggie who caught him in her arms. She hugged him close, kissing his cheeks. "You taste like cake."

"Bwent," Matt flopped toward him. He opened his arms to receive the little boy. Matt wrapped his chubby arms around his neck, then laid his head on Brent's shoulder. Brent rubbed Matt's back. The boy seemed content to stay where he was.

"I saw the two of you on the dance floor earlier," Libby said. "You guys looked good together."

Maggie shot Brent a knowing glance. "That's because, Mom, we *are* good together."

Epilogue

A year later

Placing the matching candlesticks on the fireplace mantel, Maggie stepped back and adjusted them. The task of unpacking from their move in October had taken a couple of months. With working, parenting, and being newlyweds, time had slipped by and now Christmas was only a week away.

Putting the empty box on the pile by the door, she surveyed the living room. Marilyn had found them the perfect house. A two-story brick home with a fireplace and a large bay window in the living room with plenty of space upstairs to grow. Smiling, Maggie nodded her approval.

Their wedding had been a small, simple affair at Silver Spur Ranch with family and a few close friends in attendance. After Marilyn and John's big blowout wedding, they both wanted something more intimate. Pastor Connor officiated, and Nikki and Bernadette handled the reception— except for the wedding cake. Kristen and Ranita made an extraordinary creation in honor of the new family being formed.

Though she'd been slow to unpack, Maggie had

insisted they put up the Christmas tree and decorations the weekend after Thanksgiving for Matt's sake. Glancing toward the front window, she sighed. The lights on the Christmas tree glowed, giving the living room a warm, homey feeling.

Happy with her progress, she ignored the pile of empty boxes by the front door that needed to go out. Instead, she went upstairs to retrieve a shopping bag hidden under her side of the bed. Pulling out the bag, she glanced at the clock on her nightstand. Her guys would be home soon. Her heart warmed at the thought. She never tired of referring to Brent and Matt as her guys.

Going back downstairs, she went to the closet in the foyer and dug behind the coats to find the bin that held the wrapping paper. She lifted the long tub, carrying it to the living room along with the shopping bag.

She placed a white gift box on the coffee table, then pulled the gift for Matt from the plastic bag and placed it inside. Taping the box shut, she pulled blue Christmas paper with snowmen on it from the bin and unrolled it on the table.

Once done, she repeated the wrapping process with Brent's gift. She giggled in anticipation. He'd never guess what the box contained. Not the real gift.

She chose the bows and ribbon, making sure they complemented the paper, then placed the two gifts in the center of the coffee table where they couldn't be missed.

Twenty minutes later, Matt and Brent burst into the house in a flurry of activity, knocking over the empty boxes. "Momma," Matt called, "home."

Maggie scurried from the kitchen to greet them. "How was your shopping?" She knelt to help Matt off with his shoes. "Fun. We saw a dog." Matt lifted his foot for her to remove his tennis shoe.

"It went wonderfully. We have a few surprises, but they're none of your business until Christmas Day." Brent opened the foyer closet and tossed his shoes inside. Walking to the oak console table near the door, he put his wallet and keys in the basket.

"I can't wait." She beamed. "Speaking of surprises, I have one of my own." She grabbed Brent's hand and dragged him to the living room. "Ta-da. I finished the unpacking."

"Wow, it looks great." He pulled her close, placing a kiss on her cheek.

She poked him in the ribs with her elbow. "You can't tell a difference, can you?"

Sheepishly, he shook his head. "Not really, except for the empty boxes by the door." A half-grin appeared on his lips, and she lifted onto her tiptoes to kiss it away.

Matt darted into the room, carrying one of the boxes. Placing it on the floor, he lifted his leg to climb into it but stopped.

Maggie followed his gaze. He'd discovered the presents sitting on the coffee table.

"Would you like to open a gift?" Maggie walked to the table and lifted the two presents. "I have one for each of you," she teased, jiggling the boxes.

"Isn't that cheating?"

"Maybe, but I think you should open these gifts today and not wait."

Brent raised an eyebrow, but he took the gift from

her hand. Sitting on the couch, he held the gift to his ear and shook it. "Hmm, it's not heavy and doesn't make noise, but it needs to be opened today. Is it perishable, like candy?" Brent widened his eyes.

Maggie shrugged. "You'll just have to open it to find out."

Sitting beside him, she lifted Matt onto the couch and put him between them. She handed the three-year-old the other package. "Here you go. sweetie."

Brent tore into the paper, freeing the box without much effort. Matt mimicked Brent and pulled off the bow but couldn't get his fingers under the paper to tear it.

Maggie helped by tearing one of the ends for him.

Brent laughed as the little boy finished ripping the paper off the gift, slinging it to the floor with gusto. "Okay, big man, you go first."

A smile pulled at her lips. She suspected Brent would let Matt go first. She pressed her lips together to keep from blurting out her surprise before Matt could open the box.

Leaning over the little boy, Brent popped loose the tape that secured the lid. "Okay, let's see what you've got." Brent slid open the box and pulled out a Matt-sized tee shirt. "Look, it's a shirt. It says, '*Big Brother.*'" Brent blinked and reread the shirt. "Big Brother?" His gaze sought hers. "Are you serious?" Brent jumped from the couch. "Maggie, Matt's going to be a big brother." He yelled and grabbed her shoulders lifting her to her feet. "I'm going to be a dad, again!" Drawing her to him, he squeezed her so tight she couldn't breathe.

When he released her, she asked, "So, how do you

really feel about having a baby?"

"I feel like a man who has been blessed three times over." The glow in his eyes when he looked at her matched the brightness of the lights on the tree.

Maggie picked up the package she'd given him from the couch where it had fallen and opened the lid. Taking the hat out of the box, she placed it on Brent's head. "*World's Best Dad*," she read.

"That's a lot to live up to," he said, drawing her into his arms.

"Yes, but you do it every day already." Sliding her arms around his neck, he bent to kiss her. "Merry Christmas, Maggie."

"Merry Christmas, Brent," she murmured, right before his lips touched hers.

The End

Join Bonita's newsletter, **Beyond the Page**, at www.bonitaymccoy.com

For updates, book recommendations, and fun giveaways or follow her on

Facebook@bonitaymccoyauthor

Dear Reader,

From the first word to the last, I thoroughly enjoyed our romp through Orange Blossom, Texas, and getting to know the characters in the Billionaire Bothers of Silver Spur Ranch series. It has been a three year, three book journey that had me looking up such topics as Molotov cocktails, police codes, and apartment floor plans.

I hope you enjoyed meeting Brent Thibodeaux and the warm-hearted Maggie Kemp Bishop on this return trip. Their story delighted me as they grew closer to one another and learned how to trust each other and the Lord.

Brent's experience in the military and being injured in the line of duty made me appreciate those men and women who serve our country every day through the military, police and fire brigades. Thank you for your service.

Maggie and Matt quickly became two of my favorite characters. I've added them to the ranks of the tender-hearted Nikki, the feisty Bernadette, and the three handsome heroes.

As always, I need to thank my sweet husband for encouraging me all the way to writing "the end", yet again. He's my own hero, and I'm so thankful for him. I'd also like to give a shoutout to my grown kids, all four, who make my world a brighter place.

And now I'd like to thank you, my reader. Your support and encouragement allow me to do what I love, and for that, I am so grateful. So, as the crew from Orange Blossom would say, "Thank you, kindly."

May God bless and keep each one of you along your own journey.

Bonita Y. McCoy

Bonita Y. McCoy - Author

Bonita Y. McCoy hails from the Great State of Alabama where she lives on a five-acre farm with two dogs, two cows, and one husband who she's had since circa 1989.

Her background includes a degree in Journalism from Mississippi State University as well as ten years teaching high school literature and writing classes to some of the best students, ever.

More recent adventures include publishing her Amy Kate Cozy Mystery series through Winged Publications and being a finalist in both the Selah awards and Silver Falchion Awards with that series.

The Coffee with God devotional series her Word Weavers group publishes has given her an avenue to encourage other Christians along the way.

On any given day, you can find her reading a good book, playing with her German shepherds, or drinking coffee with her hubby on the front porch swing. Of course, that's when she's not writing her next cozy mystery or sweet romance.

She is an active member of both American Christian Fiction Writers and Word Weavers International.

Sign up for her newsletter at www.bonitaymccoy.com and become part of her newsletter family.

 Scan here to see Bonita's Books!

Other Books by Bonita Y. McCoy

Amy Kate Mystery series

Twisted Plots

<u>Family Twist</u>

<u>Twisted Vows</u>

Sawyer Sweet Romance series

<u>No Room in His Heart</u>

<u>Truth Be Told</u>

<u>Seeds of Love</u>

Billionaire Brothers of Silver Spur Ranch series

<u>Billionaire Cowboy Next Door</u>

<u>Billionaire Sheriff on the Move</u>

<u>Billionaire Boss' Holiday Proposal</u>

Stand Alone:

<u>Merry Christmas Mix-up</u>

<u>Only for the Summer</u>

Contributed:

<u>Coffee with God</u>

<u>Coffee and Cookies with God   at Christmas</u>

<u>Coffee with God to Bless Your Heart</u>

<u>Coffee with God On the Road</u>

<u>Coffee with God: 31 Gratitude-Filled Devotions</u>

<u>Coffee with God: 31 Red, White, and Blue Devotions</u>

<u>Chicken Soup for the Soul: Thanks Dad edition</u>

<u>Christmas Spirit</u>

<u>Handy Tips for Homeschooling Parents: When You're Feeling Overwhelmed</u>